Words of Silence

Vincent Ball

OTHER BOOKS BY VINCENT BALL

Buck Jones, Where are You? (autobiography)

The Cathedral Tree

Patrick Downs

Regency Rebel

Writer's Block

Words of Silence

VINCENT BALL

First published 2018 by Vincent Ball.

ISBN: 978-0646-98383-7 (sc)
ISBN: 978-0646-98634-0 (e)

A CIP number for this book is available at the National Library of Australia.

Cover by Digital Print Australia

Printed in Australia, UK and USA

VB rev. date: 20/03/2018

ABOUT THE AUTHOR

Vincent Ball OAM was born in Wee Waa, New South Wales. His dream of becoming *a cowboy on the fillums* took him on an adventure that included serving with the RAAF in England in World War II, working his way back to England on a tramp steamer, and winning a scholarship to The Royal Academy of Dramatic Art, London.

He worked as an actor for 25 years (waiting to be discovered and whisked off to Hollywood!), and returned to Australia in 1973.

Vincent is a widower. He has four children, five grandchildren and one great-grandchild.

Acknowledgements

My grateful thanks once again to Peter Yeldam who was always there with his encouragement and valuable input. Robert Bartlett guided me through the 'computer speak' labyrinth to find what I was looking for and when my computer went walkabout, my friendly neighbour and computer whiz Matthew Widdup, brought it to heel and enabled me to get my manuscript to the printers at Digital Print Australia, where Cory Heneker and Steve Lewis efficiently tied up the loose ends and produced a cover for the book that made everybody happy.

And a big thank you to my back-up team of dear friends, Julia, Diana, Dorothy and Krithia, whose kind remarks and enthusiasm always kept me going when all seemed lost.

Vincent Ball, March 2018

For Diana Beevers.
A very special lady

Chapter 1

The two men could be in their late twenties. It was hard to tell as their skin had the leathery brownness that told its tale of a life in the Australian outback. They sat their horses in a relaxed, easy way, eyes screwed up against the dust raised by the cattle and the glare of the hot midday sun. At first glance they were typical stockmen, their lean frames clothed in chequered shirts, off-white trousers, elastic-sided boots and topped with a wide-brimmed hat.

They watched the herd being expertly funnelled into the holding pens by the aborigine stockmen. The nervous bawling of the cattle intermingled with the rider's whistles and the sharp crack of their stockwhips created a cacophony of noise that was typical of cattle yards in country towns all over Australia.

Jack Evans, owner of Waaree cattle station – 500 square miles of unfriendly pasture that somehow sustained his large herd of cattle – sadly surveyed the noisy dusty scene around him.

"Looks like this'll be the last time we'll be mustering on horseback Reg. But, if we're gunna compete, we'll have to be like the rest of 'em and hire helicopters and get ourselves some 'Yamaha' motor bikes." He patted the neck of his stockhorse."It's not going to be the same is it? Part of the romance of working a cattle station is the stockhorse. I dunno about you but I'm going to miss all that."

Reg Brady, Jack's friend and foreman, didn't answer for a moment as he was thinking about riding 'Yamaha' motor bikes and wondering if they'd be able to do the same job as a horse.

But as Jack turned towards him, Reg's hands and fingers began to flutter like butterflies in reply as he mouthed silent words and signed a homemade language that only Jack could understand.

"Yeah I couldn't agree with you more. I'm going to miss the saddling up of a morning with the other men. The Australian stockhorse has sort of, become part of the family haven't they?" Reg laughed a soundless laugh, his white teeth a slash in his brown face and signed, *"What am I saying, 'part of the family', it must be the heat."*

Jack shared the laugh."Yeah I know what you mean."

They continued to watch the busy scene in companionable silence, their thoughts on the future with motor bikes and helicopters.

Jack slowly shook his head and more to himself murmured,

"Yeah, it's never going to be the same again."

He turned to Reg.

"They've just about finished. I'll go and pay the men and see you back at the hotel."

Reg nodded, wheeled his horse and moved towards the town's centre.

Jack trotted over to the holding pens where his seven Aboriginal stockmen had gathered.

Peter, the head stockman spoke.

"Boss, all in now, pretty good shape. Me and men camp down by river same place last time.

"All right Peter. I'll bring some money and some beer, only no trouble now."

Peter gave him a wide grin, saying,

"No trouble boss, no trouble."

"Okay," and raising his arm to the others, Jack moved away.

* * *

The pub was crowded and Jack and Reg, freshly showered and clothed, managed to shoulder their way to the bar that ran the length of the room. After eventually getting the attention of the harassed barmen they then had to shoulder their way back through the crowd without losing too much of their beer.

"Bloody hell, it's hardly worth it, where did all these blokes come from?"

Reg handed his beer to Jack and signed,

"Looks like there's a couple of shearing gangs here" – indicating a large group of men doing a good job of noisily drinking their way through their last pay cheque." *And if I'm not mistaken they're getting to the stage of being belligerent loud mouthed drunks."*

His hand movements caught the eye a couple of the shearers, who in their drunken state were fascinated by the unusual activity of Reg's hands.

"Aye sport, "one of them yelled out, "what are yer wavin' yer hands around like a great big sheila for. You a poof or somethin?"

When Reg didn't reply, this somewhat angered the noisy

drunk who was being egged on by his mates.

"Aye I'm talkin' to you."

"Ignore him," Jack said, handing Reg his beer, "he's only looking for a fight."

Reg turned his back and did as Jack said.

That was like a red rag to a bull. The drunk was up on his feet and shouldering his way towards Reg and Jack.

Jack watched his progress saying quietly.

"Oh shit, he's on his way over, looks like trouble."

Reg casually moved towards the bar, left his beer there and turned to face the oncoming troublemaker.

Jack, as peacemaker, stepped forward in the path of the would-be assailant.

"My friend is mute. It's a sign language. It is the only way he can speak."

Hoping that the drunk would understand and maybe this would calm him down.

The drunken shearer stared at Reg for some time.

"He's a dummy, is that what yer sayin?"

"He is dumb ..." but Jack was interrupted by,

"He's a dummy!" The drunk turned to his mates calling out, "Hey, we've got a dummy here fellas!"

Reg, who had quietly been watching this interplay eased his way forward to stand directly in front of the shearer's face. He made a few small signals with his hands.

The now bemused drunk looked at Jack and shook his head as he slurringly said, "what did he say?"

Jack resignedly rolled his eyes to the ceiling.

"He said why don't you piss off."

4

Well that did it. The drunk took a swing at Reg, who easily avoided it and stepped in with a short right to the jaw and the drunk landed on back and stayed there. It was on then for young and old.

Jack and Reg could obviously take care of themselves. They'd been doing it for the past ten years in the bush pubs of Queensland. Eventually everybody was involved, most of them not really knowing what it was all about – some even trying to ignore it.

Shouts of "Get the Police" didn't have any effect and it was only when shouts of "The police are coming!" that the fighting stopped. Chairs were quickly picked up and tables righted as if it was a sort of regular routine.

A lone rather nervous looking policeman entered.

"What's going on here?"

Someone said "Nothing" – except that there was spilt beer all over the place, shirts were torn, there were bloody noses, busted lips and a tooth was lying on the bar ...

The barman called out,

"Have a drink Bill."

A schooner was passed quickly along to the policeman. He sipped his beer, while looking around at the groups of men quietly chatting as if it was a church tea party, his face registering the unreality of it all.

*

The town had quietened down. The dormitory style accommodation for the shearers were now full of snoring men sleeping off their boozing, before heading to the next shearing station at daybreak. A few lone stragglers, like me, wended their way home along the dimly lit street and in the distance the bawling and movement of the penned-up cattle could be heard waiting for the auction the following day.

In the blackness of room No 5 in the Coolabah Hotel, I could hear from down the hall a murmur of voices – male and female – the squeaking of a bed – giggles.

But in here there was only me and a gut full of beer for company. Being mute made it too difficult to get a girl – to 'chat one up' in a noisy pub? Yeah right.

I was born unable to talk and my mum kept telling me when I was a kid that it was all right to be dumb and that it didn't really matter. I couldn't talk and it didn't really matter! That was my mum for you!

Thank God for Helen Evans the wife of George Evans the owner of Waaree. She'd been a schoolteacher before she married George and to occupy herself, while her husband was with the cattle, she gathered together all the aborigine children around the station, cleaned out and decorated a small empty building and started teaching them how to read and write. My mum used to help her until I came along and Jack arrived a couple of months later.

But me being born mute didn't help my parents – I can still hear my mum and dad, fighting and shouting and blaming each other for my muteness.

In the late fifties, School of the Air was established for remote learning and it soon had the same curriculum as any other school in the state. So that SOA students weren't disadvantaged the teachers tried to tailor each package to their individual needs. Gifted students or those with learning difficulties were especially catered for and given individual learning programs.

Helen Evans had the latest radio equipment installed and school for me became an adventure as I struggled to 'keep up' with Jack and pass my exams. To counteract my muteness, she encouraged me to read. This I did. and I became an avid reader travelling the world with great explorers, adventuring and fighting battles with heroes like Wellington, Nelson and any other colourful heroic person that changed the course of history.

In the end, my mum got so fed up with me and her life on Waaree, that one morning she gave me a hug and a kiss, packed her bags and took off with a travelling rodeo rider, who happened to be passing by at the time and that was the last we ever saw of them.

With no mum around to help me, it was left to my dad, old Charlie Wright and School of the Air to fill in the gap. My dad did the best he could, but being head stockman at Waaree meant that he spent most of his time in the saddle and away from the homestead. In all that 'alone time' I developed a sign language all of my own that enabled me to 'speak' to all the aborigines on the station, who'd fall about with laughter at the antics I'd get up to, when trying to make them understand me. The only person I could really have a conversation with was Jack, but he wasn't around anymore, he'd been sent away to a boarding school in Brisbane.

With my mum gone I was more or less 'adopted' by the women in the aborigine quarters and when I wasn't doing lessons with School of the Air, I'd spend hours watching Lily – the elder of the women – painting on bits of bark. I didn't understand what all the dots that she was doing meant, and when I asked her, she told me she was of the Kalkadoon tribe and she was telling the story of the night her tribe was killed by the troopers at Battle Mountain.

It was her way of making sure that that massacre would never be forgotten.

Whenever I wasn't reading, I was with Lily, going walkabout, listening to her stories of 'dreamtime.'

"Would you like to paint?" she asked me one day.

I nodded a "yes".

Lily spoke to my father and in the next mail drop there

was a palette, sketchbooks, pencils, brushes, paints and a pile of special watercolour paper.

After that when she was putting all those dots on her pieces of bark, she'd tell me her dreamtime stories as I struggled with sketchbook and pencil to draw what I could see around me. Lily would look at my awful drawings and tell me what was wrong, but when I blobbed colours onto them to cover up all the mistakes I'd made, she silently studied the result and didn't say anything.

For most of my childhood I tried to hide my frustration with my muteness in the fantasy world I created through reading and painting. It was the only way I could cope with being different from other kids.

Over the years, Lily said, my trees and bush-land had got better and the rivers now flowed with energy and colour.

Sometimes, in the loneliness of my quarters at night I would lie in bed and think of the painting that I had created, and for a time retreat into an idyllic world of fantasy, where I lived with both my parents in the small bull-nosed cottage that sat by the river or went fishing with my dad. Other times I would be lulled to sleep by the sound of Lily's soft calming voice telling me the dreamtime stories of the Kalkadoon tribe.

Tonight in room No 5 of the Coolabah Hotel, I fished with my dad in companionable silence from underneath the willow tree on the banks by the cottage.

* * *

Chapter 2

The colour of the land leading to Waaree wasn't the centre-red that prevailed around the surrounding countryside, it now had subtle shades of grey, blue and red lining the twenty kilometre dirt road that led to the homestead.

Although it could have done with some colourful flowers perhaps, the lawns of Jack's cattle station were green and the 'flower' beds by the path leading up to the front steps of the house were neat and tidy. The two windmills that were slowly turning, beyond the big corrugated iron Queensland homestead, attested to the greenness.

The house was built on stilts, the posts bolted on to metal supports imbedded into a concrete base to deter the hungry white ants and termites that thrived in the bush. Eight steps led up to the wide verandah that encircled the whole house and two water bags hung from the rafters.

Surrounding the main house were the white stockmen's quarters, a meat house, a cookhouse, a dining room and beyond the windmills the stockyards. A landing strip, with a small hanger and the nose of a twin engine Cessna poking it's way out of the open doors, separated the house and buildings from the collection of corrugated iron huts of the blacks camp where the aborigine stockmen and their families lived.

From the air Waaree had the appearance of a small hamlet – a green oasis in the vast dryness of the Queensland outback.

* * *

Jack was having a sign language lesson as he and Reg relaxed in armchairs on the front verandah – vocalizing the signs Reg made.

"Why do I have to learn all this?" Jack complained.

"So you'll understand me better." Reg signed.

"But I understand you perfectly now."

"Not perfectly. Not the little things. Not the subtle things I say."

"Subtle? You? There's nothing subtle about you," Jack said with a laugh.

Reg gave him a friendly ' up yours' sign and Jack laughed harder,

"See what I mean."

Reg, held up his hand for silence and then signed, *"There's an aircraft coming."*

Jack was amazed at Reg's acute hearing – he couldn't hear a thing. Then he did hear the crackle of the radio from the radio room. He quickly got up and went inside.

Inside the Radio room the aircraft was already calling in.

"Hello Waaree Station – hello Waaree Station. This is Flying Doctor aircraft D for David – are you receiving me?"

"Loud and clear D for David. This is Jack Evans – is that you George?"

"Yes it is Jack. I'm on my way to 'Rooeena' – Bill Steven's place. There's been an accident. Bill's been thrown from his horse. I don't know how bad he is, but you're a mate of his, so would you stand-by in case you can help in anyway."

"Yeah, I'll stand-by."

"Thanks Jack. I call you from Bill's place – over and out."

Reg who was standing at the doorway had heard the message about Bill and signed, *"Let's hope it's not too bad."*

*

Jack and Reg waited in near silence for some time before George radioed back.

"Bill's badly injured, Jack. He's got a fractured skull, his back is broken, maybe in two places, and he was brought in by land rover, which didn't help. I daren't move him. All I can do at the moment is make him comfortable – alleviate the pain. He keeps mentioning your name. I think you should get over here ASAP."

"I'm on my way George."

*

Jack's twin engine Cessna made short work of the trip to Rooeena and he was soon sitting by Bill's bed.

Betty stroked her husband's hand and talked quietly to him – about the station, the cattle, their prize bull Blackie – anything to keep him comfortable with familiar things.

Bill opened his eyes and whispered, "Jack?"

Jack leant forward."I'm here Bill."

He beckoned Jack closer."You should have a herd like mine Jack – the best in the country. That's why I'm gunna leave Blackie to you in my will." He turned his head to Betty."You make sure he gets him love won't you."

11

"Yes Bill I will."

"There's no rush mate. I don't think we can get rid of you that quickly."

Bill started to chuckle."Yer should see him perform Jack. Boy that old Blackie is a real cracker. Why, one day I saw him perform and he's got the biggest ..."

But Betty, shaking his hand, warningly said "Bill ". . . to stop him further elaborating.

Bill closed his eyes with a smile on his face!

Jack sat by the bed and watched over his friend – remembering the good times – their growing up together – the years they spent in Brisbane when they were small kids at boarding school. It was a friendship that had been welded together through drought, bush fires, floods, humour and a zest for living. Was this how it was going to end?

The Doc indicated to Jack to step outside.

While Jack put the kettle on to make some tea he was given the bad news.

"He's not going to make it Jack. His head fracture is a bad one and his back I'm sure is broken in two places. I can move him to the hospital but that would quickly kill him. I think he would prefer to die here in his own home, among friends and familiar things."

Jack slowly shook his head."That bad eh?"

"Yeah, that bad. I've contacted base and they're getting in touch with Betty's niece in Brisbane. I thought Betty should have another female friend around for support. I left instructions for her to fly to Cloncurry where you'll pick her up. Is that okay with you?"

"Yes of course."

Jack took a cup of tea into Betty.

"Jack, if you're staying, there's two spare rooms made up for you and the Doc. I'll get some food ready later on."

"Betty, the Doc and I can take care of ourselves. Don't worry ..."

"No Jack, I'd prefer to be doing something – to be occupied."

"Okay."

It was a long night. The Doc kept an eye on Bill. Betty occupied herself by preparing food or else – holding her husband's hand as he floated in and out of a coma.

Jack wandered around the house, sipping beer and spending hours on the front verandah staring out into the blackness and remembering.

The laughter of a Kookaburra ushered in the dawn and a clear blue sky.

The crackle from the radio room "Calling Rooeena Station – calling Rooeena Station – over, "brought Jack in from the kitchen.

"Rooeena station answering."

"This is the Fying Doctor Base at Cloncurry. Mary Stevens will be arriving here today at 1.45 pm. She's a brunette and will be wearing jeans and a blue blouse."

"Read you Cloncurry. This is Jack Evans. I'll be picking her up. Thank you. Over."

"Thank you Jack. Over and out."

Jack paused by the bedroom door. Betty was still there. Her eyes were closed. She held Bill's hand in both of hers, seemingly to be willing him by prayer to come out of the deep coma that was now his constant companion.

Jack, joined her in a silent prayer, mouthed a, "Hang in there mate," and headed out to his aircraft.

* * *

Cloncurry, being the main railhead for the transportation of stock in Cloncurry Shire reflected the town's importance in its modern airport. Jack touched down and taxied towards the reception centre.

After checking in with his flight plan he hurried over to 'Arrivals'. He quickly scanned the people milling around the carousal – *for a brunette wearing jeans and a blue blouse* – ah there she is. He didn't rush over, but happily looked at what he saw. She was a brunette, about 5'6" or 7, hair to her shoulders and jeans encasing very long legs and a butt that made you take a second look or a third or maybe you didn't take your eyes of it at all – oh yes and a blue blouse.

"Mary Stevens?" brought her around to the voice.

My goodness, what have we here she thought. Confronting her was a cowboy. He well over 6ft tall, lean, brown and with a relaxed loose-limbed look that all cowboys seem to have. All he needed was a gun and he'd be straight out of the West.

"Yes," she managed to stutter.

Close up Mary Stevens lived up to what he had seen from a distance. Large green eyes in a heart shaped face free of make-up with a dimpled chin and lips that cried out to be kissed.

"My name is Jack Evans. I'm a friend of your Uncle Bills. I've come to pick you up." And he gave her a lazy crooked smile, showing his teeth to advantage in his handsome face.

God, white teeth and a lazy crooked smile! What next, she thought.

"Here let me take your bag," he said.

14

He picked up her bag and took off in an unhurried walk that had Mary trotting beside him to keep up.

"Will it take us long to get there," she panted.

"About an hour."

"You must be a very fast driver."

He looked at her for a moment before replying.

"Yeah. Pretty fast."

"How's Uncle Bill?"

"Not good."

She waited for him to elaborate. He didn't.

This was obviously a monosyllabic cowboy. He didn't say much. Just briefly answered the question and that was it.

It was only when they were standing by the Cessna that she cottoned on that they'd be flying to Rooeena.

"You're a pilot?"

"I hope so. Otherwise we're in dead trouble." *Again the lazy crooked smile!*

"Why didn't you say?"

"You didn't ask."

Such a smart arse, she thought.

She made him nervous. Her closeness was having an effect upon his body – in places where the cramped pilot seat and straps didn't help much!

As he leveled the Cessna out at about 5000ft. Mary oohed and aahed at the view below her.

"I've only ever flown in jets – never this low. How beautiful it all is. You can understand why some people love the outback."

Jack looked down at what to him was a familiar scene.

"Yes. I'm one of those people who love the outback. It's all I know really. I don't hanker after the city life. I was at boarding school in Brisbane for four years. I took on board all they taught me but I couldn't wait to get back to the station – to sit astride a stock horse – go droving, mustering, working the cattle. Just doing all the things that needed dong around a cattle station."

Here he paused and thought of his mate fighting for his life back at the station – must keep talking – keep her mind off her Uncle Bill.

"It's a hard and some times lonely life. You have to contend with droughts, floods, bush-fires and market prices. But there's a beauty about the bush. It gets in your blood and stays there. What's that saying ' you can take the boy out of the bush, but you can't take the bush out of the boy,' I think that's true, in my case anyway."

She watched his profile as he told her about his life on a cattle station and there was a simple sincerity in the words he used in describing the things he loved. She felt a wave of warmness leave her and wash over this 'cowboy' she had just met. What was happening to her? She'd only known him for half an hour!

In no time at all they were landing at Rooeena and taxiing towards the house.

Doc Ryan met them on the steps of the verandah and quietly told them.

"Bill died while you were away. Betty's still with him."

Jack shepherded Mary into the house and to the bedroom. Betty was sitting at her husband's bedside holding his hand.

Mary went over and gently disengaged Betty's hands and with her arm around her shoulders eased her out of the chair and walked her out of the room. It was then that Betty

16

started sobbing.

Jack moved over to the bedside, felt the prickles start behind his eyes as reached out and gently stroked Bill's cheek. He huskily whispered,

"It was a privilege to know you and to be your friend. We'll look after Betty for you."

He stayed, like a sentinel and watched over his mate. And while he stood there a myriad of emotions moved across his face as a kaleidoscope of images – of their times together, swirled around his brain. And as he remembered, his eyes filled with tears that soon overflowed and coursed down his cheeks.

*

Bill was buried besides two small crosses, his son and daughter, underneath the pepper tree on a knoll a kilometre from the house. It was simple ceremony attended by several people who had made the journey by plane, truck and horseback to say goodbye to their friend and neighbour. A group of aborigines stoically watched the white man bury their dead.

The Flying Doctor and the priest were the first to leave. They said their goodbyes at the graveside. Doc Ryan left medication for Betty and the reverent his blessing and prayers.

Tea, cold beer and beef sandwiches were laid out on a trestle table on the front verandah and the gathering that was left helped themselves before offering their sympathy to Betty and going about their business.

It was midday when Betty, Jack, Mary and Reg watched the last of them leave and the heat was shimmering in mirage like waves across the countryside.

Betty Stevens was the first to break the silence.

"I won't be sorry to leave here," she quietly said in a flat unemotional voice.

"You're still going to sell?" Jack asked.

"Yes. I've had enough – the heat – all those years of struggle – the droughts – the ... "she paused for a moment and dipped her head – "the loss of the children – the years of hardship and now Bill. Yes I will sell."

She reached out a hand to Jack.

"Blackie is yours Jack. I know Bill wanted it that way."

I was suddenly on the outside looking in. Well that's what it felt like. Since Mary arrived, Jack's attention was devoted to her. Not that I blamed him. She was a fine looking girl and worthy of any mans full attention. But now I had nobody to 'talk' to and I didn't like to interrupt him with a whistle every time I wanted to say something, especially when he's 'chatting up' a pretty girl. The aborigine stockmen knew the basic signs of my silent language, but I couldn't really have a 'conversation' with them.

Betty rose from her armchair.

"I'm just going to have a lie down." As Mary turned to go with her, Betty held up her hand."No Mary I'll be all right, you stay here." Mary demurred, "are you sure?"

"Yes," Betty said, "please."

They watched this now seemingly lonely figure slowly go inside.

Mary reached out a hand to Jack for comfort.

"Oh Jack, I feel for her, but it'll do her good to get away from here. All the sad things in her life happened on this cattle station. She'll leave with nothing but memories of the struggle to survive and the loss of her children and

18

husband. Not much is it after all those years."

Jack nodded and covered her hand in sympathy.

"No, not much," he huskily whispered.

This moment of intimacy that I saw, separated them from the outside world that I was part of and the old saying of 'two's company, three's a crowd' was never more apparent.

I whistled for attention, rose and wandered towards the steps.

"I'll see you two later, I'm just going for a bit of a walk." I signed, and headed off in the direction of the stockmen's quarters.

* * *

Jack flew Betty and Mary to Cloncurry to pick up their fight to Brisbane.

The mutual attraction between Jack and Mary was so strong that he didn't hesitate to lean forward, in front of Betty, to kiss her as he said goodbye.

"I'm going to miss you Mary. I've only known you three days but I think somebody like you has been in my fantasies for years."

She smiled up at this tall cowboy who was turning her world upside down.

"Well I'm not a fantasy anymore Jack. I'm real and I'll be back in about three weeks – once I get Betty settled – to prove it to you."

He smiled that lazy crooked smile of his and she shook her head and laughingly continued,

"This is all too much, goodbye Jack, and turned away.

Jack gave Betty a hug and held her for a moment.

"You take care. I'll see you soon."

19

He watched them go along the concourse to their flight.

* * *

Jack returned to Waaree, collected Charlie, who hated flying, and flew him to Rooeena, where he would act as caretaker until Mary returned to pack up Betty's personal belongings and have them trucked to Brisbane.

Life at Waaree settled down after all the to-ing and fro-ing and even Jack's distracted air of mooning around the place was accepted by the stockmen and myself as that of a man being in love and quite normal!

When Mary appeared on the scene and I saw Jack's reaction and behaviour in her presence, I knew things were going to change. It was bound to happen sooner or later. We were both getting on a bit and it was about time we thought of settling down and having a family. I know I would like to have the companionship of marriage and kids. For Jack it would be easy – he was quite a catch – owner of a big cattle station and very presentable. Me? Not so easy. Being mute, not many people spoke 'my language' and regarded by some as a bit of a freak. The only person that I could really communicate with was Jack and once he had a wife I'd move out of the main house and into the head stockmen's quarters with old Charlie Wright, who didn't understand my sign signals and we could only talk to each other with notepad and pencil.

Deep down in my sub-conscious I knew that I had been hiding my 'affliction' in the isolation of the outback and there would come the day when I would eventually have to leave Waaree, to find my own kind – in the deaf and mute world of the big cities. It was something I'd been putting off for years. I loved the bush, the outback, working on a cattle station and the thought of trying to make my unskilled way in a city, was so alien to me that I never had the courage to make the break and leave. Soon I would have no choice.

My voice is my hands and I needed to be able to talk to people, to tell them what I'm saying and feeling.

*

Jack was to pick up Mary at Cloncurry and take her to Rooeena. She'd been away three weeks and Jacks preparation for his trip to airport had had him primping and preening like schoolboy on his first date!

As I drove him to the Cessna, I signed,

"I think you've overdone the cologne."

A worried, "do you think so?"

Then he saw my grin.

"Aw piss off, "and gave me a friendly thump on my arm.

* * *

When Charlie radioed from Rooeena that Mary had finished Betty's packing, Jack couldn't wait to get in the truck to pick her and Blackie up. On this kind of trip Jack and I filled in the time with rugby songs, bush ballads, talk and companionable silences. We shared the driving and when I was the passenger I tried to watch the passing landscape with the eyes of a painter and get the 'feel' of the outback, so that when I was in my room I could maybe transfer that 'feel' with colours onto the scene I was painting.

* * *

Chapter 3

Jack, with the nose lead in front, was speaking quietly to Blackie trying to coax him with soft words up the ramp and on to the back of the truck. Mary, Charlie and myself were doing our bit and shoving from behind. The ton or so of recalcitrant beef refused to move and all the soft words, pushing, pulling and heaving was to no avail.

We all stood back exhausted by our efforts and it was old Charlie Wright who then did something we all should have thought of in the first place. He simply went off and returned with an armful of lucerne, some hay and a bucket of oats. He gave Blackie a sample as he went past him, then on up the ramp, put the cocktail of goodies near the back of the cabin of the truck, and Blackie chewing contentedly quietly lumbered up after him, so easy.

The front seat of the truck was a bit of a squash for three adults. I don't think Jack and Mary minded, the closer the better as far as they were concerned, but I felt out of it, as I couldn't 'talk' to Jack who was busy driving.

When Jack and I were using the truck we'd filled in the time with songs, mainly rugby or old bush ballads that we could remember, Jack singing the lyrics and me whistling along supplying the music! Now Mary led the singing with the up to date songs of the city. I didn't have a clue and Jack wasn't much better.

He should have been paying more attention to the dirt road we were on, as there were dips and ruts to be avoided, but he was distracted by the closeness of Mary who was teaching him the lyrics of a song, when we hit a deep rut head on. There was god-almighty bang from underneath the truck that soon lost traction and slowly ground to a halt. I jumped out and crawled underneath to have a look. The bloody axle was broken! Now what do we do! Miles from anywhere with a big black bull bellowing his head off in the back of the now stationery truck.

I led Blackie down the ramp off the truck, gave him a drink, surrounded him with his goodies and tied him to a tree – he was happy.

I whistled to get Jack's attention and signed, *"Now what do you want to do?"*

"Well, it's getting towards evening, so I reckon we should make an early camp here and then head off at first light. We'll just follow the road on foot and get out from this dense bush that we're in. Charlie will be calling Waaree every half hour and if we haven't made contact after four hours he'll call the Police who'll send out a search plane. They know we're on this road 'cos it's the only one, so I don't think there's anything to worry about."

"Sounds good," I signed, *"I don't think we should light a fire, too much dry scrub around, only needs a spark and we could be in trouble."*

We made a meal of cold beef sandwiches, washed down by water, which seems to be the staple diet of meals on the go. A good piece of beef, some pepper and salt, between two slabs on buttered bread takes some beating. I should know. I've been eating them for the past twenty years.

23

Another beef sandwich for breakfast, then with Jack and I carrying water bags and with Jack and Mary up front leading a rather reluctant Blackie we started walking. We needed to get into the open, out from underneath the overhanging trees, so that we could be seen from the air.

It was all rather pleasant actually, strolling along at Blackie's pace, the sunlight filtering through the trees, the sounds of the bush waking up, birds calling to each other, kangaroos, alert, watching from a distance. I loved the bush – this part of the day – before the heat settled like blanket over the outback and had you thinking of cold schooners and shady trees.

I watched the body language of Jack and Mary, up ahead, either side of Blackie and I shook my head in wonderment at the change that was taking place around me. I didn't realize Jack was such a tactile person, as he seem to be reaching out to Mary all the time, touching her shoulder to illustrate a point he was trying to make and she in turn would catch his hand in flight, hold it for a moment, then return it to him with a smile.

Sadly I knew my time at Waaree was quickly coming to an end. I needed to get a life and let Jack and Mary get on with theirs.

I caught the first little whiff of smoke. I stopped and looked behind me. I stared hard back along the road. Nothing at first and then faintly in the distance, smoke, a bush fire and traveling fast, leaping from treetop to treetop, crossing the road and with the present wind, moving much faster than we could walk or run.

I whistled to Jack, and the insistent tone of the whistle had him turning quickly.

I pointed behind me and he saw the smoke.

"Bloody hell," he said. "A bush fire, that's all we need. We can only stick to the road and hope for a wind change."

I gave Blackie a whack on the rump with my hat to get him going faster, but Blackie also had got the message via the smell of smoke and broke into a quick lumber with a few bellows of protest.

The wind soon brought the smoke as a traveling companion, making it difficult to breathe and at the pace we were going we wouldn't be able to keep it up much longer. Mary, a city girl, was just about exhausted and Jack, half supporting her was finding it difficult to keep up with Blackie. I let his nose lead go and went back to help Jack with Mary. Blackie deciding he wanted a change of direction did a sharp right turn and headed into a dry gully bed. Maybe he knew something, had some bovine instinct. He was a great trailbreaker and as he lumbered on we followed.

Things were really desperate now. The oxygen was being sucked out of the air and I could hardly breathe. I'd just about had it and I could see that Jack and Mary were in worse shape than me. Blackie then gave three or four bellows of what could only be described as triumph and there it was.

A small billabong already inhabited by a couple of wallabies.

Blackie went straight into the centre of the pool, which was about four feet deep and we followed. We ducked under the water to cool off and with our hats sluiced water over Blackie to do the same for him. The heat was pretty fierce now and the fire was all around us, but with three hats throwing water over Blackie and the continual ducking under the water to cool off and breathing close to the surface, we somehow survived. There was a continual hissing as burning branches landed in the pool around us which was now pretty full with a cross section of the animals of the outback, who'd called a truce for the time being and nobody was killing or biting anybody. It was like Noah's Ark – except the water was in the inside and not on the outside!

Gradually the fire passed us by, but we stayed in the pool waiting for the countryside to cool off before we ventured out. Our relief of having survived showed itself as we patted, sluiced and hugged our saviour – Blackie.

"You bloody beauty Blackie," Jack said."You saved our lives and from now on you're gunna live like a king and I'll put you with the prettiest heifers you ever did see."

"I couldn't agree more," I signed to our bovine friend, whose only reaction to my hand signals, was puzzlement – well it looked like puzzlement – but then again I wasn't sure if bulls did 'puzzlement'!

Then I heard it, the drone of an aircraft engine.

I whistled to Jack, who turned towards me. I signed, *"Aircraft coming."*

I spotted it. A Cessna, flying low, following the road we'd traveled. Soon it was circling above, a hand waving from the cockpit, they'd seen us, and then it headed back the way it'd come.

Once old Charlie Wright got the news, he'd be into one of Bill's trucks and on his way to pick us up to continue our journey with Blackie.

* * *

Back at Waaree, Blackie was already in one of the green home paddocks, getting used to the good life in his new surroundings, and Jack was preparing to fly Mary to Cloncurry on her way to Brisbane. Old Charlie Wright hadn't wasted any time. He'd refueled the truck, packed a few sandwiches, filled the water bags and had taken off and was now on the road back to Rooeena Station.

I busied myself around the homestead, doing the odd jobs

that I'd been meaning to do for months or sketching and painting from photos that I'd taken in the bush of scenes that had caught my eye. Anything to keep out of the way of Jack and Mary as the experience of the bushfire, and their brush with death, had somehow speeded up their romance and now they were more tactile than ever.

Although we had separate rooms, I felt l was intruding on their privacy and for the first time – like a hired hand. But moving out of the main house and into the bunkhouse would only embarrass Mary so I stayed put. Jack I don't think was aware of my problems as he only had eyes for Mary. Sometimes my silent gestures went 'unheard' and I couldn't very well whistle every time I wanted to say something.

Normally after a meal, when there was only the two of us, Jack and I would sit out on the verandah to have a cigarette and a bit of a yarn. The filtered light from the kitchen was enough for Jack to see my signs as I always sat near him and slightly in front, so that even in the dim light it was easy for him to read me.

Now Mary was in that position and I was really behind the eight ball. Although they included me in their conversation, any reply I made was hard to see in the half-light and Jack, a couple of times, had to ask me to repeat it. Mary didn't know what I was saying so Jack had to interpret it for her. It made me more aware of my muteness, which now became the centre of attention and an embarrassment to me. I felt I should apologise for it. But even that was too complicated, so in the end I stood up and signed that I was off to bed.

Mary rose quickly and came over to me.

"Reg, I can't thank you enough for your help on the road. Without you I wouldn't have made it."

And she reached up, kissed me on the cheek and hugged me.

I nodded and moved away.

*

Much later there was a tap tap on the door, that broke into my reverie of shady willow trees and fish that couldn't wait to be hooked – all in the idyllic land that I was creating in my painting on the easel.

I knew it was Jack's knock. I put down my paintbrush and looked up as he entered.

He wandered over and studied my painting for some time.

"You know you're bloody good at this – bloody good," he said shaking his head."You should do something about it, get people to have a look a them," indicating with his head the pile of finished landscapes in the corner of the room.

I waved away the idea as crazy.

"Anyway, there's been a change of plans," he said, settling himself on the edge of my bed and giving me a sheepish grin."You must by now have a pretty good idea that I'm very keen on Mary."

I laughingly signed, *"Yeah – a pretty good idea."*

"So I'm going to stay a few days in Brisbane, to get to know her. To be honest, I'm frightened to let her out of my sight in case I lose her. I want to marry her Reg, I just hope she feels the same way about me."

I signed, *"She's a nice girl Jack. You'd make a great couple. I wish you luck."*

"Thanks. I don't know how long I'll be away it all depends on how things go – a few days, a week maybe, who knows. Anyway you'll be in charge. I'll talk to the stockmen about the cattle and get Peter to report to you at the end of each day, but, as Charlie's away at Rooeena, I want you around the homestead in case I need to get in touch. Same routine, same signals."

"Okay, no problem." I signed.

He nodded."Good," studied me for a moment, as if he wanted to say something else, but then hesitated and came out with,

"Well, that's about it."

He rose and thoughtfully, looked at the half finished painting, gave a "Mmmm" and left.

Jack and I had a simple system on communication when he was away. It consisted of morse code and taps on the radio microphone. A morse code key had been installed about twenty years ago and I had laboriously learnt the code and after months of practice, how to use the key. In an emergency I tapped out a message that went via the radio to the post office in Cloncurry, who then got in touch with the police or Flying Doctor.

When I got a call on the radio, I tapped the microphone to let the caller know that I was there and then more tapping to let them know that I had received and understood the message. Simple.

*

Next morning I drove Jack and Mary with their baggage down to the Cessna and while Jack did his pre-flight check I loaded the bags into the back of the aircraft.

I had the feeling that this was the last time I'd be seeing Jack off on one of his flights. I don't know what it was, but everything that I was doing now seemed to be for the last time! It was as if the final decision had already been made for me to leave Waaree.

I watched them taxi down the landing strip, turn around, heard the change of pitch as the engines revved up for the take off into the wind and then they were on their way.

I waved goodbye, and only until the Cessna was just a

tiny speck in the sky did I turn away and go back to the truck.

I don't think I ever felt so alone and depressed. Maybe it was envy and feeling sorry for myself – to have what Jack had – a girl – plans of marriage – a future – and my mother telling me that being dumb didn't matter – what a terrible fucking lie to tell a kid!

*

When I arrived at the aborigine's quarters, Lily was sitting under a tree near one of the huts, surrounded by about six or seven kids and mothers. She saw me coming, said something to her audience, who upped and scattered like chaff in the wind.

She raised her hand in welcome, calling out,

"G'day Reggie, you big stranger now. Hope you paint still?"

I nodded and reached out to shake her hand, which she took and pulled me into a motherly hug against her ample bosom.

When I managed to extricate myself I wrote on the notepad I carried and handed it to her.

"While the boss is away I want to plenty clean big house."

Liliy had been taught to read and write at the Mission school when she was a child and writing notes was my way of communicating with her.

Lily looked at the note and nodded.

"Good. I get girls and we make big house plenty clean for boss and new Mrs."

Nothing much, it seemed, went on around the homestead that Lily didn't know about.

I wrote.

"Start today?"

"Okay. We start today."

The women arrived *en masse* with kids, buckets, brooms and mops. They filled the house with noise, clatter and laughter. Lily marched around like a General, giving orders, checking and organizing. She convinced the kids that it was some sort of game and soon had them cleaning up the yard and gardens.

The best thing for me to do was to keep out of the way, so I collected my painting gear, and a painting that I'd just started and locked myself in the radio room and tried to ignore what was going on outside. This eventually wasn't very hard to do, because I was soon lost in the world of colour as I tried to bring to life the idyllic scene that I'd sketched on the stretched canvas.

The beauty about painting and I imagine with writing is that you can escape into a world of your own creation and make it as you wish. In my landscape world I could always talk. Sometimes I would actually try, and using my lips, teeth and tongue, silently mouth a word I thought it should sound like. I'd heard words all my life, but I didn't know *how* to talk, how to *form* a word and being mute I couldn't tell if I'd ever got it anywhere near right. When I was a kid I'd feel sorry for myself and cry with frustration but I was in my early twenties before I chastised myself as being a bloody fool and stopped bawling.

I was mute in real life – but when I fantasized in my paintings I could talk – I'll have to settle for that.

The noise outside had stopped. I opened the door and was met by Lily.

"We finish," she said."plenty clean now." She looked over my shoulder, pushed me aside and went into the radio room.

She propped up my painting against the microphone and stood back to look at it.

Her opinion I valued – after all it was she who'd taught me.

She turned to me and enveloped me in one of her motherly hugs.

"You bloody good painter now Reggie – bloody good."

Over the years I had learnt that when lily used the word 'bloody' she was paying you the highest of compliments.

I nodded and hugged her back.

I wrote her a note.

'We'll go to the stock room now and get some baccy and stores.'

"Good" and she thumped me on the arm, "you bloody good man."

* * *

Peter, the head stockmen, reported nightly to me with a tally of calves mustered and branded. I knew by the numbers that they were doing a good days work and that things were running smoothly in Jack's absence.

Lily sent a couple of the girls up daily to keep an eye on the house and to make sure I wasn't making a mess of it!

I hadn't heard from Jack and I wondered how his 'courting' was going. If their body language had been anything to go by when they were here, they were probably shacked up by now.

That'd be nice – sex on tap – it sure as hell beats this celibate life that I'm bloody well leading!

The squawk from the radio interrupted my thoughts on sex, or the lack of it, and Jack's voice filled the radio room.'

"Reg are you there?"

I quickly moved in from the verandah and tapped the microphone.

"Great." he replied."Mary and I are married Reg. How about that. We decided we'd do it now while we were in Brisbane. We couldn't be happier and were coming home. We'll be there tomorrow some time, okay."

I gave a quick rat tat tat on the mike.

"We're both looking forward to seeing you Reg, over and out."

In a daze I wandered back outside onto the verandah.

I was stunned and hurt that I hadn't been asked to be best man. But then I realized I couldn't have gone anyway, as I was looking after Waaree while he was in Brisbane doing his courting!

I absent-mindedly picked up the painting I'd been framing and continued working on it. I now knew what I would do with it – I'd leave it as a wedding present for Jack and Mary.

A newly married couple would want the house to themselves!

I stared off into the distance my mind in turmoil.

I could move into the head stockman's house with Charlie Wright for the time being – then what?

Leave Waaree!

I'd been here all my life – I knew no other life.

I was distracted by two of the young aborigine mothers, Betty and Lana mounting the verandah steps for their daily visit of cleaning or checking up to see if I'd made a mess or not. I quickly wrote a note for Lily and handed it to Betty who read the note, squealed with excitement and they both took off back to where they came from.

I sat in my room for some time, thoughtful, bewildered and imprinting in my minds eye, this room that had been my home for so long. Slowly I took some of the pictures off the walls and put them with the large stack of landscapes that were piled in one corner of the room – over the years I'd kept all the paintings that had been given the nod of approval by Lily – *I hoarded things like a squirrel.* I started to pack my belongings.

*

I stood back and studied my painting. It was now above the fireplace in the sitting room. I thought it looked okay, as it was a cool refreshing change from the framed print of a branding and castrating scene showing pain, dust, heat and sweat, that'd been there before

* * *

Chapter 4

I watched the Cessna taxi towards the hanger and already Jack's hand was outside the cockpit waving.

I enveloped my friend and mate in a congratulatory hug as he stepped out of the plane. I was a little more circumspect with Mary and gave her a chaste kiss on her cheek.

Greetings over, we unloaded the luggage and for a stockman who always traveled light, Jack had really gone to town and brought half of Brisbane back with him! Already married life was changing him!

The welcoming spread I'd prepared wasn't the greatest. Firstly I'd made sure there was plenty of cold beer. The rest was a mixture. A tin of peanuts I'd found in the back of a cupboard, a jar of pickled onions, a damper lily had sent up and of course some sliced beef – which all together, I thought, was pretty good for a male dominated outback cattle station.

After our thirst had been slaked I stood up and whistled for attention.

I signed, and for Mary's benefit, Jack watched my hands and spoke my silent words.

"Reg says, that he hoped Mary knew what she was doing in taking on a barely house trained cattleman like me. But he feels sure that I would eventually come up to scratch and be a good husband – a little rough around the edges maybe – but a good husband! And he would now like to propose a toast to us, the newly weds.

"To Jack and Mary, my congratulations and best wishes for a long and happy life together. We make a handsome couple and may all our children be as good looking as we are, and he feels proud to know us."

I raised my can of 4X and silently toasted Jack and Mary.

Mary came over and gave me a hug and a kiss and I got the same from Jack – minus the kiss.

I held up my hand. In the distance I heard the sound of chanting and the beating of sticks on small hollow logs.

I moved to the edge of the verandah and beckoned to Mary and Jack to follow. All the aborigine women and children were in a shuffling line heading towards the house. They gathered at the bottom of the steps and formed a circle. They then started to do some sort of corroboree dance led by Lily, who had a branch of leaves in her hand and as she circled doing her dance she would sweep the branch in the dust and wave it towards the house.

Jack whispered,

"She's chasing away all the evil spirits that might be here and making sure that it's a good place for the new missus to live in."

The corroboree lasted for some time and in the end Lily raised her branch to the sky and shook it vigorously. The chanting stopped and the lubras turned to go, but Lily remained standing looking up at me. I knew what she wanted. I took a cold 4X down to her. She smiled her thanks, turned and followed the young mothers home.

I had a couple more beers and I think we were all finding the routine of Jack having to interpret and relay my signing to Mary a bit exhausting. I was never more aware of my inability to talk and for the first time apologized for it.

Jack read my signing and for a moment didn't say anything.

"What did Reg say Jack?" asked Mary.

He very quietly replied.

"He said he's sorry he cannot talk."

And what now could Mary say! That it was 'okay to be dumb – that it didn't matter – that she understood'! Nobody could understand not being able to talk, unless they bloody well *couldn't* talk.

I should never have put her in this position. The only thing left for her to do was to sympathize with me and that I'd hate. I'd been given enough maternal sympathy during my life already – I didn't need anymore.

The atmosphere was now uncomfortable. Trust me to put a damper on things.

I could hear the jingle of harness and horses in the distance – it was the stockmen returning after a day with the cattle.

I signed, *"I'll go and talk Peter and see if there's any problems. I'll see you both tomorrow."*

Jack didn't try to stop me, but I could feel his eyes watching me, as I moved off the verandah and head towards to where the aborigines were unsaddling their horses.

* * *

The head stockman's quarters, was a small tinned roofed, two bed-roomed house, with a sitting room, kitchen and bathroom. I'd moved all my gear from the main house into it, earlier on, before Jack and Mary's arrival. It was just as well that I didn't have much in the clothing line, as my pile of finished paintings and equipment took up most of the space in the room. I had thrown a sheet over the lot to keep out the dust and a chest of drawers and a wardrobe had easily swallowed my clothes. For the moment the room was neat and tidy!

The beef casserole had been in the oven for hours. I'd raided Charlie's vegetable patch and had come away with some potatoes, carrots, onions and a cabbage. All of which went into the pot that was now giving off hungry making aromas. If I didn't make a pig of myself it should last me a week.

The meal was over, the washing up done and now what!

Normally, in the big house, Jack and I would go out on the verandah for a bit of a yarn and maybe a cup of tea. But that was history now – all in the past.

I switched on the radio, listened to the news – that was too depressing, so I changed stations and got a young girl screaming her head off in what was supposed to be a song contest. I tried to make sense of the lyrics but gave up in the end and switched her off.

I mooched over to the front door and looked out. The lights were on in the big house – they were probably still having their meal – I wonder who did the cooking – wonder what they had?

Too early to go to bed and as Lily had always said *"if yer feelin' blue and sad, get busy – work – do anything to stop sad thoughts – paint – then live and dream in pretty little house you always draw."*

I set up the easel in the bedroom and put the painting I'd already started on it. I then hunted around for the box of photographs I'd taken of landscapes over the years.

Eventually I found the box and the photo I wanted and sat in a chair in front of the painting to study them both

And as I studied and lost myself in the scene that I was painting, I could still hear Lily's voice from when I was a kid.

"If you paint the bush Reggie, you must know and love it, like I do. Think like us aborigines, that way you will get the 'feel' of the trees, rivers, rocks, waterfalls and all you see around you" waving her digging stick in an encompassing sweep that took in the landscape and sky.*"Then you will know what colours to mix to give them a life that has energy and love."*

"You Christians live by that book you call the Bible. We live by this," again she pointed to the surrounding bush and sky.*"This our Bible. We got stories, sacred places, dreamtime, but it is love for the bush and the animals we hunt that let us live in land like this.'*

"We are soft now. We not hunt and our tribe not go from hunting ground to hunting ground anymore. We stay in same place and live with white man and his Bible."

I got out my palette and paints and began to mix the colours.

* * *

A semblance of normalcy pervaded over the station, as I saddled up with the stockmen at dawn, for a day of branding, castrating and dehorning calves. We'd spend the morning mustering the cows and calves into the holding paddocks before branding etc in the cooler part of the day.

Jack hadn't put in an appearance as yet – could you blame him – he was still on his honeymoon!

My night had been a mixture of success and frustration. I was pleased with what I had painted, but had tossed and turned in my bed for hours, before I finally made the decision to leave Waaree as soon as possible.

I would go to Brisbane and learn the sign language of the deaf and mute and get myself a life.

Already I was having second thoughts and as the sun came up so had the doubts – I must tell Jack and go before I lose my resolve and change my mind.

It had been a hot, tiring and dusty day with the cattle, but in a perverse sort of way I enjoyed it. Maybe it was because at the back of my mind everything I was doing now, I thought, was for the last time. Yes, I would miss it, but the inner excitement in my gut of what the future held overtook the cosy life at Waaree and opened up a vista of my own making, similar to the fantasy life that I often lived in my paintings.

I whistled sharply to let them know that I was visiting.

They were both sitting on the verandah or should I say curled up together on the settee when I arrived – *a warm enviable domestic scene.*

Jack greeted me with his standard welcome.

"Reg come and sit down and have a beer."

I nodded my thanks and moved one of the deck chairs into the light so he could see my hands.

Jack returned from the kitchen with a cold beer.

Mary was the first to speak.

"Reg, I must thank you for that lovely painting above the mantle piece in the sitting room. I think it's one of the best landscapes I've ever seen. I don't know, but, it seems to be alive. I swear that I thought I saw the river move or flow for a second. I know it sounds crazy but I did. I wish you had signed it."

"But I did." I signed.

Jack repeated the answer to Mary.

"You did. Where?"

I got up and beckoned them to follow me.

I signed to Jack.

"It's in the right hand corner."

They both peered at the painting for some time.

Mary said," I don't see any writing on ..." and then excitingly," wait a bit, yes, now I see it ... it's part of the painting. How clever ... look Jack, there, see, it looks like twigs and grass."

"Well I'll be buggered." Was all he said when he finally saw it.

It was my bit of fun as I finished each painting.

Back on the verandah I sipped my beer and mentally rehearsed what I would say to Jack about my leaving.

He gave me the opening I needed.

"Your looking very thoughtful Reg, do you have a problem?"

I nodded and signed.

"Yes. I'm going to leave Waaree and go to Brisbane to learn the deaf and mute language that's used in Australia." I paused and waited for his reaction – his face showed nothing so I ploughed on,

"I need to be able to meet and talk to people. I can't go on anymore leading this celibate life – I'm not a monk. I would like to have a wife and family – to have a normal life and I can't get that by staying here."

Jack didn't seem surprised by my news.

"I knew this would happen one day Reg and you'll be sorely missed. You've been like brother to me mate, but I

41

understand. Just you remember, there's always a job at Waaree. Anyway you're like part of the family and If you do get married, maybe you'd like to come back here. There's the head stockman's house and you'll be always welcome. Nobody knows more about cattle than you do."

"Thanks," I signed, *"But I'll see how I go first. I don't know how I'm going to earn a living, as the only thing I know about is the cattle business."*

"When do you want to go?"

"As soon as possible – in the next few days – whenever you can fly me to Cloncurry. I'll take the paintings I have. Lily always said I could maybe sell them if I ever run out of money. But I shouldn't think they're worth much."

"You've got quite a bit of holiday money owing to you. I'll sort it out and pay it into your bank account. I'll fly you out whenever you're ready."

When I told Lily I was leaving, she took from around her neck a necklace that was made with some kind of cord and had a shiny stone attached to it. She put it around my neck.

"You wear this all the time, it will look after you – you like son to me." She then gave me one of her motherly hugs.

"Keep painting Reggie and remember what I tell you about the bush. You come back some time see me. Bring missus with you. Now go."

* * *

Chapter 5

I handed the note to the girl in the Qantas ticket office. She read it looked up at me, smiled, tapped a few keys on her computer and the printer next to her whirred into action and shot out a ticket.

"That will be $220."

I counted out the money and gave it to her. She handed me the ticket.

"Have a good flight sir."

I nodded my thanks and turned to where Jack and Mary were waiting with my luggage.

"OK?" Jack asked.

I nodded.

"Right," he said, "let's take this lot over to the excess baggage check-in." Indicating a trolley laden with all my luggage and painting gear.

I was finally left with a small carry-on bag and the company of Jack and Mary. We wandered over to the entrance for boarding.

"This is it." I signed.

Mary made the first move and gave me a hug and kissed me on the cheek.

"Goodbye Reg. Good luck and keep in touch."

I nodded and turned to Jack, holding out my hand.

"Goodbye Reg," he said, taking my hand and pulling me into one of his manly hugs."Don't forget, any problems let us know. Take care."

I turned and left before I started to bawl – *I hate long goodbyes.*

The uneventful flight took no time at all and I soon found myself by the baggage carousal in Brisbane with two trolleys loaded with luggage and paintings. I saw where the customs and exit signs were and headed with some difficulty in that direction.

My first real taste of life in the big city was a long taxi queue with a busy uniformed gentleman in charge who waved in taxis as they were needed.

When I was next in line he asked, "where to?"

I handed him the note that I'd already written.

He frowned, read it, and then went into action. He frantically waved in a station wagon Taxi with a roof rack, said something to the driver, who hopped out and started loading my luggage and paintings in and on top of his cab. That done he then quickly opened the cab door and was attempting to help me in. At the same time, I was also getting a pat on the back from the uniform, who said, "he'll see yer right mate." Maybe he thought that being mute was like being an invalid! Anyway I managed to smile, nod my thanks and got a smiling salute back!

"The YMCA, is that right?" the taxi driver asked.

I nodded a "yes "and got a thumbs-up in reply. We were now both using the sign language!

The YMCA was a three-storied grey building with large gold YMCA lettering above the entrance. It was next door to 'Carlo's' a fast food café.

I handed a note to the taxi driver, which he read.

"Right. Now, if they haven't got a room, I know a place," he said.

I gave him a thumbs-up, got out of the cab and entered the building.

A young man was in attendance at the counter in 'reception'. The wall behind him was covered with pigeonholes with keys dangling out of them. He looked up as I entered.

"Good afternoon sir. How may I help you?"

I handed him a note.

He didn't open it for a moment but nervously kept looking at me. Maybe he thought that this was some kind of hold-up and the note said, *"This is a stick-up, open the safe, I've got a gun pointing at you."*

I gave him an encouraging smile and nodded towards the note.

He then read what I had written and a dawning look of relief came over his face as he studied me for a moment – *was he checking to see if I was really mute!* Then the young man, whose name was 'Fred', according to the name tag on his shirt, shook himself back to earth and said,

"Yes sir, we do have a room and your painting gear can be stored in the basement with the left-luggage."

I nodded a "thank you "and indicated, by using my homemade sign language that I'd be back with the luggage.

45

"Understood sir."

The taxi driver helped with the baggage and the three of us took my landscapes down into the basement storeroom, and as I paid and tipped my very helpful driver, he said, handing me his card.

"My name's Mick Maloney. If you ever want a cab mate, give me a bell. I'll be glad to help."

I shook his hand, smiled my thanks and he left.

"Now sir, if you'd like to fill out this for me," said Fred the receptionist, indicating a 'signing in' form on the counter.

After all the regulations had been taken care of, he handed me a key with the number 26 on a disk attached to it.

"I suggest you leave it at the desk here when you go out sir. You'd be surprised as to how many keys get lost."

I nodded that I understood.

I caught the lift to the second floor and by the time I found my room I was stuffed. All the traveling, nodding, smiling, thumbs up and signing was as tiring as a long day in the saddle.

The room was neat and tidy. It had a large single bed with a bedside table, a wardrobe with a full-length mirror, table and chairs, an armchair and a cupboard containing a small refrigerator and a tray with an electric kettle and teabags etc. There was a door that opened to a small bathroom with shower and toilet.

A print of a landscape on one of the walls was the only decoration. I studied it for some time. Mine were better.

I put the kettle on for a cup of tea and flopped on the bed while I waited for it to boil. *This would now be my new way of 'boiling the billy'.*

* * *

Fred was on duty next morning when I arrived at reception and was all smiles as he greeted me.

"Good morning sir. I hope you slept well?"

I smilingly nodded and handed him a note. He read it and pointed to a large board, which had slots for pamphlets, brochures and maps that was on a wall on my side of the counter.

"You'll find maps of Brisbane and what you need over there, sir."

Eventually, armed with a street map of Brisbane, I set out to find The Deaf Institute.

Walking the streets of Brisbane, on my way to the bus station, was an education in itself on the behavioural habits of the pedestrians who walked its pavements. *Why was everybody in such a hurry!* They all had a determined look on their faces as they rushed from one set of lights to another. Waiting for the green to cross the road was the only thing that slowed them down.

435 Compton Road was an unprepossessing building on one level. It was a drab brown in colour and the thought of being ensconced in this dreary building, didn't do anything for my morale. Anyone coming to this uninviting place for tuition, already had enough problems on arrival.

I opened the entrance door and was struck by the silence. Two groups of people were animatedly talking and laughing, their hands fluttering like the wings of birds as they nodded, pointed, waved and gesticulated at a speed that I found mind boggling and nervous making.

The décor inside was in complete contrast to the outside. Whites and yellows prevailed and vases of colourful flowers stood on the occasional tables, giving a cheerful ambience to the whole of the reception area.

I walked over to the girl behind the counter and handed her a note I'd written back at the YMCA.

After reading what I had written, she regarded me for some time before she spoke.

"Mr Brady, we don't often get students your age for the beginners class, but we never turn people away. Leave this with me for the moment. Meanwhile I'll get you to fill out this application form. Also I'll give you a letter to Centrelink. You'll be entitled to a grant to offset your tuition fees here. I'd sit over at one of the tables, much more comfortable."

I nodded my thanks, collected the form and a pen and moved away.

By the time I returned the completed form I felt like a book that had been well and truly read. My soul had been laid bare and there was nothing left to disclose.

I carried a folder with the name Joanne Newton on the outside to room number 4. I tentatively knocked, gently opened the door and stepped inside.

The person in charge of the class was a slim brunette, about 5'6", with a no nonsense hair cut that shone and floated around her head like a halo and when she laughed she threw back her head and shook it like a puppy. It was a husky, infectious throaty noise that showed her very white teeth and I could see it very much pleased the class and the person who had made her laugh. Well why shouldn't it! She made a very attractive friendly picture standing there on the dais with her hands raised and wiggling her fingers in a sign of clapping

She looked over in my direction and signed to the class in front of her." Now I have to meet a new student, I'll see you all next week." and indicated for me to come forward. The class as they filed out looked me over, some smiled and nodded, some signing "hello" – I think. Their hand movements were so quick it was difficult for me to read them.

Up close Joanne Newton was, to quote that much used description, *'knock down bloody gorgeous'*. Well for me anyway. Her smiling brown eyes swept over me like a warm breeze and the smile that reached her mouth exposed a dimple in her right cheek. Her whole demeanour said ' welcome.'

All I could do was to stand there like a stunned mullet with a dopey grin on my face.

Jo Newton was pleased with what she saw – he looked like the 'Marlborough Man'. He was a tall, lean, brown, stockman, complete with, would you believe it – giggling to herself – a lazy crooked smile.

I handed her the folder, which she perused for a couple of minutes.

"So, you can hear?" she said.

I was surprised that she could talk. I nodded my head.

"Well that makes things easier. My name is Joanne Newton. I'm to be your teacher and everybody calls me Jo. May I call you Reg?"

I nodded.

Just then there was a knock on the door and a head poked itself around the now open doorway.

"Jo, would you see me before you go."

"Right Joan," she replied.

Again I was surprised!

She could hear and talk! Joanne Newton was normal and this put her in a category that was beyond my reach. The disappointment I felt suddenly was a shock to me. *That I should feel this way because some one I had just met was neither mute nor deaf – did I want all people to be like me? I* shook my head in bewilderment.

She was thoughtfully watching me.

"Are you all right Reg?"

I nodded.

"Reg, can you do anything else apart from nodding. Can you speak with your hands, do sign language?"

"A bit." I signed.

She watched me with an enquiring look!

"Would you like to elaborate?"

Suddenly I was all thumbs and fingers in hands that now became very clumsy as I tried to tell her that I had taught myself, with the help from School of the Air and that Jack my boss was the only one that could really understand me.

And my new teacher stood there with a smile on her face watching me struggle.

I'll call him my 'Marlborough Man' she thought watching Reg Brady give his own homemade version of a sign language that was a bit of everything. She got the gist of what he was saying but was distracted by the animation on his face as he mimed the words that he was trying to convey. Such a handsome man and being mute didn't distract from his attractiveness one little bit. She shook her head. Oh for God's sake Jo Newton do concentrate on being a teacher and stop perving on your new student.

She held up her hand.

"Whoa that's enough."

I gratefully stopped.

"Well Reg, you have a lovely private sign language that I think only you and your friend Jack would understand, but I'm afraid that it doesn't conform to 'Auslan', the universal sign language of Australia. Which means that you'll have to unlearn a lot of it. It'll make things a little more difficult for you but I'm sure," here she paused and gave him the benefit of an encouraging smile, "you can cope with that."

With her as my teacher I felt I could cope with anything!

"While you are here, you will learn to finger spell, develop a vocabulary of basic conversational signs and how to structure a sentence. Meanwhile," she returned to her desk and gathered some papers."I want you to study these over the weekend." And she handed me some foolscap pages with sketches of the sign language used in Australia.

"I'm starting a new class of five students on Monday, the youngest is 6 and the eldest is 7. They are all deaf and mute. Very rarely do we get mature students such as you. As you can hear, they would only slow you down, but I would ask you to sit in on the their classes to begin with. It will give you an idea of how we work and the difficulty of making contact with small children that can neither hear nor speak. I only work with them for three hours as we have found that their concentration only lasts about that length of time. Then in the afternoon I will work with you. How does that sound to you?"

"Fine," I roughly signed, *"and if the kids don't mind an old man being with them, I don't mind."*

"Splendid." *She suddenly had a picture of her Marlborough Man with five small children sitting on his lap.*

"What's so funny?" I signed.

"I just had this lovely picture of er ... no no it was nothing ..."and to hide her confusion quickly returned to her desk.

"Do you want to ask me any questions Reg?

Yes I thought, I'd like to ask you out, but that was a big no no and would have to remain as one of my fantasies where Joanne Newton, my teacher, was concerned.

"No, I'll be right." I signed.

I paused and shuffled the papers she'd given me.

"I'll get off to my room now," I clumsily signed, *"and start learning these new signs. I'll see you Monday Jo, bye,"* and I made for the door.

Jo Newton looked around the empty classroom – *"off to his room."* It sounded so lonely. She sighed and started to collect her things.

On my way out I stopped at the reception desk and wrote a note that I handed to the receptionist.

"Yes, I have the cards of a couple of boarding houses that have taken students from here. They do breakfast and dinner and I understand are quite reasonable. They're both in Compton Road, which will be very handy to the school, "she said, producing two cards and handing them to me.

I smilingly signed a, *"thank you,"* and left.

* * *

Chapter 6

Monday morning, and I was up early to do some shopping. It was my first day at school and I needed to have the right gear. I located an 'Office-works' and by the time I left that establishment, I had, as always, my sketch-pad and pencils, plus a school bag, notebooks, erasers and various other things that the young lady behind the counter thought that I might need. The only thing missing it seemed to me was ' an apple for the teacher'

I'd spent the whole weekend practicing signing the alphabet in front of the mirror until I'd got it right. Some of the letters I already knew so it wasn't all that difficult. Dexterity and speed was another matter, but I did put in the hard yards and fuelled by Carlo's junk food from next door managed to survive without a heart attack!

Five small children were sitting in chairs grouped together in the front of the classroom, Jo was behind her desk busy with papers, and as I entered they looked up at me with the wide-eyed look of rabbits suddenly caught in the headlights of a car. I tried to smile and wave a hand in an attempt to say 'hello' but I couldn't get past the empty lost look in their eyes as they silently watched me. I stood rooted to the spot – *I can't take this I thought – cattle I can handle – but small helpless children, that were isolated by their afflictions to a world of complete silence was beyond my capabilities. I knew what it was like to be mute, but these poor kids were deaf and mute!*

"Good morning Reg," snapped me back to reality and I quickly signed a greeting to Jo.

"Are you alright?" she enquired.

I nodded.

"Then come and meet your new class mates."

I moved over to the group of children as Jo came around from her desk.

She moved in among the children, like a hen with her chicks, pinning a nametag on them as she did so. I could see them visibly relax as she made contact.

"Reg I want you to stand in front of each child to be introduced. I will articulate and enunciate their name and yours so that they can watch my lips, teeth and tongue and imitate me. I will do it several times."

The first little girl that I stood in front of had a name tag on her that said 'My name is Amanda and I am 5 years old'. Jo stood by my side. She pointed to the small girl while saying "Amanda" then to her own mouth, indicating for her to watch as she repeated the name.

Interest showed in Amanda eyes and she tried to imitate Jo's slow enunciation of the word, gaining more confidence as she did so and slowly after several attempts a slight smile began to form on her lips and a look of wonderment began to effuse her features as she pressed her tiny hand on her chest and mouthed 'Amanda'. Jo nodded her head and clapped her hands and the little girl's smile spread wider and became a laugh as she kept mouthing 'Amanda' with her hand pointing to her chest at the same time.

Jo turned and pointed to me."Reg" she articulated, and Amanda, bless her, cottoned on right away and tried mouthing 'Reg' while pointing at me. Soon she was pointing and mouthing both names and practically jumping out of her skin with excitement.

"Put out your hand Reg as in a handshake and smile."

This I did and Amanda looked at it for a moment, then shyly put out her small hand, which I took in mine and gave it a gentle squeeze and a bit of a shake. She did the same, but it wasn't enough for her now and she laughingly pumped my hand as if I was a long lost friend.

Jo was watching us both with a smile of satisfaction on her face that said she had been amply repaid for her infinite patience and sympathy in imparting what knowledge she had to this little girl.

I surreptitiously brushed away a threatening tear that was on the verge of getting out of control.

After the same routine was carried out with John, Luke, Dorothy and Carol, I was wrung out like a dishcloth. The satisfaction that I felt, as I watched the children now intermingling, pointing, mouthing, laughing and behaving like normal children, made me thankful that I had been part of the process.

"Thanks for your help Reg. You being here made it so much easier."

I shrugged away the compliment and signed,

"You were great."

"All in a days work."

"That I don't believe."

I watched the kids for a moment and then signed,

"I think I'm in love."

"Amanda?"

I nodded.

"Big softie," she said, as the first of the parents came though the door to collect their offspring.

* * *

The session with the kids had taken three hours. It was now just after 12 noon.

I had two hours to fill in before my lesson with Jo.

Leading off from the reception area there was a rest room/kitchen for students. It had an electric kettle, toaster, a small fridge, cutlery, cup, saucers mugs etc.

I put the kettle on and delved into my school bag for the two cheese sandwiches from Carlos and a tea bag that I'd taken from my room.

I idly picked up my sketchpad and began to draw.

I sensed somebody was standing behind me and looking over my shoulder. I started to close my book, but a hand touching my arm stopped me, and Jo's voice said,

"Please Reg, don't shut it. Let me look, please."

The time now was 1.55. I'd been sketching for nearly two hours and I still hadn't got it right. The face on the pad in front of me was that of Amanda. I had tried to recapture the look of achievement, joy and wonder that I had seen on her sweet face, when she'd mouthed the names, pointed and laughed, while making her first sudden incursion into the silent outside world.

"How beautiful," Jo whispered.

I shrugged and gave a depreciatory wave of my hand.

"Don't put yourself down Reg Brady. Learn to be gracious, and accept a compliment when it is well meant."

I was being chastised and at my age I didn't like it.

I turned and looked up at her, but any resolve I had fell by the wayside as I came under the influence her big brown eyes that were now brimming with tears.

"May I have it?" She huskily asked."I would like to use it in my classes."

At this moment I would have done anything to please this unique woman, who, earlier today had brought so much joy and hope to five little lost souls.

I carefully cut out the sketch and handed it to her.

Jo's, "Thank you Reg" brought me out in goose bumps.

Now, maybe I was reading too much into it, but it was the way she said it, that – I don't know – probably wishful thinking on my part – but I felt there was something there ... something different ... even ... sexual ... Oh for God's sake Brady don't kid yourself. Stick to the fantasy world you create on paper and leave the real world to other people. Well I can dream can't I?

I sat at the front desk in the empty classroom waiting for my first lesson in signing. I must say it felt a bit strange being the only student. But, then, I did leave it a bit late in life before starting to learn didn't I.

Jo entered the room – *do I stand or what* – I started to rise ...

"Reg it's very sweet of you, but it's not necessary for you to stand when I enter a room."

I did a confused nodding and sitting at the same time!

My big Marlborough Man looks like a small nervous boy on his first day at school she thought – how sweet! She mentally slapped herself on the wrist – now think as a teacher.

"I want you to run through the alphabet for me – concentrate on getting it right, not on speed."

I started signing. She stood in front of me. When I had finished, she said,

"Now I want you to watch me and next time you do it – at this speed."

I then watched Jo clearly and slowly sign the alphabet. Her hands were so expressive in forming each letter that I had no trouble in knowing what they were.

"When I raise my hand I want you to repeat that letter until you get it right."

I signed 'A', she raised her hand and I signed it more deliberately – she let me go on. 'B' got a pass and so did 'C'. Maybe I got a bit cocky because after that it was disaster. Finally and I think slightly hysterical I finished.

"Right. Now let's do it all again."

We did. She was a hard taskmaster but her method was paying off – I was getting better.

"Now I will do the alphabet and I want you to read what I sign and repeat it."

I nodded.

And that's how the lesson continued until Jo looked at her watch and called a halt. Two hours had gone by and I felt drained. Cattle mustering was a piece of cake compared to this.

"Reg most of the hard work is done at home. You must practice what we've done today and in that way you'll progress so much quicker. Also "returning to her desk, "I'll give you a sheet of words and signs to familiarize yourself with."

Homework already – on my first day!

She handed me a sheet of paper covered in words and signs – bloody hell, there seemed to be hundreds of them!

"Are you up to it?"

I nodded – *lost for words!*

She raised an enquiring eyebrow.

I got the message and slowly signed a Y E S.

She smiled a "Good. I'll see you tomorrow morning then," and returned to her desk.

I packed my school bag, smiled a goodbye to the top of Jo's bent head and ran headlong into a crowd of students coming in for their next lesson. A lot of silent confusion took place and I helped retrieve a couple of books that had been dropped by two of the girls in the group.

Their appraising looks and signed "thank you" didn't go un-noticed by Jo, who had looked up at their entrance. *I must keep an eye on my Marlborough Man, she thought – keep him out of the clutches of predatory females – they seemed to be everywhere!*

* * *

I made good use of the rest of the afternoon.

Armed with a letter for Centrelink and the two addresses of the Boarding houses in Compton Road. I set out first to check the boarding houses No 368 and 341 as they were within easy walking distance from the school.

No 368, was a two-storied red brick building with a big sign that said.

Harben House Full board Weekly terms.

No Vacancies.

I pressed on to No 341, which was similar to 368, except

for the sign that said,

Full board Home Cooking Family Run

This looks more promising. I knocked on the door, which eventually was opened by a bustling smiling matronly lady drying her hands on her apron. There was a smudge of flour on her cheek.

"Hello dear, can I help you?" she said.

I handed her a note.

After reading it she studied me for a few moments before speaking.

"I'll have a vacancy in weeks time, if that is suitable. What would you be wanting, full board, bed and breakfast?"

I quickly scribbled another note.

"Breakfast, a packed lunch and dinner, and you'd like to put down a deposit." she read from my note.

"You're a very business like young man aren't you."

I pulled out my wallet and handed her three one hundred dollar bills – *I was making sure I'd get the room when it became vacant.*

"Come with me Dearie and I'll give you a receipt and get you to fill out your particulars. Depending on how you want to pay, but I'll give you the weekly, fortnightly and monthly tariffs to choose from. The rooms are not serviced, so you will be responsible for your own cleaning. The sheets are changed once a week, but any laundry that's you want done is collected by the local Laundrette. My name is Sandra Wicks but everybody calls me Sandy."

By the time I'd given Sandy my particulars and did the same again at Centrelink, *several times,* I felt that everybody in Brisbane now knew that Reg Brady had hit town!

* * *

After another rushed 'heart attack' cholesterol filled meal from Carlo's I was ready to do my homework. I'd only been one day at my new school and already the amount of work was piling up, which left no time for anything else except 'swat'.

But I didn't know *how* to swat! I never 'swatted' at the cattle station. Any spare time I had was spent with Lily learning to paint.

But I did learn that morse code!

I sat in front of the mirror for one hour, and remembering what Jo had told me, repeated and practiced what I had done that day.

Then for the next two hours, I studied the list of words and signs that I'd been given, until my brain, that had never been asked to do so much in one go, called it a day and refused to remember a thing. I was getting so confused I had to stop.

I made a cup of tea. *Tea! I needed a beer – must get some in.*

The 'benchmark' for my learning was the picture of the group students I had seen that day and the easy fluent animated language of their hands as they talked and laughed. God, how long is it going to take me to get like them! Years – what a depressing thought!

* * *

Tuesday morning and I was already late for school. It was my first taste of a peak hour traffic jam in the city, and Compton Road once more had ground to a halt. We were nose to tail all the way and moving at a snails pace. It seemed to me that I was the only one on the bus that was getting agitated – maybe all these commuters were used to it!

When I opened the door of room No4 all eyes turned to

me.

Jo smiled and nodded. I did the same. Then I turned to my classmates and they made my day. Gone was the lost look of yesterday and in their place was a friendly smile of welcome. Some of them mouthing Reg and pointing at me, others putting out their little hand to be shaken, but they were all animated and connecting with each other and me.

I could have wept.

Jo, watching all this, dipped her head and got busy reading!

I scribbled a note and handed it to Jo.

"You're late for school and you've brought me a note?"

"*Sorry I'm late, traffic jam.*" she read.

I smilingly nodded.

Dear God, there's that lazy crooked smile again! Is he doing it purposely as a sort of flirting approach knowing how it affects me?

She snapped out of her reverie.

"This morning Reg I'm going to start to teach the class the alphabet. I think you'd be better occupied by studying those words and signs I gave you. You can do it here, outside in the garden, in the rest room or wherever, but *your* lesson starts at 2 o'clock."

I retreated to the rear of the room and found the corner seat furthest from the group up front and started to memorize the words and signs. But it was no good. I couldn't concentrate. It was the 'silence' that disturbed me and it kept bringing my eyes up to watch Jo and her pupils.

Jo's face had an expression of patience, compassion and understanding as she stood in front of her class and mouthed the letter A, while her hands in movements of clear silent gestures showed them the right way to 'say' the first letter of the alphabet.

From my angle there was something sad about the scene. I needed the quick fix of being able to see the other side – the dawning look of understanding on the faces of my little classmates.

I collected my things and quietly left the room.

*

The garden around the Institute was in need of a bit of TLC but I found a tree with a couple of benches underneath it and set to work.

I'm sure there must be a special way of learning the sign language. After all the years of research, teachers, teaching, students and lessons, surely somebody by now must have figured out 'the best way' of doing it. Whatever it was nobody had told me, so I ploughed on with my own method.

Being a stockman and spending so much time on your own, I think teaches you be independent, self reliant and the ability to focus on what you are doing at the time, as there's was always the chance of making a mistake and being injured.

I don't know how long he'd been sitting there, but I became aware of his presence when I turned my head to the right to get the crick out of my neck, from having it in the one position for too long.

He was sitting on one of the benches with his back against the trunk of the tree watching me. He was about my age, smaller and wearing a baseball cap, back to front. There was a cigarette dangling from his lips. He looked like an aging delinquent.

He gave me a friendly wave and nod. I did the same.

That was all the encouragement he needed and he got up

and strolled over and sat on the end of my bench.

His hands did a quick flutter of signing – I didn't have a clue of what he said – it was all too quick.

I scribbled a note and handed it to him.

After reading it, he indicated he'd like to write something. I handed him the notepad and pencil.

I read,

"Why didn't you learn to sign when you were a kid? You're a bit old to be starting now aren't you!"

Everybody keeps telling me how old I am – I'm not that bloody old!

"I know," I signed.

He studied me for some time and then signed that he'd like to help me.

"You want to help me?" I managed to roughly sign.

He gave a deprecatory shrug, nodded and grinned.

If anybody needed help I did – so why not!

I smilingly nodded "*yes* "and signed a *"thank you."*

He reached out for the pad and wrote.

"My name is Ted Tyson but everybody calls me TT."

I wrote.

"My name is Reg Brady and everybody calls me Reg."

We shook hands.

He was hopefully my first friend in the silent world of the deaf and mute.

He picked up the sheet of paper with all the words and signs that Jo had given me, gave it a cursory glance and then reached out and took the pad and pencil and wrote the word 'MY' – it was the first word on the page. He then mouthed the word and at the same time slowly formed the sign with his hands. Being so close to me he was easy to follow and imitate. I noticed then that his hands and fingers were long and delicate and I'm sure had never done a days manual work in their lives. Then he stopped signing and indicated for me to continue mouthing and signing while he rolled himself a cigarette.

After he lighted the cigarette, he wrote the next word 'NAME' and we went through the same routine again until we were on word no 12 before he called a halt. I breathed a sigh of relief and just when I thought we'd finished he started throwing signs at me in no particular order without mouthing the word. And that's how we continued until he thought I'd done enough – my brain couldn't take anymore – and I had missed lunch. It was time for my lesson with Jo.

TT stood up, shook my hand, signed "see you tomorrow" gave me a grin, a casual wave and strolled off, leaving me to collect my things and get to my next lesson.

I shook my head in bemused wonderment at what had just happened.

Who was Ted Tyson or TT as everybody called him?

Jo gave me the benefit of her million-dollar smile when I walked into the classroom and that made me think of romantic things that only existed in my fantasy world.

Her question of "How did you get on, do some good work?" brought me down to earth.

"Yes, I think so." I signed.

"Good. Now I will call out a word and I want you to sign and mouth it at the same time. Alright?"

Jo then proceeded to call out the words in the order they

were on the sheet. I got everyone right, there were a few stumbles, but passable. She then picked the words out at random, still no mistakes.

She paused and studied me for some time.

"Reg, have you been taking lessons from somebody else? You're signing is so fluid and clear, which is quite amazing after only one lesson."

Should I tell her about TT? Would it get him into trouble?

I wrote on my pad and handed it to her.

"You had some help from a chap you met in the garden," she read.

I nodded.

"Does this er 'chap' have a name?"

"TT" I signed.

Jo understandingly smiled and nodded her head several times, as if she knew the reason why I had progressed so quickly.

"TT was one of the best students ever to attend this school. He was streets ahead of everybody else and all without any apparent effort. He was quite brilliant in fact. Even better than most of the teachers who were teaching him!

"He is also a crook, a thief, a con man and a lovable rogue, who is permanently out on parole as no prison has the facilities to cope with a deaf and mute villain. He reports to a parole officer once a week and he lives alone with his mum, whom he adores."

She paused and shrugged her shoulders.

"We have, all in our time tried to 'save' TT, but he thinks of himself as a 'free spirit', a modern day Robin Hood, who only takes from the rich to give to the poor and doesn't want to be 'saved' by all us do-gooders out here."

I was too nonplussed to reply.

"Maybe you can repay him a little for his help by quietly keeping a eye on him. He's not past redemption. There's a lot of good in TT and I should imagine he would be very loyal person."

Jo finished her assessment of my new friend and raised an enquiring eyebrow.

"Well?" she asked.

I was still trying to come to terms with the fact that my 'teacher' this morning was a crook!

I shook my head in a noncommittal way and signed, *"I liked him and he helped me, he ..."* and I tailed off lost for words.

"Then continue to like him Reg. Maybe he's lonely and needs a friend."

I nodded.*"Maybe we both need a friend."* I signed.

My Marlborough Man is lonely, and so am I sometimes, thought Jo. The obvious thing would be to ... don't go down that track Newton – just concentrate on your teaching.

"Right Reg, we'll start with a new lot of words and signs."

We worked for a couple of hours, but I think I was too distracted to get the full benefit of Jo's teaching. Half my mind was on TT – *who apparently was a thief, a con man and a likeable rogue – but also a bloody good teacher.*

"I think we've done enough for today," said Jo, and thoughtfully studied me for some time.

She often did that 'thoughtfully looking at me bit'. I wonder what she's thinking!

"Reg, use your own judgment about TT. Don't listen to other people."

She smiled.

"See you tomorrow."

I bathed in her friendliness and smilingly nodded and left.

As Jo watched his retreating back she could still feel the warmth of his lazy crooked smile!

* * *

Next morning, after spending about ten minutes with my small schoolmates, I went out into the garden.

TT was waiting for me.

He was sitting on a circular seat that was around a tree. He was leaning against the trunk, his knees hunched up with his arms around them, and the inevitable cigarette was dangling from his lips. He gave me a casual wave as he got up and ambled over and sat near me on the same bench.

"Good morning Reg," he signed.

"Good morning TT." I signed.

I busied myself with my school bag, getting out the list of words and signs, determined to carry on as normally as I could.

I looked up. TT was silently laughing and he signed, "you know don't you?"

I gave him what I thought was a 'not understanding look' and signed,

"Know what?"

"That I'm a crook."

"So?" I casually signed.

"So, does it make any difference?"

"No, why should it, I still have my wallet." I wrote, in an attempt at humour.

The way TT shook of his head, gave me a pretty good idea of what he thought of me trying to be humorous and signed.

"Very funny."

I wrote,

"TT, I must do some work. I've got a lot to get through, and the sooner I learn the sign language the sooner I can get rid of this bloody pad and pencil and talk to you in signs."

He reached over took the pad and pencil from my hands, picked up the list, gave it a glance and wrote the word CAR on the pad. For the next two hours he taught me, drilled me and force-fed me with words and signs until

I was felt so punch drunk that I called for a halt – it was lunchtime.

I delved into my school bag and brought out two brown paper lunch bags and a thermos. I put one bag in front of TT.

I opened up mine and started to eat the ham and pickle sandwich. TT was still staring at his bag with a strange look on his face. I indicated, 'eat.'

He looked up at me, and there was an unusual shiny look about his eyes. I ducked my head and concentrated on my lunch. When I next glanced up, TT was happily munching away on his ham and pickle sandwich.

A cup of coffee, rounded off what turned out to be, a pleasant, relaxing lunchtime break. TT had insisted that we try to communicate without the use of pad and pencil. Amidst a lot of laughter we somehow did.

This strange, deaf and mute person, of doubtful occupation, brought a breath of fresh air into my life that subconsciously I was missing, and his company was a learning curve of expert advice, help and friendship that money couldn't buy.

Every morning for the first week TT was in the garden to greet me, and every morning he would make me converse, without pad and pencil, for at least a half an hour, with what I had learnt the day before. Between him, Jo, all the recapping and my willingness to learn, my progression had Jo shaking her head in disbelief.

"Reg, you are now putting limited sentences together, and only after one week, which is amazing. Pass on my congratulations to TT for me would you."

I nodded a *"yes."*

I felt that my relationship with Jo was now on a different level. I don't quite know what it was, but we seemed to be more relaxed with each other. Maybe it was the intimacy of working so close together, and my distraction sometimes of thinking, while Jo was mouthing words, 'I wonder what it would be like to kiss those lips' which was taking me, for a moment, out of the fantasy world and into the real one.

Dare I ask her out? Rejection would put an unbearable strain on the, one on one, relationship of teaching. It would hang over our heads like a dark cloud. Learning would be difficult and the easy friendly relationship would disappear and in it's place there would be tension. At the moment every thing in the garden was 'sweet'. What is that old saying, 'if the fence ain't broke don't mend it' Ah shit!

*

During one of our lunch breaks, TT relaxed and told me, with pad and pencil, about his life. He said he lived with his mother, who was a floor supervisor at Russell's, a big departmental store in the city, and every afternoon he cleaned the flat and cooked the evening meal."I can never repay her for her life of sacrifices that she's made on my behalf "he wrote." When they found out that I was deaf and mute, my dad walked out and left us – he couldn't handle the fact that he had fathered a 'freak' – my mum, bless her, learnt the sign language."

He smilingly shook his head and started on a fresh page."After the meal at night we usually watch a foreign movie with sub-titles. I try to get her to go out to meet people. She needs a partner, but I always feel that I 'cramp her style' as she always puts me first. You must come for a meal one night and meet her." He paused and grinned at me, "and I'm not thinking of you as a father-in-law."

* * *

Chapter 7

There's a song somewhere with the lyric, *'Saturday night could be the loneliest night of the week.'* Well Friday night would give it a run for its money!

It was now Friday night and I needed a break from learning, Carlo's junk food and my room at the YMCA – but where do I go and what do I do? My own company I was used to, but tonight I missed the presence of Jack, Jo or TT – people I could talk to. I was bloody lonely and feeling sorry for myself.

I caught the bus to down town Brisbane and wandered its brightly lighted crowded streets. I shop windowed at all the best shops, ate a Chinese meal in a smart restaurant, knocked back a couple of prostitutes who approached me and by that time I'd had enough.

I caught the bus back to the YMCA and walked to the nearest pub where I bought a six-pack of 4X and came back to my room.

I sat on the edge of the bed next morning and surveyed the rumpled clothes and empty beer bottles intermingled on the floor around me, and wondered where the night had gone and had I done anything that I should remember.

After a cup of coffee and a shower I felt better. But I still had the same problem – what to do, as an empty Saturday and Sunday loomed up in front of me!

Decision made – I would do something about my paintings – find out if they're worth anything.

I collected the key for the storeroom from Fred at reception and went down and selected two of my paintings that I thought would be suitable. Fred helped me out with two big plastic rubbish bags with ties to protect my samples and I was ready for my foray into the art world.

From a 'What's On' pamphlet I found there was an water colour art exibition at 140 Weller Road, Tarragindi, a bus ride from Adelaide street – *get on at stop 24 and get off at stop 44 and from there a short walk to the Art Gallery.* It all sounded so simple on paper, but the doing of it was another matter. It seemed to take bloody hours before I actually got there.

The Art Gallery building was quite impressive. It turned out to be the official art gallery for water colourists in Queensland.

I felt self-conscious lugging my two big paintings in their rubbish bags around with me, and the lady at Reception eyed them suspiciously as I handed her a note.

She looked up at me after reading it and now in place of suspicion there was the dreaded look of maternal sympathy on her face. Sometimes it's a hindrance – today it helped.

"There are special days for assessments, but If you'd like to wait here a moment, I'll see if I can find someone who might be able to help you," she said, and disappeared through a door behind her.

I filled in the time looking at some landscapes in the reception area and as I studied each painting I could feel the prickles of excitement covering my arms and neck. These landscapes were good and the asking prices were $5.000 each.

But I could already hear Lily voice saying, "Reggie, your paintings bloody side better."

"Mr Brady would you come with me, Mr Wright will see you."

She led the way through the door behind reception and announced me to a middle-aged man with long hair and sporting a bow tie. He was sitting behind a cluttered desk and rose as I entered.

"Thank you Helen." he said, and waited until she left before turning to me.

"How can I help you Mr Brady?" he asked.

I quickly scribbled a note and handed it to him.

"Well, lets have a look at them shall we," he said in rather a kindly condescendingly way – already preparing his path to let me down lightly.

I looked around the room to find a spot where the light was right for them to be seen to their advantage. I put two chairs up against the wall and placed my painting on them and stepped back.

Mr Wright watched all this with a long suffering look at my fussy preparation, and then the kindly condescending look slowly disappeared from his face as he saw the paintings. Something else took their place. He walked forward and closely studied each landscape. Then he moved back and stood looking at them.

"Who is the artist?" he asked.

I indicated *"Me."*

"What school did you go to Mr Brady?"

I wrote a note and handed it to him.

"You were taught by a aborigine lubra on a cattle station up north," he enquired unbelievingly?

I nodded a *"yes."*

"You are an unknown artist Mr Brady and that will affect the value of your work. I wouldn't attempt to put a price on them. I'll wait for my colleague to arrive, he's an expert on landscapes and will be able to give you a better idea as to their value," he said, looking at his watch."He should be here in about twenty minutes."

Mr Wright, again studying the paintings, was shaking his head and muttering to himself, "taught by an aborigine on a cattle station – unbelievable."

He turned to me.

"I think I need a drink Mr Brady, would you care join me?"

I grinned a *"yes."*

"What – whisky – beer – coke?"

I indicated – beer.

He handed me a 4X and mixed himself a large scotch with ice and water.

"By the way, my name is Arthur, "he said.

I wrote *'Reg'* and showed it to him.

"Cheers Reg."

I raised my drink and mouthed *Arthur.*

I think Arthur felt that as I was mute, it was up to him to do all the talking and that he did. He told me all about the gallery, its aims, its aspirations, its problems."We always have money troubles Reg and we are always looking for sponsors to fund our schools and promote an awareness of water colour painting. We want to make it available to all classes, especially the poor and the disadvantaged."

The door opened and in walked, I presumed, was his colleague.

He was about 60, with close-cropped hair, a limp and a walking stick.

"Morning Arthur, "he said "and? "with an enquiring look at me.

"Reg Brady, George. Reg has a couple of landscapes he wants you to look at."

"Oh, so where are they?" looking around."Ah I see them."

He limped over to my paintings and looked at them.

Arthur sipped his scotch and I took a nervous pull of my beer.

George bent down to get a closer look and made a couple of noises that weren't words just sounds.

"Who painted these?" he asked.

"Reg, here." replied Arthur.

"Did he now."

"Yes. Reg is mute, but he can hear."

George turned his full attention on me.

"Who taught you young man?"

I quickly wrote on my pad and handed it to him.

"An aborigine lubra on a cattle station up North," he read, and shaking his head in disbelief, continued, "I think I'm wasting my time here teaching."

I wrote.

"What do you think, are they any good?"

"No they're not good young man, they're much better than 'good'."

I gulped some more beer.

"Have you seen the landscapes we have on display here?" George asked.

I wrote on my pad and showed him.

"Yes and I think mine are their equal." he read.

He nodded his head, gave a "Mmmm "and said," you're not shy in coming forward are you Reg."

I wrote,

"My teacher Lily taught me to think and love the bush and it's animals like an aborigine, then you will know how to paint them with the right colours that will give them life and energy, she said. I have tried to do that." George read, "and very successfully."he added.

Arthur poured himself another scotch and as he swirled the ice around with his finger he said.

"I would like to frame them and put them on display to see what reaction we get. What do you think George?"

George promptly replied, "I agree."

"Would you be prepared to allow us to act as your Agent while your paintings are on display here. Our commission would be ten per cent plus framing. How do you feel about that Reg?"

I think I smilingly nodded a *"yes"* several times.

I was beginning to feel like Noddy – I couldn't believe all this was happening to me.

"Right. I'll give you a receipt for the paintings and we'll get cracking. Call in, in a couple of week's time. The paintings will be still on display."

I left with the receipt and the lingering bemused look of two landscape-painting experts.

I was on a 'high' as I made my way back to the YMCA. My depression was gone and with it that 'feeling sorry for myself' bit. Even the thought of another artery sealing meal at Carlos didn't depress me.

I worked until late Saturday night with an enthusiasm that had been triggered off, with what I thought had been, a successful attempt to raise money, which would allow me to continue to study full time until I became proficient in signing.

With the help of Jo and TT, I now began to see a light at the end of the dark tunnel that had confronted me when I first made the decision to leave Waaree. I repeatedly mouthed and signed with a determination to show them that their help and support in me wouldn't be in vain.

Sunday was spent protecting my 'hoard of goodies' in the basement. Armed with a large roll of brown wrapping paper and Sellatape from Officeworks, I numbered and photographed each painting so that they could readily be identified. Then dusted, wrapped and sealed them separately. I now handled them more carefully. No more casually tossing them about. There were sixteen stretched canvas paintings. I stacked them gently together in four batches and carried them upstairs to my room, where they would be safe from prying eyes and sticky fingers.

* * *

Chapter 8

Amanda, bless her, was the first to greet me as I walked into the classroom on Monday morning and the others weren't far behind. Their animation and intermingling with each other and me, after only one week of tuition, said much for Jo's ability as a teacher – she had these five little lost forlorn souls of a week ago now behaving like normal children.

Each morning, she would sit behind her desk with a slight smile on her face and watch my classmates and me as we mouthed, signed and high-fived for the half an hour before classes started.

And each morning I fell a little deeper in love with Joanne Newton.

Did she have a boyfriend? Was she living with somebody? I couldn't believe that this beautiful creature was alone. I would've thought that the men would be lining up to date her and they probably were. Yet sometimes when I caught her watching me there was a look in her eyes that I didn't understand – I don't know – it made me want to scream with anger and frustration because I couldn't talk and felt I wasn't good enough to ask her out.

Her, "alright Reg it's time for classes," had me shepherding Amanda and Co, with a final high five to their desks. Jo and I smilingly nodded to each other and I left the room.

TT, as usual was waiting for me, propped up against a tree, with a cigarette between his lips and a ready smile when I appeared.

He signed, "Morning, did you have a good week-end?"

I nodded and signed, *"You?"*

"Yeah, pretty good."

We sat on a bench together ready to work.

TT watched me and raised an enquiring eyebrow.

"Well?" he signed.

I looked at him, not understanding.

"Well, what?" I signed.

"Well, tell me."

"Tell you what?" I signed.

"Will you stop farting about and tell me what happened over the weekend?"

Was the inner excitement of my painting news showing! Until I heard from George and Arthur I didn't want to tell Jo or TT about it.

God, if my inner feelings were so obvious, Jo must have a pretty good idea how I feel about her. I was such a lousy actor – talk about wearing my heart on my sleeve! But now there was TT to deal with.

I wrote,

"Nothing happened over the weekend, except that I went down town Friday night, had a Chinese meal, bought a six pack of beer, drank them, went to bed. Saturday I went to an art exibition, had a meal at Carlos, worked until late at

night and Sunday I packed up ready to move to the boarding house today after class."

"Boarding House? You didn't tell me!"

"Did I have to," I signed.

TT slowly shook his head and signed,

"No, I suppose not."

TT drew on his fag and studied me.

"Want a hand?" he signed.

"No thanks TT. I haven't got much. I'll just catch a cab from the YMCA." I wrote.

"Which one is it?" he mouthed.

I scribbled,

"Mrs Wicks, 341 Compton Road."

He wrote,

"You'll like it. Give Sandy my regards. She runs the place with her mother who helps with the cooking."

For the next two hours we worked and TT pushed me along until *he* was satisfied and signed, "that's enough" and gave me a wink, mouthing "Good."

It was like getting praise from Lily. TT's "Good" had the same value as Lily's "Bloody Good."

Carlos had packed chicken rolls for lunch – even *his food* was getting better. I seemed to be on a roll of good fortune, but I wondered when the axe would fall.

*

Jo's million-dollar smile greeted me when I entered the classroom. *Everybody was greeting me with a bigger than usual smiles today. Was my body, unbeknown to me, exuding some sort of bonhomie that triggered off these smiles of welcome – was I wearing my heart on my sleeve again!*

"Did you have a good weekend Reg?" Jo enquired.

I nodded a *"yes."*

"Good," she smilingly replied, "because today I want you to form sentences without reference to the lists that I have given you."

"I understand." I signed.

For the next two hours my memory was put to the test recalling what I had learnt from TT, Jo and my swatting, but I did make up sentences. Sometimes I got some of them wrong, which were quickly corrected by Jo who nodded and smiled encouragement when I was struggling.

Sitting so close to her as we worked and smelling her fragrance, created an intimacy that sidetracked me sometimes and I would drift off into fantasyland to lose myself in the depth of her brown eyes and just every now and again I thought I could see an answering reply – or was that just wishful thinking on my part!

When Jo raised her hand to call a halt, she didn't speak for some time. She just looked at me.

Was she waiting for me to say something? Was she aware of my dreaming, my wishful thinking? I knew that this was the time to ask her out, but again my courage failed me. Being mute had given me an inferiority complex that I was finding bloody difficult to overcome.

"Very good." she finally said.

The moment had passed. Jo dipped her head and busied herself with some papers.

* * *

Fred, at the YMCA, phoned the friendly taxi driver who had delivered me here and he said he'd be arriving in about twenty minutes. I was all packed and ready to go to my new abode at 341 Compton Rd.

Mick Maloney, my cabbie arrived and between the two of us we loaded my belongings into his cab. I thanked and said goodbye to Fred and promised Carlo next door that I'd be in for a meal now and again.

Sandy answered the bell at her boarding house and Mick and I carried all my gear up to a big light airy room in the front of the house. I thanked and tipped Mick for his help.

"Don't forget Reg, anytime mate, give me a bell."

After Mick departed I sat in the middle of my room and looked about me.

I was pleased with what I saw. There was a wardrobe, a chest of drawers, two bedside tables, an armchair, a table with two matching chairs and to top it all off, a small room with a toilet and washbasin – luxury.

I rearranged the furniture to my liking and unpacked what little I had into various drawers and cupboards.

Finally I set up my easel and got out my old sketchbook.

My years of going walkabout with Lily in the wet and dry seasons around Waaree, looking for likely scenes that I might paint, filled its pages. Each sketch had a couple of colour photographs of the landscape clipped to it and notations of why Lily and I had chosen that particular scene at that time, hoping that they would jog my memory when I came to paint it. And through Lily's eyes hear her soft voice talking about the 'feel' of that particular landscape.

I needed to get back to my painting. I missed the therapeutic balm of losing myself in the colours and fantasy of the little world that I created with paint and pencil. Also, now there was the added need – knowing they were worth money – to keep my hand in and continue to paint.

Tea was at 6.30.

There were five men seated around the table when I arrived at the dining room. Sandy was on hand to introduce me. She told them that I was mute, but could hear. I shook hands with Pandit, a colourful Indian wearing a turban, and then, there was a Lance, a Peter, a Jerry and a Terry and they all regarded me with a look of sympathetic interest that openly said – *the poor bugger, he can't talk.*

The meal, which consisted of a large helping of beef casserole and vegetables, followed by banana custard for dessert, was slightly hysterical as my fellow boarders got confused with deaf and mute. They'd get half way through giving me signs to pass the salt or pepper etc, realise their mistake and then shout at me as if I was deaf.

I didn't write a note when I wanted the butter. I just pointed, nodded and smiled.

I spent an hour, after the meal, sketching the landscape that I had chosen and then I began my nightly ritual – two hours of signing and mouthing in front of a mirror.

*

Next morning at breakfast I passed on TT's regards to Sandy and asked her to pack two lunches, as TT was helping me with my signing.

"There's a lot of good in TT," she said, "and he needs a friend to keep him on the straight and narrow."

She smilingly shook her head.

"He once brought me a beautiful silver cutlery set that he thought I might like. It was practically brand new and worth quite a lot of money. I said 'no,' it would look out of place in my boarding house.

When I asked where he'd got it from, he was very vague," she sighed and added."Then he was arrested, found guilty of breaking and entering and placed on parole. Give him my regards."

*

The days dovetailed into each other and TT's hard earned "good" and Jo's smiling nod of approval daily, kept my nose to the grindstone.

It was two weeks since I had taken my landscapes to the Art gallery and tomorrow being Saturday, I was off to see them, framed and hanging I hope in the Reception area of Brisbane's main centre for watercolourists.

I tried to do some study, but it was no good. My mind was going through so many 'what ifs' about my paintings, that's all I could do at night after tea was fiddle about with my landscape on the easel.

*

I just stood there, with my mouth open catching flies, while gazing at my paintings, now beautifully framed, hanging on the main wall in the Reception area of the Art Gallery. I didn't realise that framing would make made such a vast difference. My landscapes suddenly looked very expensive.

There was a small stand with a notice on it that said.

Landscapes

By

R Brady.

If only Lily was here to see them – bless her – I owed her so much.

"What do you think Reg?" Arthur asked. He and George were beside me. I'd been so rapt in just looking that I hadn't noticed their presence.

All I could do was nod and smile several times.

85

"You need to sign them Reg." George said, "I noticed several people looking for your name on the paintings."

I didn't tell him that they were already signed. I don't know why, but some instinct stopped me. I nodded and wrote,

"Can I borrow some paints?"

"Yes, come with me and I'll get you some," said George.

I signed my name in the bottom right hand corner of each painting. They were unobtrusive but clear and melded in with the colours surrounding them. I got a nod of approval from George.

In Arthur's office I was given a beer, George mixed himself a gin and tonic and Arthur stirred his whisky, ice and water with his finger. I waited for one of them to tell me the news, if any.

"Cheers," George said, raising his glass and drinking. Arthur and I did the same.

"Well Reg your paintings have caused quite a stir." George said."We've had three offers to buy them and two orders or commissions for two more landscapes. I told them all I'd talk to you."

"How much are they offering?" I wrote.

"One offer from a private buyer was for $6.000. An agent I recognised offered $7.000 for each painting and another agent offered $15.000 for both paintings. Those two agents I know are working for Art dealers. If they are offering that kind of money for an unknown artist, then they must think they'll get more at an auction or from showing them in their own art gallery."

My mind reeled at the amount of money I was being offered.

"I suggest we accept the commissions and play hard to

get with the other offers. I'd prefer to sell them to a private buyer who wants to keep them in his home and enjoy them." George continued.

I agreed with him there but was he turning down all that lovely money on offer!

"What do you think Reg?"

I was too bewildered, nonplussed *to* think. All I could do was shake my head in wonderment. I wrote.

"You're my agent. I'll leave it up to you."

George smilingly nodded his head.

"Don't worry Reg, that's just their first offer. We won't lose you any money. We might even make you some more."

I shrugged and tried to give him a nonchalant look and failed miserably.

"The other thing Reg is, we'd like to run an article on you in our Art magazine. Any publicity we do while your paintings are on display will be a great help. That's if you're agreeable."

I nodded a *"yes."*

"If you've got the time now, Arthur will take a photo of you and get some information about your upbringing and life on a cattle station etc, another beer?"

I mouthed and signed a *"yes* "to both.

I left Arthur with a shortened version of my autobiography and headed back to the boarding house. I was bursting to tell somebody the good news and the only people I *could* tell were TT and Jo, but I didn't know where they lived, so I settled for two letters, one to Jack and the other to Lily, giving them all the details about the school and paintings.

Saturday night, and there was nothing to do except 'swat' and paint.

What must it be like to have a regular girlfriend and be able to work hard all the week, knowing that at the weekend you can relax and take your girl out dancing or to the pictures or even just stay at home and watch television together!

And what if that girl is Joanne Newton! I've known her for only three weeks and in that time she has filled my mind with dreams and fantasies that can never be fulfilled. How do I settle for some one second best after meeting someone like Jo!

Is there a clone of her out there somewhere, who just happens to be mute and is looking for a soul mate – I doubt it.

I was obsessed with Jo. She was in my thoughts most of the day, then I'd go to bed thinking of her and when I awoke she'd still be there in the forefront of my mind. I was finding it hard to concentrate on what I was supposed to be doing and that was remembering the signing and mouthing of the lists of words that she kept giving me.

But to get her nod of approval I think I worked my butt off. I could only suppose that the extra effort I put into my 'swatting' was making up for my wishful thinking and daydreaming.

I worked hard at my signing and mouthing for a couple of hours and then spent the rest of the time painting before hitting the sack.

More of the same on Sunday, I was beginning to hate the weekends.

* * *

TT signed.

"You paint?"

I nodded and wrote, *"I have two paintings on display at the Art Gallery."*

TT's surprised look went along with his signing,

"You're an artist, well, well! Why didn't you tell me all this before?"

I wrote, *"I was waiting to find out if they were any good or not before I told anybody."*

"And are they?" he signed.

I nodded a *"yes"* and wrote, *"The chaps at the gallery seem to think so."*

He grinned and signed,

"Then I'll go and see them."

*

Jo's reaction was similar to TT's.

"You're full of surprises Reg. A water colourist and they're on display at the Art Gallery! That's a very prestigious gallery to have them hung. Where did you learn to paint? – I mean who taught you?"

I wrote, *"Lily, an aborigine dot painter on bark taught me at the cattle station."*

Jo didn't speak for a moment she just unbelievingly looked at me with her moist lips slightly apart – *oh to be able to kiss them closed.*

"How long have you been painting?" she finally asked.

"Since I was a little boy." I signed.

She nodded her head slowly.

"After seeing your beautiful sketch of Amanda on the first day here at school, I shouldn't be really surprised."

I wrote, *"I hope to be able to sell them and have enough money to stay full time here at school."*

I grinned and signed, *"With you as my teacher."*

Jo studied me for some time.

Had I gone too far!

Then she gave me a small inclination of her head and smilingly said,

"Thank you kind sir for the compliment."

I wrote, *"I would like to celebrate with the two people who have been helping me since I've been here, you and TT. Would you consider coming out to dinner with TT and myself?"*

Jo didn't hesitate. She smiled her million dollar smile and said, "Reg, I would love to have dinner with you and TT. When did you want to go?"

I signed and indicated, *"Whenever it suits you."*

"What about Friday night this week then?"

I nodded a *"yes "*and wrote, *"Do you have a favourite restaurant, I don't know any in Brisbane?"*

She thought for a moment.

"Yes. I know one. I'll book a table for three shall I?"

I signed a *"yes"*.

"If you give me TT's address and yours I'll pick you up around about 6.30. Okay?"

"You have a car?" I signed.

"Yes," she smilingly replied, "I'm a big girl now."

I was on cloud seven, or is it nine, for the rest of the day, because I understood that that was the place where all lovesick people go. I'd never been there before but I was besotted, obsessed or whatever the right word is with Joanne Newton and it was a state that I found was a full time occupation as it seemed to affect everything I did. She was always there in my thoughts, dreams and fantasies and if this was what being in love was like, how long would it last – I couldn't think straight!

TT reaction next day was predictable.

Even his hands seem to match the unbelieving look on his face as they signed,

"You invited Jo out and she accepted?"

I nodded.

He quickly wrote,

"You're the first student to date her. They all tried but never succeeded."

I wrote, *"But it's not like a real date, it's a sort of celebration and there'll be the three of us remember."*

"Yes, but you can hear. I'll feel like a bloody chaperone," he signed.

"Don't be bloody silly. It's next Friday night, are you coming?"

"Of course I'm bloody coming, I wouldn't miss a free feed."

* * *

Chapter 9

For the next three days, I sort of went through the motions of normal behaviour. I don't know about the other two but apart from this coming Friday night there was little else on my mind as I struggled to remember signs and words. My two teachers were patient with me and I hope a little understanding. TT was as always – cool – with the inevitable cigarette dangling from his lips and Jo had that slight smile of sympathy on her face as she watched me struggle.

Why was I getting my knickers in such a twist, there were going to be three of us for God's sake! It was no big deal. It wasn't like as if it was 'one on one,' just Jo and me.

I'd already been to the bank, checked that my best shirt was clean, my pants pressed and that there no stains on my tie – now the thing is, should I wear my wide brimmed stockman's hat – some people said it made me look like John Wayne! Well that wouldn't be too bad would it – John Wayne!

*

I was the second one to be picked up and was relegated to the back seat of Jo's small Mazda, my knees crunched up near my chin.

"Do you have enough room back there?" Jo asked.

I nodded and gave a *'thumbs up'* to the rear view mirror.

TT, sitting in the roomy front passenger seat, acknowledged my presence with a nonchalant wave of his hand.

On the way to the restaurant Jo and TT carried on a conversation that was way beyond my comprehension. TT's hands were fluttering like butterfly wings and Jo, driving, would reply with one hand, glancing every now and again at TT.

She called out to me.

"TT was just saying that he's going to see your paintings tomorrow. I want to see them to, so I said I'd pick him up. Do you want to come with us?"

I nodded and gave a *'thumbs up'* to the rear view mirror.

TT and Jo continued to 'talk'! That Jo could drive and carry on a conversation with a deaf mute showed how skilled she was in signing.

My only contribution had been two nods and a couple of 'thumbs ups'.

'Coopers Family Restaurant' was tucked in between an Asian food store and a Mini Mart. The faint glow of red shaded lamps shining through its front windows gave it a warm inviting look.

The entrance of an attractive woman, escorted by two tall men, one of whom was dressed like a cowboy and looking like John Wayne, caused quite a stir and made a few women forget what they were actually doing as thoughts not becoming a lady flashed through their minds and brought a warmth to the lower part of their bodies that had them squirming in their seats.

Jo was on first name terms with the young lady who showed us to our table and as I took off my, what suddenly now seemed a very large cowboy hat, she reached out her hand.

"I'll take your hat sir," she said.

I nodded and smiled a *"thank you."*

We now became the 'cabaret act' for Coopers Family Restaurant. The fluttering of TT and Jo hands, their mouthing and smiling as they talked to each other, and Jo's repeating to me what she and TT had said not only intrigued the whole of the paying customers, but me to. They were both so relaxed in what they were doing that they could have been normal people having a normal conversation.

I'd be like that one day – but how long is it going to take me to get there!

Everybody preferred 'red' so I ordered a bottle of Shiraz from the Barossa Valley. The food was good and the only time the restaurant returned to being 'normal' was when TT and Jo's hands were occupied with knife and fork. As Jo was driving, she only had one glass of wine. TT and I managed to take care of the rest.

I think TT would be a cheap drunk, as after only two glasses of wine his signing became rather flamboyant and he often looked like he was flagging down a train!

It was a pleasant evening and Jo and TT were good company. Not that I had much to do with what went on, but it was just nice to be with the two people whom I considered were now my friends. They were cushioning my entry into the new life I had chosen and for that I owed them 'big time.'

I was the first to be dropped off.

Did Jo do that purposely! Was she afraid to be left alone with me so that she wouldn't have the embarrassment of having to turn me down if I made a pass at her – make a pass at her! What am I thinking about – I haven't got the guts to make a pass at her!

Why do I always have these bloody negative thoughts where she is concerned anyway!

But tomorrows another day and once again the 'three' of us are going out together! This time I hope to be centre stage with my paintings.

* * *

I still didn't make the front seat – *but thinking about it –* what would I do up there anyway! I couldn't sign and carry on a conversation with Jo, as I didn't know enough words and signs to do that. Best leave that to TT.

The Art Gallery, when we arrived was quite crowded. There was a group of people standing around my paintings with Arthur in front talking to them. He spotted me, said something to his group and they turned as one and looked at TT, Jo and myself.

He came over to greet me.

"Reg, would you do me a favour and meet my art class and maybe sign the Art magazine that they have."

I indicated Jo and TT to him. Jo came to my rescue.

"My name is Joanne Newton and this is Ted Tyson."

"Arthur Wright." he replied, shaking their hands.

"Reg, do you mind," nodding in the direction of his class.

I followed Arthur over to meet his students.

His students watched somebody that looked the "Marlborough" man, amble over to meet them, and when he arrived they were confronted by a 6'3" lean, brown, Australian cowboy, with a lazy crooked smile that had the ladies all of a twitter and the men thinking 'I must get one of those hats'

Arthur introduced me.

"This is Reg Brady, the artist that painted those landscapes behind you. Reg is mute but can hear. Now, if you want to he'll sign the art Magazines you have."

A young girl stepped forward and offered her open copy up to me.

I stared at a large photograph of myself, superimposed over a landscape and to one corner, a hazy, vague, kneeling figure of an aborigine lubra dot painting. The caption read.

A SILENT TALENT FROM THE OUTBACK

The article covered the two centre pages of the Magazine. Arthur had done me proud.

I signed all the copies for the art class.

Jo and TT were studying and discussing my paintings. Their hands fluttering like bird's wings and the enthusiastic animation on their faces, as they mouthed the words, reinforcing what they signed. All I could do was stand and watch two experts silently talking to each other.

Then Jo saw me watching. She laid her hand on TT arm to get his attention.

She walked over to me, stood on tiptoes and kissed me on the cheek.

"They are beautiful Reg," she whispered.

TT reached out both his hands, and nodding his head in approval, clasped mine in a firm handshake that said it all.

I couldn't have been more chuffed.

But there's got to be something wrong, somewhere, Its all been too easy!

I've only been in Brisbane for five weeks and already I've made friends. I'm progressing well at the deaf and mute school and my tuition fees are being paid for by a grant from Centrelink. Two of my landscapes are on display at a prestigious art gallery with people queuing up to buy them and to top it all off, I'm living in a nice boarding house!

So it's all been too easy. Maybe it's all a dream and I'll wake up and things will go back to being normal. Or maybe the stone that Lily put around my neck is working overtime and I've got the whole Kalkadoon tribe looking out for me.

The only fly in the ointment is being mute, which has me on the back foot where Joanne Newton is concerned. I would have to sign the words or write her a note to ask her out and that would only highlight my disability.

Jo was shaking my arm.

"Reg, you've got that faraway look in your eyes again." She looked up into my face and softly asked.

"Where do you go when that happens?"

How do I tell her that I go to a fantasyland that I create in my mind, where the world is perfect and I can talk to her, as she is part of it, and shares with me the idyllic existence that my dreams are made of!

I looked down at this lovely woman and at that moment my love for her was so overwhelming that it took all my self-control to stop myself from taking her in my arms and holding her.

I apologized with my look and signed,

"Sorry, I was thinking of what you said about my paintings. I'm pleased you like them."

I looked at my hands. I had signed without thinking.

Jo was also looking at them.

"Reg you have just used your hands, without any prompting, for the first time."

She smiled up at me.

"Is there no end to your talents Mr Brady?"

Jo watched her Marlborough Man sheepishly shrug his shoulders and give her a slow lazy lopsided grin – her heart did a somersault and renewed thoughts that brought a hot flush to her rebellious body and a becoming blush to her cheeks.

"I'm sorry but may I borrow Reg for a moment."

Arthur Wright, with an apologetic air, was suddenly by my side and he led me to his office.

"Coffee, drink?"

I shook my head.

"Well Reg, the amount of money being offered to you, an unknown artist, is unbelievable. In all my experience it's never happened before. Anyway, we've accepted the two commissions on your behalf, at ten thousand each. Are you agreeable to that?"

I numbly nodded my head.

"Now the offer for both paintings on display has gone up to twenty two thousand. What do you think?"

I cannot believe this is all happening to me. At this rate, with the stack of paintings in my room, I'm sitting on a gold mine.

I wrote, *"What do you and George think?"*

"We were hoping to sell them to the private buyer, but he hasn't come back and upped his offer. I think we should wait for another week. If he doesn't contact us by then, we'll sell to the dealer. I don't think we'll get a better deal."

I nodded in '*agreement.*'

"That's about it. I'll let you get back to your friends. Oh

and here's a few of the magazines you may like." He handed me some copies of 'Art Gallery'.

"I indicated that I'd like four copies."

I wanted to send one each to Jack and Lily.

Arthur said, "Of course," and handed me the magazines.

"The two commissions – they both said they'd like something similar to the ones on display – all right?"

I signed a *"thank you"* and went back to Jo and TT. They were, as usual, chattering away like crazy and now the centre of attention from the art group, who were fascinated by a display of the deaf and mute language from two experts.

I gave them each a copy of the magazine. TT flipped through his until he came to the centre pages and pursed his lips in a gay cod look and signed,

"Oooh ... whose a pretty boy then?"

What did I expect!

Jo was of no help.

"Please Sir, will you sign my book?"

I resignedly shook my head, took each of them firmly by the arm and marched them out of the Gallery.

TT said he had to go home and prepare a meal for his mother who apparently worked every other Saturday. That would leave just Jo and me!

Now what are you going to do Brady!

After dropping off TT at a small neat house on stilts, not far from Brompton Road, the problem was solved by Jo making me an offer I couldn't refuse.

"Reg would you like to come and have a BBQ at my place. Nothing special. I thought we could cook a few sausages and a couple of chops that I have – make a salad – have a bottle of red wine – I'll run you home afterwards. What do you say?"

She said all this with an open inviting smile on her face that was free of any coyness or innuendo.

I nodded a *"yes"* and wrote, *"Can we stop off at a bottle-shop, I'd like to get some wine."*

"Reg, I have plenty of wine, besides I'll be driving you home, remember."

"But I want to bring something," I signed.

"Reg, it's my little celebration for your success – now behave."

I shook my head and smilingly raised my hand in defeat.

Jo's place was similar to TT'.s. It was a small blue Queensland house, which had a white picket fence and the doors and windows were picked out in white. It was as pretty as a picture. A neat garden with lawns and colourful flowerbeds either side of a path that led up to the front steps attested to Jo's pride in the place.

I stood and looked up at the house.

"I like your home and garden," I signed.

"Thank you. I spend a lot of time in the garden. I find it therapeutic, after spending so much time at the school with impaired children. It helps me to unwind and ease the stress that builds up while I'm teaching."

One forgets about the teacher. All you're concerned about are your own problems. Jo does it all day. I've seen the look on her face sometimes when she's with the children. She becomes emotionally involved, and I can see her struggling with them, willing them on, as they try and reach out from their silent world to be heard.

Her front verandah, looked like the one at Waarree. It

had a couple of armchairs and a table with magazines and books between them but there weren't any waterbags hanging from the ceiling.

Glass sliding doors opened into a large open plan sitting room with a fireplace. Colourful rugs were scattered over the polished wooden floor and to one end there was a small refectory table, to seat six. Two armchairs and a long settee faced a television set that sat besides the fireplace. It all looked very cosy and inviting.

An archway led to a modern kitchen with a centre island. More sliding doors opened onto a deck with an extended awning.

A wooden table that had bench seating either side of it, two armchairs and a four burner BBQ with a small table beside it completed the furnishing.

The view from the deck looked out over a park with rugby posts and a bunch of kids kicking a ball about.

I went back into the kitchen. Jo was bent over looking into the fridge and I must say the view from here was much better than the view from the deck.

Jo stood up and gave me a look, shook her head and said,

"Men!"

How did she know that I had been looking at 'her bending over,' was it so obvious. Could she tell by just looking at my face!

She handed me a plate with some sausages and chops on it.

"Maybe you'd like to start the BBQ, you'll find tongs, forks and oil, on a shelf in the BBQ."

I trotted off to do what I was told.

I got everything going and the six sausages and two large chops were now on the hot plate cooking.

Jo came out and handed me a glass of red wine.

"Cheers and welcome to chez Newton."

We clinked glasses and drank her toast.

I nodded and indicated my approval of the wine.

"Some friends brought me a case of Shiraz back from the Barossa Valley."

"They have good taste," I signed.

"I'll tell them you approve," she quietly said, but I could see that her mind was on other things as she slowly rubbed the edge of her glass against her moist open lips.

There was just a moment there when we looked at each other. For me, it was a little moment of magic, which was eventually broken by what I thought was Jo's quietly reluctant,

"I think I had better make the salad."

Or was that all just wishful thinking again on my part.

I'm no great shakes as a cook, but the snags and chops turned out okay. The salad that Jo put together with an oil and vinegar dressing, plus a crusty French loaf and butter made an enjoyable meal.

The rest of the Shiraz slowly disappeared as we ate and drank in a companionable atmosphere that was free of any sexual tension. Jo was just good to be with. We were both relaxed and I put away my note book and tried to speak to her only by signing – when I ran into trouble she was there to help me – my muteness, it seemed, not being a great problem.

When she suggested a cup of coffee I knew then that I'd not be staying for breakfast. Just as well I suppose! How could our teacher – student relationship continue on it's present level, if I'd be thinking of what I did to her body the night before, while she was trying to get me to sign the sentence 'Could you direct me to the bank please' It wouldn't work. My mind would be reliving moments of ecstasy that had nothing to do with where the bleedin' bank was!

After a chaste kiss on my cheek and her,

"I've had a lovely time Reg, and once again congrats on your paintings, you're very clever. I'll see you Monday – night."

She drove off to her blue and white cottage – I watched her go.

Then I let myself into Sandy's boarding house.

* * *

Sunday was a reality check after Saturday's euphoria at the Art Gallery. I sat in front of the mirror and practiced my signing and mouthing for three hours in the morning and then after lunch lost my self in the landscape on the easel, trying to remember the feeling that I had when Lily and I had gone walkabout and found this scene that I had eventually photographed.

"Stand still Reggie – and look about you." she had called out."*See the trees, the river, the movement of the branches. Let the feeling of the bush get into your mind. Watch the colours – see how they change and the shadows over the water and listen Reggie – listen to the sounds ..."*

I could still hear the love in her voice as she stood beside me and quietly talked about the bush.

"Think like us Reggie, be a white Kalkadoon and you'll get it right."

I mouthed, *"I'm trying Lily, I'm trying..."*

* * *

Monday morning, first thing, was high-five time with my young classmates. Amanda had taken it upon herself to be leader of the pack and had organized them to show me how much they had learnt.

I didn't understand exactly what they were doing, but they seemed to know, and the little signals they were giving each other, plus the looks on their faces while they were doing it, was enough to tell me that they were actually 'talking' to each other.

I gave them a round of applause when Amanda indicated 'finished'.

Jo watched all this with a slight dreamy smile on her face.

How well my Aussie cowboy scrubs up of a morning, she thought. He looks quite edible down there with the children – all bronzed and shiny as if he'd been polished – and why didn't she indicate that she would have liked him to stay last night – and how lonely her bed had been when she crawled into it.

She shook her head and all those thoughts scattered, as she became Joanne Newton 'teacher.'

"Thank you Reg, that was nice. I'll see you after lunch."

I nodded, signed, *"goodbye"* and left.

*

No TT waiting as usual – maybe he'd got bored with teaching me and had found better things to do.

I set to and started signing and mouthing words, but it wasn't the same without TT. I'd been spoilt over the last few weeks and it made me realize how much help he'd been. Also, I missed his larrikin attitude and cynical take on the world. Well, could you blame him! He'd got the shitty end of the stick, when they delivered him as a deaf mute baby instead of a normal one. I know how I felt just being mute!

I was further distracted by his arrival.

He signed "Good morning" and wrote on his note pad.

"I had to report to my Probation officer."

I gave him an understanding nod.

"I'd like to sleep with her," he signed.

I didn't know what to say to that so I kept quiet.

He kept writing,

"I'm working on the angle that she may like something different, 'an exotic experience' – a silent root, so to speak – me being deaf and mute – what do you think?"

I tried to keep a straight face – I hadn't heard that old-fashioned word 'root' in years.

I slowly signed,

"Well, I must admit it's a new approach, it might work."

"Yeah, that's what I think," he signed, thoughtfully nodding his head.

There was no smile on his face – he must be serious!

Suddenly he looked up and grinned.

"Work" he signed.

And that's what we did for the next two hours.

* * *

Chapter 10

Each day melded into another with a sameness that was beginning to pall. I needed a break from the daily routine at the school and boarding house – I missed the bush, the horse riding and the comradeship of the other stockmen. I missed Waaree.

Lily had instilled in me a love for the outback and I longed to go 'walkabout'. To recharge my batteries and find landscapes that I could lose myself in 'my' dreamtime, as I followed her advice, listening, looking and feeling the magic that surrounded me.

I needed a little house on wheels – *a campervan to escape the city at the weekends would solve my problem.*

I scoured the Motor Mart section of the Saturday morning papers and came up with one possibility.

Campervan VW Kombi. Good condition, pop up roof, 2Lt, fuel inject, automatic, air con, sound system, twin batteries, fridge, cooker, NRMA inspect report, low klms, power pt, $8500. No offers. Ph no. 8426 7198, evenings.

Now I had a problem – how do I phone them!

Jo was the only person who could help, but I couldn't remember her address, so I'd have to wait until Monday – by that time the van would probably have been sold. I didn't have a choice – so I waited.

After a distracted Monday morning of study with TT, I finally handed a page of my note pad to Jo. She read what I had written.

"Well of course Reg. I'll gladly help. What about if I come around to your place at about six o'clock, I can ring from there?"

I nodded my agreement.

"Now to work," she said.

*

Jo arrived at six and used the phone in the hall. I stood beside her.

"Hello, I'm ringing about the campervan advertised in Motor Mart. Has it been sold?"

"I see … Yes we would, just a moment," she said, turning to me.

"Would you like to see it now?"

I nodded a *"yes."*

"Yes we would … one moment."

"Reg, a pad and pencil."

I handed them to her and she wrote down the address.

"Thank you … yes we should be there within the next half hour, bye."

"Well', turning to me, "he said he'd had two offers but they were below the asking price. Whether that's true or not we don't know. Anyway we're off to see it now"

I told Sandy I wouldn't be in for a meal and we left.

Jo knew the suburb of the address but not the street. While she drove, I made use of the street directory that was in the side pocket of the door.

46 Parker street, and there it was, a yellow VW campervan.

"Looks good." Jo said.

We got out of the car and walked around the van. It looked a well maintained vehicle and the owner had given it a good wash and polish – it practically shone.

A mature gentleman was slowly making his way down the front steps of 46.

"Hello, are you the people that just rung up?" he asked.

"Yes we are," Jo replied.

"My name's Bert Hughes." He came through the front gate and handed her the keys.

"Take it for a spin and see what you think."

"I'm Jo Newton and this is Reg Brady."

We shook hands with Bert, and Jo handed me the keys.

"Off you go then."

She didn't offer to come with me.

Two special sheepskin-covered Recaro front seats were a bonus – there had been no mention of them in the advert.

I drove around the block a couple of times, tested the brakes, the windscreen wipers, the indicators – everything seemed to work alright and the engine and automatic transmission gave me a smooth ride.

I returned, parked it and put up the pop-up roof.

Jo joined me.

"Well, how did it run?"

I gave her a thumbs-up.

We checked the fridge, cooker, batteries – everything was clean and tidy and there was room for another sleeping body in the roof area.

I looked at Jo with an enquiring look that asked the question.

She nodded.

"I like it Reg, I don't think you'd do better for a second hand Campervan. It has everything you need. They have even left you all the cutlery and things. It's fully equipped ready for the road."

Bert was waiting by the gate.

"Reg would like to buy it Bert at your asking price."

"What, no bargaining, no hassle," he smilingly asked?

"No Bert, no hassle."

She turned to me.

"Deposit?"

I pulled out my wallet and handed her two hundred dollars.

"Bert, may we leave two hundred dollars as a deposit and we'll be back tomorrow with a bank cheque for the remainder. Would that be alright?"

He had by now a fixed smile on his face and nodded first to Jo then to me, each time shaking our hands and saying "deal, deal."

He kept looking at me. I think he was waiting for me to say something.

Jo helped me out.

"Reg is mute Bert, but he can hear."

Bert, bless him, couldn't help the wave of sympathy that washed across his face and he shuffled uncomfortably, and as he moved off, he murmured something that sounded like,

"I'll get you a receipt then."

While he was gone I put down the roof and locked up the van – I didn't want anyone stealing *my* campervan.

Jo tapped my arm.

"I think you'll be very happy in your little house on wheels."

I wanted to hug this beautiful woman who seemed to speak my thoughts as I formed them, my muteness being reduced to a minimal inconvenience when I was with her.

I signed, *"Let's celebrate by going out for a meal, please?"*

Jo studied me for a second.

"Pretty please," I quickly signed.

She smiled and nodded.

"Yes, let's."

Bert was there by our side with the receipt.

I jubilantly took it, and Jo said, "See you tomorrow Bert," and we took off for out celebratory meal.

As we headed back into the city I thought that life doesn't get much better than this. I'd got myself a campervan and I was taking the girl I love out for a meal.

"Do you like Italian," Jo asked.

I nodded.

"We'll go to Beterelli's then, I often go there."

I didn't mind where we ended up – I was with Jo – that

110

was enough.

Beterelli's, left you in no doubt as to what the most popular drink was. Empty Chanti bottles, as decorations, were everywhere. Most of them converted to lamps that sat on the tables, giving off a subdued flattering red glow, that I'm sure the ladies loved, and created an ambience of intimacy, with just enough light to see what you were eating.

Unfortunately for me, because of the dim lighting, Jo had difficulty reading my signs when I wanted to 'speak', so I moved my chair closer and was practically sitting on her lap by the time I finished signing. This I didn't mind!

My problems caused a lot of giggling. Maybe it was the amount of Chanti I was knocking back, but I was on a high and Jo caught my mood and joined me. The spaghetti meal just slipped by, along with a lot of laughter until the bottle was empty.

As Jo drove me back to my digs I was hoping that I had consumed most of the wine. The law came down pretty heavily on those caught drink driving, and I wasn't sure how much Jo had had.

She nudged my arm.

"Stop worrying. I'm alright, I've only had two glasses."

How did she know that I was thinking about that!

Do I give off some sort of vibe that she can read?

If I did, then she must know that I love her!

* * *

Next day after classes Jo drove me over to Bert's to pick up the van. He was waiting for us on the verandah, in the company of a stooped grey haired lady with a walking stick.

111

He introduced her as Rose his wife.

I handed over a Bank cheque for $8300 to him.

He didn't even look at it, just gave me a sad smile, the registration papers and said, "Thank you," and Rose burst into tears.

I didn't know what to do. I looked at Jo, who instinctively stepped forward a placed a comforting arm around Rose's shoulder.

"She just loved that van," Bert said.

"She even gave it a name, she called it 'Aloha.'" He lovingly looked a his wife, "we had such happy times together in it ..."his voice trembled and trailed off and for a moment I thought he was about to tearfully join her.

"But arthritis and old age has caught up with us, and now we're swapping Aloha for a nursing home." He reached out a hand to his wife.

"Every trip was like an outdoor adventure, wasn't it Rose dear, it kept us young ..."he paused for a second, shook his head slowly and quietly said,

"Now it'll be Bingo and Indoor Bowls I expect – not quite the same is it!"

He looked from Jo to me.

"You two enjoy your time with Aloha, it'll keep you young too."

I felt terrible. I felt like I was stealing the family pet. What should have been a happy occasion was turning into a sort of Irish 'wake', the 'body' on view being a yellow campervan!

I nodded and gave Bert, what I hope, was an understanding smile.

Jo answered.

"We'll do that Bert," and she stretched out to firmly shake his hand.

"Now we'll be off, and we will take good care of Aloha for you."

I also shook his hand and accepted the frail shaking fingers that Rose tentatively put forward and gave them a gentle squeeze.

* * *

I drove to school the next day, partly because I wanted to show off my new acquisition to TT, but mainly because I loved driving it – the automatic transmission giving me a smooth ride, as I sat up high in the driver's seat and looked down on the other vehicles – it made me feel good!

I wasn't sure if TT was liking 'my pride and joy' or not. He casually walked all around it – kicked the tyres – *of course* – opened the side door – put up the roof – then crawled all over it pulling open drawers and cupboards as he did so.

I eventually got his grin, nod of approval and a thumbs up.

Now that that was sorted out it was back to work. I offered to drive him home after the class but he said 'no' he'd rather have lunch with me and find his own way home – I was also getting his nod of approval.

* * *

Chapter 11

I had spent too much of my life resenting and regretting what I was and I'd used it as an excuse not to do things. I found out regret's a waste of time. I was stuck with being mute and you never knew when you're life was going to end anyway, so I went with that old saying of "live for today for tomorrow we die," and headed for the campervan.

I stared at the bell. All I had to do was push it – *easier said than done!*

I leant forward, pressed it and I could hear the chimes echoing in the house. I waited.

Eventually the door was opened and Jo, with a towel wrapped turban style around her head, looked at me with a surprised enquiring,

"Reg!"

I slowly signed, hoping my hands would convey all the yearning that I felt for this girl.

"I just wanted to see you."

What Joanne Newton did see was every woman's dream. He was a mixture of John Wayne and the Marlborough Man and he was standing on *her* doorstep looking like a small boy and saying that he wanted to see her – her heart did a back flip!

"What about Reg?" she managed to stutter.

I shrugged and slowly and longingly signed.

"I just wanted to see you Jo, to be with you, that's all."

What girl could resist that!

There was no preamble to his simple declaration. And as he stood there wearing his heart on his sleeve, she felt a little weak at the knees as her rebellious body reacted to the vibes that emanated from his presence.

"Do come in Reg, I'm just out of the shower. I'll put some clothes on. Make yourself comfortable, I'll be back in a sec."

It was then that I noticed she was in her dressing gown.

Left alone on the sitting room, I nervously had time to collect my jumbled thoughts and slow down my heartbeat that had been doing a rhumba in my rib cage.

What do I say to her now?

There was a moment there in the doorway when the mood was right for me to tell Jo how I felt about her but that moment was past and the mood broken. Now what!

Jo swept back into the room, still wearing her turban, all shiny and scrubbed, free of make-up and looking about sixteen years old.

"Sorry about that," she said."Shall we have a cup of tea, I'll put the kettle on."

I followed her into the kitchen, where she busied herself with the kettle, plugging it in and organizing cups and things for tea. I couldn't 'talk' to her as her back was towards me.

"Right that's done," she said, moving out onto the deck and unwinding the towel from around her head. She stood in the sunshine, shook her head and fluffed out her hair to let the sun do the drying. I watched all this, intrigued.

I was unused to the company of women and seeing what they got up to in their bedrooms.

"I hope you don't mind me doing this Reg, but I've been catching up on the housework. The weekends are the only chance I have to do it. Oops there's the kettle."

I followed her back into the kitchen where she prepared the tea.

"How do you like your tea?"

I signed, *"Milk, no sugar."*

Finally, I had my tea, Jo had hers and I followed her out again onto the deck and we sat in the sunshine. She looked over at me expectantly.

I smiled at her. I know I was expected to say something – but what with all the tea making, hair drying and the moving backwards and forwards to the deck, it had somehow cooled my ardour a bit and put us now on a different level of awareness.

The moment didn't seem right for my declaration of love to the girl toweling her hair in the sunshine.

I hesitantly signed,

"I just wanted to see you Jo. I can't use a phone, so I had to come over without warning. I er wondered if you'd er like to come on er a picnic in Aloha?"

Jo stopped what she was doing and stared at me – it was not at all what she had expected to hear.

"You want to take me on a picnic?"

I sheepishly nodded a *"yes" Picnic? Where had that come*

from!

She studied me, slowly resuming her hair drying and giving me a smile that broke my heart said, "I'd love to come on a picnic with you Reg,"

Then with all the enthusiasm of a child – *because that's what she looked like with her scrubbed features and hair glinting in the sunlight.*

"Where shall we go?"

I was so busy restraining myself from rushing over and taking her in my arms, that where we should picnic had never entered my head as I'd only thought of it a moment ago!

I signed.

"We could drive out into the countryside, pick up some food on the way and stop at any place that took our fancy. What do you think?"

Joanne Newton knew now, as she watched her Marlborough Man that she was in love with him. In a matter of weeks, of working closely with him, watching the animation on his face as he signed, his lopsided grin, his deprecatory manner and the look in his eyes, that brought her out in goose bumps, as he watched her sometimes, all added up to what she wanted in a man and Reg Brady was that man. It was time to do something about it.

"I think that's a good idea, but nothing too big, just tea and biscuits. Then we can come back here and have a BBQ."

"Come back here and have a BBQ" swirled around in my head as I tried to come to terms with what she had just said. Tonight I would tell her how I felt.

Mount Coot-tha was only about eight or nine kilometres from the city centre and offered, so the brochure said, an attractive' breathing space' for city dwellers. There were a lot of picnic areas to choose from and eventually we ended up at J.C. Slaughter Falls with a view across the city and Moreton Bay.

We found ourselves a good spot in the sunshine, popped up the roof, put the whistling kettle on and settled in our collapsible canvas chairs and waited for the whistle.

Our first picnic, and we dined in style, on tea with long life milk and shredded wheatmeal biscuits – *I really do know how to treat a girl!*

But I don't think it mattered about what we ate as our friendship was suddenly on a different level. Ever since Jo had mentioned the BBQ all I could think about was the evening and I got the impression that that was on Jo's mind as well. It was as if we had both decided to do something about our relationship and tonight was the night.

She had made the first move with the invite now it was up to me!

We filled in the time by wandering about – attracting some attention from the other picnicers with my 'talking' – looking at more views, reading plaques of information of what we were seeing and generally behaving like two people having a picnic! I was just happy to be in the company of this beautiful girl and didn't really mind what we did.

*

I sipped my glass of red on Jo's deck and watched the two big T-boned steaks sizzle on the BBQ. After years in the bush, I had found that there was no great mystique about cooking meat. You just burnt it one side, turned it over, burnt the other and it was done.

Jo was busy in the kitchen making salad and other bits and pieces to go with the steaks.

By mutual consent we'd had enough of 'picnicing' and

had made our way back to her house.

All that we were doing now was a preamble to what was to come later. In what form that would take was anybody's guess, but I had run so many scenarios through my mind that I was now more confused than ever!

I refilled my glass and went into the kitchen signing,

"The T-bones are ready."

Jo thrust two filled bowls into my hands.

"Right, take those," and followed me out to the deck.

All that fresh air had made us both very hungry, and we didn't say much as we did justice to my well cooked steaks and Jo' delicious salad. That and a couple of glasses of red wine will take some beating as far as meals go.

We reclined in the deck chairs – and dozed – repleat.

Jo's, "help me take the things in Reg," brought me wide-awake and on my feet. We cleared the table and took the things into the kitchen.

I watched her stack the dishes, rinse and dry her hands.

She turned and regarded me for some considerable time and then she kept it all so simple and real.

She came and put her arms around me and looked up at me as if she was asking to be kissed. When the girl you love wants you to kiss her for the first time, that's what you do. I leaned down and gently placed my lips on hers, which were soft and warm and all my dreams and fantasies came true as I lost myself in the touch of her lips and the overwhelming love that swept over me as her body melded into mine. I could have stayed like that forever but desire took over and I leaned back and signed,

"I love you Jo."

"And I love you Reg," she huskily replied.

I led her by the hand to her bedroom, and it only took her seconds to get out of her clothes and stand there, naked, watching me while I was still trying to get my pants off. She had the beautiful firm body that I knew she would have and everything about her lived up to my fantasies. Thank god my manhood, fuelled with the energy of a big T-boned steak, didn't let me down and rose to the occasion at the sight of her smooth naked body.

I lifted her up and carried her the few feet to her bed and gently placed her between the sheets and silently climbed in after her. I couldn't whisper endearments as I made love but I hoped my gentleness and the feeling that I had for her were relayed through my hands and body as they stroked and caressed her until she arched her back, called out my name and we climaxed together.

I held her warm body to mine as we dozed off and when I opened my eyes again the moonlight was shining through the open window. I looked lovingly at the girl nestling in my arms. The fantasy of sleeping with her had been realized, but I had never thought it would be like this. All the dips and curves and softness of her body seemed to fit into mine and as she slept I softly traced without touching her, the endearing features that made up Joanne Newton's face and my love for her completely filled my heart.

The moonlight flickered across her face and gave Jo an ethereal look as I kept watch over her. I was happy to just look, but her snuggling closer, wiggling and hand movements under the sheets brought everything alive and we happily made love again.

*

Jo was at the kitchen stove, wearing jeans and a roll necked sweater that made her look like a teenager. She must have heard my entrance and turned around giving me that million dollar smile of hers.

"Would you like some scrambled eggs on toast?" she asked.

I nodded and signed, *"Great."*

I could hear the rain beating down on the corrugated iron roof, a sound that always brought me pleasure, as it often foretold the beginning of the end of the dry season at Waaree and the bringing of life to the land and new vegetation for the cattle. Here it brought cosiness to the kitchen and we ate in companionable silence, Jo not asking questions while my hands were busy with a knife and fork.

It was the first time I'd ever 'stayed for breakfast' with a woman. There'd been other women in my life but only to satisfy a physical need. I'd never had a relationship that lasted more than a night and because of my 'muteness', I was considered 'different' and I usually had to pay for it. Nobody I'd ever met showed any real interest in me. But Jo was different. She was my teacher and had quietly refused to be pushed aside by my deprecatory attitude and had given me the confidence and encouragement to court her with my hands, that had caressed the words with a new and warm expression that spoke I hope with a feeling of love and tenderness.

As she finished pouring the coffee she looked up at me.

"What are you thinking about? You have that far away look on your face again."

I studied this beautiful girl with the no nonsense hair cut that had come into my life. She was neither deaf nor mute and yet had shown me a tenderness and understanding that had knocked aside my inferiority complex and had me behaving towards her as an equal with all my faculties.

Being what I was, I had learnt earlier on in life that if you didn't wish for too much, you weren't so hurt when you didn't get it. But it never always worked out that way, because it's only human nature to want more, to want something that's better, to stretch out for something that is beyond your reach.

I signed,

"I was thinking about you actually. I can't get over how lucky I am to have met you and I worry that it's all a dream and you'll disappear with a puff of wind."

I reached out for her hand and Jo to reassure me, clasped mine in both of hers.

"I'm real Reg and it's not a dream."

I moved around the table and enfolded her in my arms. I held her tightly and as her body responded I felt such an overpowering wave of love and emotion for this beautiful creature that the prickles started behind my eyes and unashamedly I cried.

We held each other until I sheepishly stepped back and signed.

"Sorry about that but I er ..."

"Never feel ashamed or apologetic for shedding a few tears Reg." She tilted her head to one side and looked at me.

"So what are we going to do now?"

I shook my head.

"I don't know," I signed, *"I'm not a religious man, because I always thought that God didn't treat me fairly when I was born. He made me dumb and I was too young to have sinned. I was being punished for no reason and I never forgave him for that."*

I reached out, touched this dear girl's face and held it for a moment. I then signed slowly, with all the loving care that I could focus into my hands.

"I love you Joanne Newton. Maybe he could even things up now by making me, in your eyes, acceptable to you."

"Oh Reg, I don't need Gods help in loving you. I am quite capable of doing that all by myself and that I do unreservedly."

Here she gave me a gentle smile.

"Still it would be nice to have him on our side, so don't be too hard on him. I think he's tried to make up for it by giving you a special talent with your painting."

Why are we talking about my bloody painting and 'my special talent'? I'm talking 'love' and Jo is now talking about 'my special talent'!

My painting was what I only did to escape the frustration of being mute. It was something I'd been doing all my life. I didn't know then if the end results were any good or not and I didn't care. I'd never showed them to anybody except Lily, whose "bloody good' was all the praise I needed, and I was always content to fantasise and live for a time in the bush cottage that I had sketched and water-coloured or from the same painting, fish from the river bank under the shade of the weeping willow tree. I suppose that is why I had kept a lot of them. They were part of 'my' dreamtime and I was loath to throw them out. But now I'm told, by the watercolour experts, that I do have a 'special talent'

"Well any time he wants to make a swap, a voice for a special talent, that's okay by me."

Jo's arms went around me."Oh Reg, don't be bitter. Let's count our blessings. We have each other and that's not a bad start is it?"

Mollified, I held her tightly and nodded my head against hers – *no, it's not a bad start.*

"As I said. What are we going to do now?" she whispered.

I signed,

"I don't know. All I do know is that I love you and want to

spent the rest of my life with you. But I have nothing to offer."

I paused for a moment and then slowly and with some difficulty I tried to explain to her with my hands how I felt,

"Working on a cattle station is the only business I really understand and that's no life for somebody like you Jo. Maybe at the beginning I'll be able to make a living selling my landscapes, but that's all very iffy. I might be popular now – new boy on the block and all that – but who knows – in a couple of years things may change ..."

I was interrupted with, "Reg, I was brought up on a farm so I know all about the bush and anyway I don't think your landscapes are a passing fancy, besides it takes two to tango. Remember I'm a qualified teacher, under contract to the Queensland government, so there'll be my contribution to the family coffers."

She paused for a moment and sidling up towards me, gave me the benefit of her smile and rather cheekily, I thought, said,

"We even get paid for maternity leave now."

I was too gob-smacked to say anything for the moment. All I could do was stare at her – *family coffers – maternity leave! I think I'd just been proposed to – wasn't I supposed to do that?*

"Well? She queried, raising an enquiring eyebrow.

I looked down at my hands that would do the talking, hoping maybe that they knew how to answer her question. My gut reaction was a big 'yes'. It was like a dream come true.

"Well?" she asked, this time more firmly.

I signed, "Was that a proposal of marriage?"

The corners of Jo's mouth twitched and she nodded her head vigorously.

"*Yes, I accept your ...*" I smilingly signed, and that was as far as I got, as Jo's body hit mine in a embrace that nearly bowled me over. And her garbled words of, "oh, you beautiful man come with me," were propelling me towards the bedroom!

* * *

The sunlight peeping through my window curtains heralded the beginning of another day. It was Monday, and after a momentous weekend I felt good, as it's not often that one gets a proposal of marriage from the girl you love. I curled up and for a moment luxuriated in the memory of our love making as we tried to do an injury to our exhausted bodies in celebrating our engagement.

Eventually the smell of coffee from downstairs got me out of bed. I showered and did what I had to do, then headed for the dining room.

My fellow boarders were all there, Pandit, Lance, Jerry, Terry and Peter and I was greeted with a chorus of "Good mornings" and "Mornings."

I nodded and smiled at each in turn, then busied myself with porridge and having breakfast.

"Your famous Reg," said Lance.

"There's a photograph and nice bit in the paper about your paintings at the Art Gallery."

I nodded, smiled and gave him the 'thumbs up'

They were all used to my signing now and no matter what they said to me they always got back a nod, a smile, a 'thumbs up', a shake of the head or a mixture of the lot.

Sometimes that's what I got back from them and then you'd have five or six people sitting around the dining room table, all nodding and smiling with the odd 'thumbs up' thrown in. They thought they were helping me out by speaking my language!

* * *

Joanne Newton had me so bewitched with the tone of her voice and the look in her big brown eyes as she daily taught me, that for the love of me. I sometimes couldn't even remember what she had said. And now on top of all of that will be the memory of our lovemaking!

How are we going to concentrate and cope with that during our lessons!

Amanda and her group were already seated as I entered the classroom and my entry brought them out of their chairs and heading towards me with their little hands outstretched for a 'high five' or a handshake.

It was the usual morning ritual of contact before we 'talked' to each other with signs, gestures, nods and smiles. Somehow it always worked and we did, for a half an hour, make a form of contact. It made me feel like the Pied Piper.

I looked over at Jo behind her desk. She must have sensed my look and raised her head, and I thought she had a dopey 'I love you' look on her face as she smilingly nodded in my direction. I returned the nod and the smile.

Jo's heart missed a beat as her Marlborough Man gave her a dopey lopsided grin that said, "I love you." How is she going to cope with watching his hands sign during classes, when she'll be remembering how they so sensitively caressed her body while he was making love to her!

*

TT was waiting for me.

He was propped up against the big gum tree in the garden, rolling a cigarette and wearing his baseball cap on the right way round – why was that now!

It took away the delinquent look and gave him an air of

126

respectability.

He signed a greeting, which I returned.

My time with TT had speeded up my learning and I could now, with some help from him, carry on a limited conversation.

He signed, "What did you do over the weekend?"

I felt a jolt of guilt. Being so obsessed with Jo, I had forgotten about TT who I owed so much. I should have taken him out in the van at the weekend. It was my chance to repay a little of what I owed him.

"I took Jo out on a picnic," I signed.

He didn't bat an eyelid and slowly finished rolling his cigarette, lit it, blew the smoke into the air and signed, "And?"

"And what?"

He gave me a lascivious look.

"What happened?"

If I started lying now it would never stop. Apart from Jo, TT was the only friend I had. The least I could do was be honest with him.

I slowly signed.

"I told her that I loved her."

TT didn't fall about with laughter, but studied me for a moment, nodded and gave me a smile of understanding.

"How did she feel about that?"

I struggled with my signing, but in the end I couldn't cope and wrote,

"She said, she felt the same about me. I stayed with her for the weekend and one day we hope to get married. When that happens I'd like you to be my best man."

TT was nonplussed, stunned and a look of bewilderment washed across his face. He was a convicted thief, permanently out on parole and a respectable person, for the first time, had confided in him and reached out a hand of friendship.

I watched TT struggle with his emotions as he kept re-reading my note pad, and there was a shiny look in his eyes as he thrust out his hand and firmly shook mine, nodding his head vigorously before quickly turning away.

I busied myself with my books, but not before I saw him try to surreptitiously wipe his face on his sleeve.

For the next two hours I barely thought of the weekend – I didn't have time. For some reason, TT was pushing and badgering me as he relentlessly hammered me with words and signs. It was as if I was cramming for an exam. There was a look of grim determination on his face as he worked and he only lost it when he signed.

"Enough," and all in one movement, grinned, winked and indicated with his head, my bag.

He wanted his lunch.

Sandy, bless her, knowing that one of the packed lunches was for TT, had always added a little extra 'something' for him and I had become used to seeing him finish off his meal with a nice piece of sponge cake with icing! It was her way of making him feel special.

*

As I walked into the classroom I knew we were in trouble.

Jo and I just looked at each other and smiled.

Her smile said "I love you" and I hope mine said the same.

How do we now get back on to a teacher student relationship?

She got up from behind her desk and came over to me.

"How are we going to make it work Reg?"

I quickly wrote on my pad,

"We've got to make it work Jo, otherwise I'll never be able to talk to you."

She nodded.

"Let's give it a try shall we," and moved over to the desks.

We assumed our normal student teacher position and started the lesson.

Maybe I didn't learn as much, to begin with, as I usually did, because of the distraction of once signing, "I love you" instead of ' I'd like to go," and after that moment of weakness on my part, it took us some time to get back to where we were before. But as we worked it was slowly getting easier to concentrate, and after two hours our relationship was more relaxed – without too much sexual pressure – and our teacher student relationship was practically back to normal.

"I think we'll be fine from now on Reg," said Jo, packing up her books.

"Yes I think so to," I signed, *" Shall I see you tonight?"*

Jo regarded me for some time before replying.

"I don't think that's a good idea. We should try and keep it as it was before and only 'see' each other at the weekends. Otherwise you'll never do any homework or painting and I'll never get any work done either."

I was stunned.

I wrote,

"Isn't that a bit drastic?"

She reached out her hand to me – *which I grasped like a drowning man* – and said rather imploringly,

129

"No Reg. It's the only way it will work."

I knew she was right, as I'm not one of these strong minded stoic people who can just push their emotions into the background and 'carry on' as normal With her, I wouldn't be able to keep my hands off her beautiful body and from what I remember of yesterday, she'd be doing the same to mine.

I nodded in agreement and as nonchalantly as I could manage, signed,

"Well, I'll see you tomorrow then."

And it nearly broke Jo Newton's heart to watch him go.

* * *

Chapter 12

I counted them again. There were only fourteen of my paintings in the room. There should have been sixteen. I knew I wasn't making a mistake because I had double-checked them after I'd chosen a couple to take to the Art Gallery.

I was going to submit one of the sixteen as one of my commissions – the other one I was painting – that was how I was suddenly, now, finding two missing!

How did somebody get into my room and steal them?

I always locked my door!

I checked the window and there were no marks of a forced entry!

Whoever it was must have known about them, where they were and their value. Who could that be?

The only people who knew were Sandy, my fellow boarders, Jo, TT, the Art Gallery people, Fred from the YMCA and Mick Maloney the taxi driver.

So now what do I do?

I didn't need to check to see which ones were missing, as I'd recognize my paintings anywhere. Besides, I could always identify them by their photograph and my hidden signature.

I needed to talk to somebody – to get some advice – but who?

TT's larrikin image suddenly appeared before me.

Now why did I instantly think of him?

Was it because he knew about such things as 'stealing'?

Of course it was.

* * *

TT slowly read the pages of notes that I had handed to him. Then he lifted his head and thoughtfully regarded me before signing,

"What make you think that I can help?"

I wrote, *"If I go to the police now everybody will be under suspicion and questioned. With your track record you'll be No 1 suspect and also it'll cause a lot of anger among the boarders. I don't want that. I thought we might be able to, somehow, quietly go about finding out what happened to them.*

Besides, I needed to talk to somebody and you and Jo are the only friends I have in Brisbane."

TT watched me for a moment and then signed.

"Right. Lets go then."

"Go where?" I signed.

"I want to see your room."

"Now?"

"Yes now, no classes today." he signed.

*

TT was like Colombo, the detective you see on television as he checked out my room – *the scene of the crime.*

I noticed he never touched anything with his hands.

He used a screwdriver to probe and prod with as he moved about.

I thought it was an odd thing to carry – a screwdriver!

"I've seen enough," he signed, "I'd like you to take me into the city and drop me off. I want to see some people."

He looked at the easel with a sheet covering my painting.

"Do you mind If I have a look?"

"No." I indicated and removed the sheet.

TT studied my painting for some time. Finally, nodding his head, he looked at me, gave me a 'thumbs up' and walked out of the room.

The area in the city that TT directed me to was in need of some TLC. Leaving your car unattended here for a couple of hours was an open invitation to having it stripped. All you'd be left with would be the chassis.

A group of men loitering on the street corner, all wearing baseball caps, on back to front, watched us approach.

I parked the van and TT jumped out and slouched over towards them. I then noticed that TT's cap was once again on back to front. That and the slouch gave him the slovenly look of an aging delinquent and he melded in perfectly with this gang of men that greeted him with high fives and much back-slapping.

He turned and indicated for me to leave. I drove away.

* * *

Working by myself back at the school made me realize how much I depended on TT to keep me focused and guide me through the lessons.

I don't think I learnt anything in the two hours of distracted study that I tried to do. My mind was on stolen landscapes – and to help me – TT's foray back into the world he was trying to leave. His parole officer would have a fit if he knew that TT was possibly associating with known criminals.

I broke for an early lunch and ended up eating mine, and half of TT's – I needed a lot of 'comfort food' it seemed.

*

I told Jo about the stolen landscapes and TT's offer to help.

She thoughtfully said, "I always said he'd be a loyal friend and he's jeopardizing his parole and his efforts to go straight in helping you. Whether he can or nor remains to be seen. Maybe it would have been wiser for you to have gone straight to the police."

I nodded in agreement and signed, *"Maybe you're right."*

"Do you have any suspicions?"

I shook my head and signed, *"No. I always lock my door. The only other person that has a key is Sandy,"* then I had a thought, *"but I don't always lock it when I go to the dining room."*

Jo sagely nodded her head, "I should think that's when it happened then. It has to be one of the boarders."

We looked at each other appalled.

Whoever took them would need some sort of transport and Lance, the traveling salesman, had a van that he needed to carry samples and office supplies of stationary around with him for his customers. There was a possibility!

How can I behave normally at mealtime when I know that one of my friendly fellow diners is a thief and has pinched my paintings!

"Reg, we can spend the whole afternoon playing at being detectives, but we must try and do some work. So why don't you come around and see me after classes. Then we can talk about it some more. But for now, let's work."

Jo went into her teacher mode and very business like said,

"Right. We wont try and learn any new signings, we'll recap on what we've done."

The thought of seeing Jo tonight cheered me up and we did work quite well, until the door opened and in poured the students for her next class.

* * *

The sound of chimes, were silenced by Jo opening the door.

She didn't speak, but just looked at me, smiled, extended her hand to take mine and we led each other into the bedroom, where – savouring every special moment – I began to slowly undress her. Our impatient bodies had other ideas at the speed of undress and the anticipation and desire of well remembered sex took over, and within seconds our clothes were littered all over the carpet floor as we tumbled, body and limbs entwined, naked, onto the bed.

To say that our sex was frenetic would be doing it an injustice. When you're mute, it's difficult to whisper endearments as you need your hands to do the talking and at this particular time mine were busy! It wasn't necessary to speak anyway, as all our love making was done was with loving caresses and long lingering strokes, like a well rehearsed orchestra that only reached it's climax when Jo shuddered in my arms and I silently called out her name.

I kissed the top of her head as she snuggled up to me. I was so full of love for this person in my arms that I didn't know how to fully express it or how to really show it. I just lay there in a soft and tender mood and held her.

Her muffled,

"I'm hungry." confused me for a moment – *food, I thought at a time like this* – and then I realized I hadn't eaten.

I extricated my arms and signed, *"What would you like?"*

"There's steak again, I'm afraid, in the fridge. You cope with the BBQ and I'll cope with the rest."

Having been given my orders, I rolled off the bed and hunted around the bedroom floor looking for my clothes. Jo just slipped on a dressing gown and headed for the bathroom, with me not far behind her.

We sipped our mandatory glass of red wine while we prepared the food, shyly grinning, touching and pecking at each other in passing.

Steak, salad, crusty French bread and red wine for a meal will take some beating!

I had a funny thought though. Does this mean that every time I make love to Jo I get a steak!

If so, we'll need to have a lot of cattle in the back yard!

With all our senses satisfied we got down to the nitty gritty of my stolen landscapes. It was two days since I had left TT with his 'friends' in the grubby part of town. Nothing since then had been heard of him. What he was up to was anybody's guess, but I just hoped it was nothing that would get him into trouble with his Parole officer.

Jo and I tossed ideas backwards and forwards but we

needed TT's 'expert' opinion of what to do without going to the police.

It was eight o'clock when Jo said, "Right. Off you go then darling. I have papers that need marking and I'm sure you have things to do to."

How can she be so strong-minded! She's right of course, but still ...

It was only when I was driving home that I remembered she had used the word "darling" for the first time. There had been a natural permanency about its use and it made me feel good.

* * *

TT, sitting at one of the benches in the garden of the school was a welcome sight when I arrived next morning.

He acknowledged my appearance with a casual wave of his arm and I noticed that his cap was, peak to the front.

He handed me his notepad and indicated, "read."

I read.

"Two unsigned landscape paintings passed through the hands of an art 'fence' I know last week. They were taken off his hands by a shonky dealer."

"What's the dealer's name?" I signed.

TT shook his head, grinned and signed,

"My friends don't hand out names. They don't dob each other in."

I read some more.

"The paintings are 'hot', so each person handling them takes a quick profit and gets rid of them."

"What do we do now?" I signed.

The answer was already written.

"We wait until they're put on show in an art gallery. It's the best way for the dealer to get a better price. He'll put a fictitious name on them and hope he quickly gets a buyer. He won't want to hang onto them for too long in case he's caught with 'stolen' property.

We need to get hold of them before they're sold to a private collector, who'll just put them up on his sitting room wall and then we'll never find them."

I was appalled at the idea of keeping tabs on all the art galleries in Brisbane.

"How do we go about that?" I signed.

TT wrote,

"First. We see your Art Gallery friends. We'll need Jo to do the 'talking' for us. The paintings were unsigned, so how are you going to prove they belong to you. They'll have another name on them and it won't be yours?"

"When we find the paintings I will show you." I signed.

TT gave me a puzzled look, shrugged his shoulders and signed,

"Okay then, lets try and do some work until we see Jo."

TT had a way of getting me to focus on working and all my concentration was needed as I struggled with 'remembering' and 'signing' as he pushed me without letup for two solid hours. The world of stolen art and shonky dealers was pushed into the background and for the moment, it was more important to me, that my hand movements spoke to and satisfied TT.

* * *

Jo was surprised to see TT and they greeted each other with such a flurry of hand movements that me realize how far I had to go to reach that level of communication. They kept talking.

Eventually Jo spoke,

"TT has told me about the paintings. He suggests that we go and see Arthur and George now. He said you did some good work this morning so you won't be missing out on too much if we cancel our class. We can use my car."

* * *

Arthur and George didn't bat an eyelid as they listened to Jo. I expected them to be at least intrigued, nonplussed or even gobsmacked – *but nothing* – they just sipped their drinks and regarded us like it was an everyday happening.

When Jo finished our tale of woe, Arthur nodded and spoke slowly so that Jo could relay what he was saying to TT.

"It's just another variation of what we've experienced over the years. Whoever took the paintings knew where they were and their value. All fingers point to one of your boarders. Reg does any of them have a car or van?"

I nodded a *"yes"* and wrote, *"Lance is a traveling salesman and has a van."*

"Then I should think that he's the most likely one. I doubt if the thief would take the risk of openly carrying two large wrapped paintings around with him. Somebody would be bound to remember seeing him. He would need transport."

TT came in with some signing that Jo translated.

"TT says the only person who knows who it the thief is, is the 'art fence' and he of course won't finger the thief. The weak link is the 'lookout' the fence employs. It's usually somebody hanging about in the street, who gives warning if police are in the area."

"How would you get him to talk?" enquired George.

139

Jo relayed the question to TT, who shook his head, shrugged his shoulders in a non-committal way and casually puffed on his cigarette.

I didn't believe him for one single moment.

"But how do we go about finding the paintings?" asked Jo.

"All the Galleries are constantly in touch with each other," said Arthur, "we're like second hand car salesmen. If we have a client that's looking for a particular kind of painting and we haven't got it, we check with the other Art Galleries to see if they can help us out. I'll get on the phone and alert them to what we're looking for. They'll let us know right away if anybody turns up wanting to exhibit watercolour landscapes."

"The dealer probably feels secure because they were unsigned," said George."Now signed with a fictitious name, they weren't painted by Reg here but by the person who's name is now on them and it's going to be difficult to prove otherwise!" giving me an enquiring look.

Now what do I do? Reveal my little secret? Sitting in this room with me were the only friends I had in Brisbane – if I can't trust them who can I trust!

"Are my paintings still on exhibit?" I signed to Jo who relayed the question to Arthur.

He nodded.

"Yes. They're still on show in reception."

I indicated for them to follow me.

Maybe my ego is getting a little inflated now, but my two paintings did look good up there on the wall of the Art Gallery.

I stopped in front of the first one and inwardly smiled as I remembered the idyllic hours of fantasy that I'd spent fishing underneath its weeping willow tree.

I turned to Arthur and wrote, *"Do you have a pointer – a long ruler?"*

He nodded."Just a moment," and went over and delved behind the reception desk and came up with a long cane.

"I use it for my classes," he said.

I wrote, *"I want you all to follow my pointer."*

I then traced, by using twigs, leaves and bits of grass at the base of the tree, my name.

"Good Lord," whispered George, "how very clever."

"It's so obvious. Now that you've pointed it out, it stands out like a beacon," said Arthur.

TT just looked at me and shook his head in a way that said, "you smart bugger."

Jo squeezed my hand.

"It's my little secret," I wrote, *"can we keep it that way?"*

They all nodded – still looking at my landscape – a ' yes.'

Jo dropped TT off at his home and as we continued on our way back to the Institute I indicated for her to pull over.

She did so, enquiring,

"What do you want to do?"

"I want to kiss you, that's what I want to do." I signed.

"Here?" she asked, looking around at the shoppers passing by.

I nodded, and Jo smilingly offered up her face to be kissed.

* * *

Was I being paranoid, but there was a nervous look about Lance at breakfast time. He avoided meeting my eye and usually he was the chatty one at the table. Because he had transport, he was now No1 suspect, and his behaviour, it seemed, suddenly had 'guilt' written all over it.

If he was the thief, he was obviously new at the game and not your cool hardened criminal. Proving it of course is another matter!

* * *

Jo dreamily watched her Marlborough Man mingling with Amanda and Co in their morning get together.

A rosy tint suffused her cheeks as she remembered the busy shopping area, yesterday, where she had stopped the car. Then, as Reg kissed her, from a group of teenagers, coming the whistles and hoots that signaled their approval. Housewives, out doing their daily chore of shopping had also paused to gawk and when Reg finally turned and gave them a small bow with a *'thumbs' up'* – he received an enthusiastic round of applause.

She had wondered as she drove away if any of those women shoppers were thinking,

"My old man never kisses me like that in public."

* * *

No TT this morning!

Maybe he had to check in with his Probation Officer, or maybe he was out and about with his cronies from the sleazy part of town – leaning on the fence's 'lookout' to get some information. Maybe!

I struggled with my work, finding it all very boring on my own. No TT to push me, and no TT to please.

He strolled in around about 12 o'clock, in time for lunch.

I didn't ask him where he'd been and he didn't offer to tell me. Whatever he'd been doing had made him hungry and when he'd finally finished a piece of Sandy's fruit cake and

142

rolled himself a fag did he sign,

"Well, don't you want to know where I've been?"

I tried to casually shrug an *"okay."*

He handed me his notepad.

I read,

"A white van with the sign OFFICE SUPPLIES on the side was in the area, and a man was seen carrying two large wrapped packages from it into the 'fences' shop."

I indicated that, *"Lance, the traveling salesman had exactly the same white van and lettering."*

"He's our man then," signed a grinning TT.

TT had made it all look so easy.

"What do we do now?" I signed.

TT wrote,

"If we call the cops, it might alert the people who have the paintings and they might panic and destroy them, that you don't want. I suggest we wait and see if we can get our hands on your landscapes. Then we can sort out our friend Lance."

He was right of course.

* * *

Chapter 13

It's Friday night and this is bloody ridiculous I thought, as I mooched around my room – which lately had become like a prison cell. Jo and I love each other and we're going through this enforced separation because we don't think our relationship, teacher and student, will work if we're living together!

Who's bloody stupid idea was that?

We should be together, enjoying our young lives, instead of wasting them by being separated.

So stop whinging Brady and do something about it. Like what?

Yeah, like what?

Like, tell her you want to get married for God's sake. Put your foot down – wear the pants for a change.

Yeah, bugger it, I thought – thinking about it – that's what I'll do. Buy a ring and go and see her.

*

On Saturday morning, armed with my little gold band, I

pressed the bell.

Jo opened the door and a look of surprise passed across her face as she saw her visitor.

There was a no nonsense look about him today. His Stetson was jammed squarely on his head and there was an aggressive attitude about him that said, 'don't mess with me.' And as he walked past her into the house, he looked as if he might have been heading for the 'OK Corral!'

"Did you want to see me?" she tentatively enquired to his back.

I turned and went straight for the jugular.

"I want to marry you," I signed, *"I'm sick of this separation. I love you Jo and I want to be with you."*

Her knees felt a bit wobbly as she replied,

"When did you have in mind?"

"How about Monday lunch time at the Registry office."

"That was a short engagement." Jo managed to stutter – *trying to humour the beast.*

I wasn't going to be put off by her attempt to be funny.

"If Monday's too soon, then the day after. Phone and make a booking. I've got the ring." I signed.

"You've already bought the ring?"

I nodded.

"Will it fit?"

I delved in to my pocket and handed her a little black box.

Jo looked at the gold band nestling in its bed of velvet and burst into tears.

I just don't understand women. I thought she'd be happy!

There she was, sobbing away, while trying to get the ring out of the box and making a mess of it. Finally, blindly, handing it to me. I took the ring out and offered it to her.

She shook her head and held up her left hand. I slipped the ring on her third finger and it fitted perfectly, which brought on a new wave of crying and a sobbing,

"I've got nothing to wear."

The picture of this beautiful woman 'starkers' at our wedding had me enfolding her in my arms, and I held her while her happy tears soaked my shirt.

*

The phone call to the Registry Office slowed everything down.

First of all we had to make an appointment to see them – to arrange a date for the wedding!

The documents they required to see at that interview were our birth certificates and eligibility papers.

Also, when there, we would apply for a marriage certificate and they'd process our fee payment.

I'm sure my birth certificate was in that box of papers that I had brought with me from Waaree.

Jo had no idea where hers was.

She made an appointment for the following Saturday morning.

Well, so much for my initial burst of macho positive action, which was now being slowly eaten away by the bureaucratic machinery of the Brisbane Registry of Births Deaths and Marriages!

We would not be man and wife for at least another two weeks!

I stayed with Jo over the weekend to celebrate our upcoming marriage.

* * *

TT's reaction to my news on Monday morning was as I expected.

Cool, with an underlying sense of pleasure, when asked to be best man, which even he couldn't completely hide.

I had a sense of guilt in not asking Jack. I knew he would come even if it was inconvenient, but I owed something to this young man sitting opposite me, that I would have difficulty in ever repaying. In some small way, asking him to be my best man was like telling him how highly I regarded his friendship.

Jo's parents were killed in a road accident when she was four and had been brought up by her Aunt and Uncle. They had succumbed to cancer when she was eighteen.

Like me, she had no relatives.

But she was going to have a maid of honour she said, a girl from one of her classes. A deaf mute just like TT. Her name was Bridget Rose.

Well I hope Bridget Rose was an attractive young lady, because that might help to get TT's mind off getting into the knickers of his Probation officer, which wasn't a good idea at all!.

My musing's were interrupted by Jo hurrying towards us.

"I've just had a phone call from Arthur." She said and signed,

"There's two new landscape paintings on show at a small gallery in Fortitude Valley, here's the address."

I looked at the piece of paper she handed me. 'The One Stop Gallery' it said.

She continued,

"He suggests we get over there as soon as possible to have a look at them. We could go at lunch time in my car."

TT came in with a flurry of hands.

"TT wants to come as well. He said it takes a crook to know a crook!"

What can you say to that!

*

It was a small neat building surrounded by lawns and flower beds. There was an understated 'quality' look about the place and the sign, 'The One Stop Gallery' was carved out in polished wood and nestled above the front door.

A bell tinkled as we entered. The interior was filled with period furniture, neatly arranged for easy viewing. The subdued ambience of the place gave it an expensive air, not in keeping with the possibility that it might be a place that exhibited stolen paintings!

I looked around the room. Except for a few large framed hunting scenes, there were no watercolour landscapes on the walls.

A neat smallish man approached us.

"May I help you," he enquired.

Jo replied, "Yes, we were wanting to look at some watercolour paintings. Do you have any on exhibit?"

"Yes. If you'd like to follow me, we have a special room for our paintings."

He led us to a door marked, 'The Gallery'.

The Gallery was a very large room sparsely but tastefully furnished giving the viewers plenty of space to move around and comfortably view the paintings.

My two landscapes enhanced their surroundings and beckoned me over to them like a flashing neon sign.

The three of us stood in front of my paintings.

"Are they yours Reg," asked Jo.

I nodded a *"yes."*

"What do we do now?" she asked and signed.

TT came in and 'spoke' to Jo with fluttering hands.

"TT says, we tell the owner of the Gallery that the paintings are stolen and we can prove it. We then simply take the paintings down off the wall and suggest that he call the police. Who will then accuse him of being a receiver of stolen goods and possibly close him down."

I had the feeling that TT had been in a similar situation before and knew all the answers.

Jo asked, "What do you think Reg?"

"I agree with TT," I signed, *"let's do it."*

The neat gentleman that had initially approached us stood nearby.

He politely smiled at us as we moved towards him.

JO gave him her million dollar smile and asked,

"We don't know your name sir. Mine is Joanne Newton, this is Reg Brady who is mute and the other gentleman is Ted Tyson who is a deaf mute."

He looked from me to TT, in a bemused sort of way. No doubt checking to see if Jo's information was correct. Then he reached out his hand to be shaken by one and all, saying,

"My name is Gavin Hamilton. I am the owner of The One Stop Gallery."

"Mr Hamilton, did you know that the two landscape paintings that you have on display here are stolen?" Jo asked.

Gavin Middleton was nonplussed for a moment.

"Stolen. What do you mean?"

"Exactly what I say. The two paintings hanging on your wall were painted by Reg Brady here and not by the R Roberts whose name is now on them. They were stolen from Mr Brady's room a couple of weeks ago."

"Then why didn't Mr Brady ... he stopped and a dawning light washed across his bewildered face." I thought I recognised you. You're the Reg Brady I read about in the Art magazine aren't you. You have paintings on display at the Art gallery ... of course ..." shaking his head, "the style is exactly the same."

He looked at me closely and rather tentatively asked,

"You are that Reg Brady aren't you?"

I nodded a *"yes"* and produced my Driving Licence to show him.

He barely looked at it.

"Who brought the paintings to you Mr Hamilton?" asked Jo.

Our Gavin was still in a state of shock and it took him some time before he answered.

"Ah ... they arrived by courier. I had a phone call from this R Roberts saying that he had these landscapes and wanted to sell them. He wanted me to have a look at them and if I thought they were any good to put them on display to be sold. He said he couldn't bring them over himself but he'd send them by courier. He gave me an answering service as his contact number. I have a select clientele. I don't deal in stolen art it's not that kind of Gallery. I accepted them in good faith." shaking his head, "I should have known better."

He slowly looked at the three of us and quietly said,

"You must believe me."

I did.

"We are going to remove those paintings now Mr Hamilton," said Jo, "and take them with us. You can call the police if you want to, that we don't mind, as Mr Brady here can prove that the paintings are his and the police then may accuse you of receiving stolen goods and close you down. I don't think you'd want that now would you?"

A bewildered Gavin said,

"No of course not, but proof – the paintings have been signed by R Roberts, how ..."

I held up my hand and stopped him and Jo came in with,

"Have you got a pointer or long ruler Mr Hamilton?"

"Eh, yes" and off he trotted to a desk and came back with a long piece of cane, which he handed to me.

"Now, watch the end of the pointer," said Jo, "and see how the leaves are forming the letter R, then those twigs the letter B ..."

"Yes I see it," Gavin said excitingly.

"Now that you point it out it's very clear. How very clever Mr Brady – and there's the letter R formed by those roots ..."

"Not many people know about these signatures and Mr Brady would like it kept like that."

"His secret is safe with me," said Gavin Hamilton, "Now, I'll call R Roberts and tell him what's happening to his landscapes."

While he was away TT and I took down the paintings and we carried them out into the reception area where Gavin was on the phone.

On seeing us he hung up and came over.

"I'm sorry this has happened Mr Brady. I assure you that I am an innocent party to all this."

I nodded and held out my hand.

A surprised and grateful Gavin Hamilton grasped it and firmly shook it saying,

"Maybe at some future date you'll allow me to exhibit some of your paintings here Mr Brady."

I nodded a *"yes"* and Jo came to my aid with,

"That's a promise Mr Hamilton."

On the way back to the school I still didn't make the front seat, and was jammed in the back with the two big canvases, while up front, TT carried on an animated conversation with Jo.

"TT said I've got a hidden talent," said Jo laughingly over her shoulder, "he said I should join up with him and we could be another Bonnie and Clyde. I've told him, no, I haven't time, I'm getting married."

"Good." I signed.

* * *

Jo and I on Saturday morning fronted up at the Brisbane, births, deaths, and marriages registry in George Street for our interview appointment.

The Registry Office was in a Heritage building and the interior was in keeping with the outside, giving it an ambience of old world charm where you could find the documents that told you about your beginning, your middle and the end of your life.

A Registry Wedding is an affordable way to get married.

So said the brochure on the reception counter. It made it

sound like a sale. Maybe they were on special this weekend!

A girl with a clipboard called out our names and Jo and I were ushered into a room where a young man introduced himself as Graham and from then on it was all business.

We shuffled papers backwards and forwards, signed documents, cheques and produced birth certificates, ID's and eligibility papers. We could have been buying a lounge suite instead of signing up to be man and wife.

Eventually we were booked in for the following Saturday at 11am. We were told quite firmly by Graham, "not to be late" as a wedding was scheduled every 30 minutes and if you were late you stuffed up the whole system." Well he didn't use those words exactly, but that was the gist of what he implied.

Graham shook our hands, wished us luck and we were shown the door.

Jo said she wanted to do a "bit of shopping" on the way home.

Well, that "bit of shopping" found me sitting uncomfortably on a rather delicate embroidered chair surrounded by knickers and bras' in a very up-market store in the centre of town, while Jo paraded in front of me in the latest creations for my approval or disapproval. Which was a waste of time really 'cos Jo to me always looked good in anything.

Besides, I was distracted by the proximity of all those flimsy knickers. They were so small, that the minute bit in front wouldn't cover the important parts and the rear was a 'thong', like a piece of string which would disappear and er hide nothing! Obviously for ladies who wanted an all over tan on their cheeks!

As Jo swirled in front of her Marlborough Man she was suddenly aware that he wasn't paying her any attention at all and had a thoughtful, puzzled look on his face while gazing at those horrible knickers.

Jo's,

"What do you think Reg?" brought me guiltily back to reality and nodding my approval.

Jo, now proudly carrying two discreet coloured shopping bags, which told everybody in the know, that this young lady only shopped at the best places.

I suggested a junk-food type of lunch.

"You mean like chips and things?" she asked.

I nodded a *"yes."*

She thoughtfully looked at me for a time.

"Okay. If you're game so am I."

I directed her to Carlo's, who didn't let me down. He surpassed himself and as Jo surveyed her now empty greasy plate, she asked,

"Do you mean to tell me you lived on this kind of food for a whole week?"

I proudly nodded a *"yes."*

She just shook her head in wonderment.

I was dumped off at my boarding house, as Jo so painstakingly explained to me on the way there, "that spending more time together at her house, would take away from the occasion of next weekend, as the days would meld into each other and the wedding night would just be like any other night of the week."

There'd be no more trial runs before the wedding.

I didn't agree with her there – but I didn't tell her that.

After a farewell kiss and her, "I'll see you on Monday for

class."

I watched her drive away and then mooched indoors.

*

I knocked on the kitchen door, which was then opened by Sandy with the accompanying mouth watering smells of home cooking.

"Reg, do come in and met my mother." and she led me over to a matronly lady, sitting, peeling apples at the kitchen table.

"Mum, this is Reg Brady, the gentleman I've been telling you about. The one who paints, Reg, this is my mum Ellen."

I nodded and smiled a hello.

Ellen smiled and said.

"Nice to meet you Reg," and went back to her peeling.

I handed Sandy a page from my notepad on which I had written.

"Sandy, I'm getting married next Saturday to Joanne Newton, my teacher at the school. I'm sorry it's such short notice, but I'll pay rent until you find another boarder. We would like you come to the reception at the address over the page."

"Don't worry about paying me rent Reg, as I have two people waiting for a vacancy. Now lets have a nice cup of tea and some apple pie."

*

What a lousy way to spend a Saturday night. I thought, as I chastely sat at my easel and signed and wrapped my canvases ready to be stored tomorrow in Arthur and George's strong room at the Art gallery.

They were to be my Dowry and for the time being my

future income. They needed to be taken good care of.

Keeping them at Jo's place, where there was no daytime surveillance wouldn't be good idea, and as TT pointed out," any thief worth his salt will eventually find a way to break into a house, no matter how much computerized security it had."

I had the feeling that TT knew what he was talking about as he might have had some first hand experience, so I didn't question it!

Some times I would pause, in the wrapping of a landscape, and try to remember when I had painted this particular one, which would trigger off a myriad of thoughts and memories that would take me back to Waaree –to the comradeship of the stockmen – the smell of horses, the jingling of harness – the movement beneath you as you rode your stock horse daily, billy tea around the camp fire and dreamtime with Lily, they were the good memories that crowded my mind and made me hanker for my life as a stockman.

Then there were the droughts, the floods, the fires, the hard baked earth that you slept on, the dry dusty grit that got into every pore and orifice of your unwashed body and the unrelenting sun beating down on you from a cloudless sky. Those were the bad times and yet ...

One day I would take Jo back to Waaree.

* * *

I was up early next morning packing my paintings into the campervan before heading off to the Art Gallery.

Pandit was the only one at the breakfast table, the others taking advantage of it being Sunday and sleeping in.

Pandit, who took himself very seriously, didn't really have a sense of humour, and was unaware that his English made him sound like Peter Sellars. He couldn't understand why sometimes his fellow boarders all fell about with laughter at some simple thing that he had said and he innocently began to believe that he was a natural comic!

I didn't want to disillusion him, as that might stop his continual chatter, which was rather pleasantly funny to listen to, as I ate my porridge. It was like having the radio tuned into the Goon Show!

I left him with a smile and a page of my note pad that said,

"Have a good day," and soon found myself driving slowly past Jo's place on my way to the Art Gallery – doing it for no other reason, except that for a brief moment, I was near her and that made me feel good.

Arthur was waiting for me and together we took the landscapes down to a cellar type like room, which was continually at an even temperature for the protection of the paintings stored there.

"I can't get over how many canvases you have," said Arthur."You could have a one man exibition, but that would be a mistake as it would flood the market and reduce the value of your landscapes.

I think it's best if we take two now for your commissions and store the rest here and filter them out one at a time or when you need money. That way they will retain their value, and most probably, as time goes by, increase in value. What do you think?"

I had taken on board all he had said and numbly nodded approval.

"Also, we've received payment for the two paintings on exibit here. There's a cheque for $18.000 waiting for you in the office."

My mind was swamped with the enormity of what was happening to me.

And it had all taken place without any great effort on my part. There had been no hassle, stress, angst or dramas. The only one, had resolved itself and that was mainly because of TT's involvement.

Since I left Waaree, It has been like a walk in the park.

I was even marrying the girl I love, for God's sake, who was also my teacher. I was getting a sort of double whammy, and here I am now blithely storing a small fortune into a strong room, while being told there's a cheque for $18000 waiting for me upstairs!

It's all been too easy – which had me giving Lily's stone a gentle rub before looking over my shoulder waiting for the shit to hit the fan – but maybe, just maybe, that excreta might miss the fan – wouldn't that be something!

* * *

Ever since Jo, TT and myself had found out that Lance was the thief, I was aware how furtive and guilty he now looked. He wasn't your hardened criminal and was obviously very new at the game.

Guilt, *to me*, was stamped all over him and especially at the meal table where his behaviour had undergone a complete change. Once he had chatted animatedly, while he ate, to his fellow boarders, regaling them with tales of the odd people he had met on his travels as a salesman.

Now he paid full attention to his food, saying little and not once lifting his head and looking directly at me. Nor did he hang about and chat after the evening meal as he usually did, but after a mumbled 'excuse me" beat a hasty retreat out of the room.

I must do something about our friend Lance!

Later that night I knocked on his door, which was opened by a very nervous Lance.

I handed him a page from my notepad on which I had written,

"I know you stole my paintings Lance. Can you give me one good reason why I shouldn't call the police?"

While he read it I could actually see him turn pale. He looked up at me with a helpless look on his face and whispered,

"Come in Reg."

His room, smaller than mine, was neat and tidy, everything 'just so.'

If he was a crook he was a very neat and tidy one.

He indicated the chair for me to sit on. He sat on the edge of the bed.

I waited.

Lance squirmed and wriggled as if he was trying to escape the invisible bars that held him prisoner. Then, just above a whisper, he said,

"Yes, I stole your paintings Reg. It was spur of the moment thing that I deeply regretted. I tried to get them back, but I was told by the 'fence' that a dealer had bought them and he refused to give me his name."

He stopped.

I waited.

He continued,

"This may sound like a big sob story, but I was desperate. I needed money to pay the Medicare gap for a lifesaving operation on my wife. The money has already been passed on to the surgeon. I have the receipts and documents of the procedure to prove it."

He hesitated.

I waited.

And he pleadingly continued,

"I beg you not to call the police. If you do I will probably be sent to gaol and I will lose my job. I need to around to support my wife after the operation. If you give me the chance, I will somehow pay you back for those paintings Reg. Please don't send me to gaol ..."

His voice faded away and he dipped his head ...

I waited.

He then looked up at me with a face that had all the right emotions of a desperate man asking for mercy.

And I felt like one big shit. Why did I have to put him through all of this!

It wasn't necessary.

What do I do now! Nail him to a tree or let him get on with his life!

He spread his hands wide.

"I don't know what to say anymore. I will leave the boarding house. I won't embarrass you at mealtimes ..."

I stopped him there and quickly wrote,

"There's no need for you to leave Lance. I've recovered the paintings, so all's well that ends well. I'm getting married next week, so I'll be the one that's leaving."

"How did you ...

I held up my hand and indicated, *"don't ask* "and turned to go.

At the door I held out my hand.

Lance looked up at me in surprise with eyes that were swimming with tears, then at my hand, which he grasped in both of his and shook it firmly, unable to speak.

160

I left before I started bawling too.

* * *

Jo and I were like two greyhounds waiting to jump out of the starting traps. There was an inner excitement in both of us, that our bodies could barely contain as we worked and waited out the week leading up to our wedding.

I don't think I learnt very much this week. My mind was on other things, mainly Jo and these vibes were escaping and having a disturbing effect on my teacher, who kept telling me, "to stop looking at her like that because it was making her hot and bothered and she was losing concentration."

I wasn't aware that my lust was showing!

Then it was Friday.

I'd already been packed for a week. I think I was trying to hurry the week along, but you know what they say about watching and waiting for a kettle to boil!

I rechecked my wedding clothes for the umpteenth time. Why I bothered I don't know as I only had one good set of clothing, a western style like suit that made me look like John Wayne – so I was told.

It was all intact and clean. The smell of mothballs still lingered a bit, but by tomorrow it should be gone.

My last evening meal was a sparse affair as Pandit was the only boarder eating in that night. The brickies always knocked off early on a Friday and ended up in the pub. Royce, the Uni student shacked up with his girl friend every weekend starting Fridays!

So I had the 'poor man's' Peter Sellars all to myself and he excelled himself.

His final words to me were,

"You have one very good life Reg. May the God's look

161

kindly on you and your wife and may your many children be healthy and strong."

He then put a red dot in the middle of my forehead and gave me an Indian style like blessing while reciting some exotic incantation in a voice that would have made Peter Sellars proud.

I left with a smile on my face and a red dot on my forehead.

* * *

Chapter 14

I was up early Saturday morning loading all my gear into the van ready for the 'off' – the start of my new life, as that of a married man.

Those three words ' a married man ' kept tumbling through my brain as I tried to get used to the thought of my new status – as that of a married man. A man of responsibility, a man of substance!

Already I was putting my new life into the idyllic world that I always created in my landscapes. Jo would now be happily living in the little house by the river and I would be fishing and daydreaming from underneath the weeping willow tree!

And of course, in this perfect world, the fish were biting.

I arrived at Jo's and sat for some time just looking at my new home, always a welcoming sight as it housed the person I loved. How lucky I was to have found her and how lucky I was that she returned my affection.

Talk about landing on your feet Brady.

I started to unload the van of my worldly possessions and carry them up the steps. This wouldn't take long as I seemed to possess so little.

On my last trip Jo appeared at the top of the steps.

"Welcome to chez Newton Mr Brady," she called out.

How well my cowboy scrubs up, she thought. He looks like every girl's dream.

I was halfway up the steps when I heard her voice.

I paused and looked up at her.

God she was beautiful. My hands were full, so the only thing I could do, was to take the last steps two at a time, drop my luggage, sweep her into my arms and kiss her. And this I did.

After some time, she managed to prize herself loose and smilingly say.

"And now you've gone and mussed up my make-up."

I signed a, *"couldn't care less,"* and made another move towards her.

She backed away saying, "No more, now be a good boy and come and meet Else."

Else was in the kitchen, where we nodded and smiled hellos. She was a motherly, middle-aged lady surrounded by enough plates and cutlery to feed an army. I had invited one guest, Sandy. Jo had gone the other way and invited the town!

"Now let's put your things in the guest room," said Jo.

I raised an enquiring eyebrow, *The guest room?*

"Yes, only for your luggage. You're in the other room. Now make yourself a cup of coffee. I have things to do."

I then was aware she was in her dressing gown.

I made some coffee and wandered out onto the deck, where there were more utensils on trestle tables.

On the field behind the house a game of rugby was taking place between two, by the look of them, under 7 teams. I thought I'd barrack for the team in blue.

I was on a roll of good fortune and my team was too. They were leading 18-10 when Jo's, "I'm ready," spun me around.

And there she was in her wedding dress.

It was pink, and she had a perky little matching hat at a rakish angle on her head.

I don't think I've ever seen anything so beautiful.

I couldn't move. I just stared at her with my mouth open in wonder.

She reached out her hand.

"Come on cowboy, let's go and do the deed."

Dreamlike, I took her hand and we left for our wedding.

* * *

The sun was shining, it was a beautiful day and the Heritage building that housed the Registry Office sparkled. It was as if it had been given a good clean for this special occasion or maybe that was my wishful thinking as everything I saw today looked cleaner and brighter.

We were shown into a waiting room where TT was in an animated conversation with a petite young lady and he was eyeing her as if he'd just been served up his favourite dessert.

They stopped mid-signing and watched us approach them and I could tell by the look on their faces that they approved of what they saw.

TT shook my hand and gave me a sly grin, before turning his attention to Jo. "Reg, this is Bridget Rose, my Maid of Honour," Jo said and signed my name to her.

I nodded and smiled *"hello"* and Bridget Rose stepped forward and pecked me on the cheek, while TT enviously looked on.

The three of them then began an earnest conversation. Their hands fluttering like butterflies and all signing it seemed to me, at the same time!

How they took in what the others were saying and joining in themselves was beyond me!

A young suited man entered the room and quietly enquired,

"The Brady Newton wedding?"

I raised my hand.

"Would you all please follow me." and he led us towards a door.

I slipped the ring to TT and in return got a cheeky grin and a dig in the ribs.

An admonishing look from Bridget Rose quickly wiped the grin off his face.

The room we entered into had the ambience of a small chapel. It was tastefully decorated in neutral colours and the simple furnishings of an antique table and two chairs gave it a feel of quality that would enhance any ceremony that took place in it.

Faint music could be heard in the background and maybe it's my imagination, or wishful thinking, but I thought there was a slight smell of incense!

A pleasant faced woman of about 40 entered from another door.

"Good morning ladies and gentlemen and welcome to the Brisbane Registry, for the marriage of Reginald Brady and Joanne Newton," she said and continued with,

"The place in which we are now met has been duly sanctioned according to law for the celebration of marriage. We are here to celebrate their union and to honour their commitment to each other. Today both will proclaim their love for one another. We celebrate with them and for them."

"My name is, Rachel Leaver, pointing to a name tag on her blouse and I am your celebrant."

She paused for a moment and looked at the four of us and smilingly enquired,

"Now, who are the lucky couple?"

Jo and I stepped forward.

"Rachel, Reg is mute and Edward Tyson and Bridget Rose are both deaf mutes," said Jo

Rachel wasn't fazed at all by this, she said, "that's no problem. I will phrase my questions to Reg in such a way that he only has to nod or shake his head and will you sign for me now when I'm speaking to Edward and Bridget?"

Rachel turned towards TT and Bridget Rose.

"If any Person present knows of any lawful impediment to this marriage they should declare it now."

Both TT and Bridget, watching Jo, shook their head.

She said to Jo and me.

"Please sit down."

Rachel had an un-preachy friendly voice that somehow still conveyed the solemnity of the occasion as she talked to Jo and me of the marriage that joins two people in the circle of love. She said, "it's a commitment to life, the best that two people can bring out in each other. It offers opportunities for learning and growth that no other opportunity can equal."

Jo turned to TT and signed to them what Rachel had just said.

Rachel quietly went on to say,

"When two people pledge their love and care for each other within a marriage they create a spirit which binds them closer than any spoken or written words. Marriage is a promise written in the hearts of two people who love each other and it takes a lifetime to fulfill."

She talked of the solemn and binding character of the vows that we would exchange and many other things with a sincerity and simplicity that could not be bettered in any Cathedral or Church or by any ordained priest, parson and vicar in the land.

She stopped, and smilingly said at Jo and I,

"Would you please stand."

I now took my vow.

"Will you Reginald Brady take Joanne Newton to be your lawful wedded wife, to be loving faithful and loyal to her for the rest of your married life?"

I nodded a *"yes."*

TT on cue came forward with the ring and I slipped on Jo's finger and as I did so,

Rachel softly said,

"I Reginald, give you this ring, as a symbol of our love. All that I am I give to you, all that I have I share with you. Jo, I promise to love you, be faithful and loyal, in good times and bad. May this ring remind you always of the words that you have heard today."

I watched Jo take her vow and I was so full of love for this special person, who against all the odds, had decided to make her life with me. How could I ever make it up to her?

"It now gives me great pleasure to tell you both that you are now legally Husband and Wife. Congratulations. Ladies and

Gentlemen this is the conclusion of the marriage ceremony. Will you please come forward and sign the Register."

This was done and it was all over.

I was now a married man.

There were hugs and kisses all round and then just before Rachel left she took my hand and Jo's in both of hers saying,

"Just love each and you'll be fine."

A gentle squeeze and a lady that I'll always remember had gone.

* * *

Jo drove us back to her house and this time I made the front seat. My first perk of being married, and from here I could watch her and luxuriate in the knowledge that we were man and wife.

"You've got that soppy look on your face again," she said

I signed,

"I know, it's my, "I love you look." You better get used to it. I'll be wearing it a lot around the house."

She reached out and gave my hand a squeeze.

I looked around to see how TT was getting on. All his attention was concentrated on Bridget Rose, who was watching him in a bemused unbelieving way as his hands flashed in front of her. God only knows what he was telling that sweet innocent looking girl.

There were several cars in front of Jo's house when we arrived and the verandah at the top of the stairs was heaving with people and on seeing us they frantically waved their arms and silently shouted a welcome.

All those people waving, signing and mouthing congratulatory messages and there was not a sound.

169

It was the first time I'd ever been in the company of so many deaf mutes and I found it frightening. But it was now my world, so I'd better get used to it.

We were shepherded out onto the back deck where Jo held up her hand to get everyone's attention.

She then began to tell them about the wedding ceremony. At one point she indicated for TT to take over and he did so with alacrity. The intrigued wedding guests were now treated to a flamboyant exhibition of signing by the infamous TT, as he embroidered, enhanced and turned our simple ceremony into something that would have made Grace Kelly proud.

Bridget Rose looked askance at him when he had finished. The admonished TT gave her a sheepish shrug and a grin.

I watched them for some time and the sweet innocent Bridget Rose was using all her looks and smiles with an artifice that woman have been using for centuries to enslave their men, and they were all still working as TT followed her around like a puppy on a lead!

I had my hand shaken by all the men and was kissed by all the women. I was told of my good fortune and informed by some," that if I didn't look after Jo, I'd have them to answer to." Some even managed to sign and hold their glass or stubby at the same time!

Else and the caterers did a good job in feeding everybody and a waiter circulated to make sure everybody's glass was topped up.

The party went well and now the alcohol was starting to take affect and people were beginning t leave. This was accelerated by Jo's appearance in her 'Honeymoon Dress.'

She looked absolutely stunning.

The caterers and Else had packed up and left and the last of the guests were carefully negotiating the stairs on their way home. Eventually with a final farewell wave they disappeared down the street.

Jo and I were left alone.

I took her hand and led her into the kitchen, where I kissed her thoroughly and sat her down.

I then delved into the back of the fridge and came out with a bottle of Moet champagne that I had hidden there for this special occasion. I found two flutes. Popped the cork, filled the glasses and handed one to Jo.

I raised my glass and we toasted each other and many other things until the bottle was empty.

Jo then reached out for my hand.

"Come on husband mine, let's go on our honeymoon."

And she led me into the bedroom.

* * *

The sound of birdsong finally penetrated my sleep and brought me half awake. Jo was curled into my back, spoon fashion, and I was loath to move in case I disturbed her. I needn't have bothered, a murmured,

"Whose turn is it to make the coffee?" brought me around, and I enveloped her in my arms and the coffee was put on the back burner for quite some time!

This made us late for school on our first day as a married couple, so we showered together to save time, weaved our way around each other in the kitchen getting our breakfast and finally packing up party leftovers for lunch.

We drove in tandem to school.

The scene that greeted us as we entered the classroom slowed us down.

Amanda, John, Luke, Dorothy and Carol were wide-eyed, in a tableau like group in the centre of the room.

Amanda had a bunch of red roses practically bigger than herself and the others were joined together by holding a long daisy chain of flowers.

She shyly came forward and with a heartbreaking smile, this deaf mute child offered up the red roses to Jo. It was such a poignant moment as Jo accepted them that I could feel the prickles start behind my eyes and I impulsively swooped down and swept Amanda up into my arms and hugged her fiercely.

I took her over to the group and squatted down to their level and as I did so they laughingly ran around and around me winding their daisy chain of flowers around my neck and shoulders as I unashamedly cried.

*

There was no TT when I went out into the garden.

I didn't mind. It was a chance to slow down and catch my breath.

I shook my head in wonder. Two days had elapsed since I was last here and in that time I'd got myself married and had been on my honeymoon!

Talk about Speedy Gonzales!

The honeymoon had only lasted two nights and one day but it was a honeymoon that I will always remember. There were no lows only highs as Jo and I in the euphoria of love, lust and hunger and in no particular order, made the most of our time before school started on Monday.

I'm not sure as to where we spent the most time, kitchen, bathroom or bed, but I have a feeling it was in bed, making love and chomping our way through leftovers, except for the time when I insisted I take time out to fire up the BBQ and cook a steak. Something to give me energy and strength to see me through the night I said.

My wife agreed, as she didn't want me to overdo things because we had the rest of our lives ahead of us.

So we have! In my rush to do things I'd completely forgotten about that!

Then there were the tender moments of just holding each other for hours and dozing, luxuriating in the knowledge that tomorrow we'd both be still there, with me counting my blessings, and maybe not feeling so bad about the bloke upstairs keeping score.

TTs arrival was a subdued one.

I signed a hello and a, *"how are you?"*

"Fine." he replied.

"Nice," he signed, indicating the flowers around my neck.

"Yeah, the kids."

"How did you get on with Bridget Rose?" I signed.

He regarded me from under hooded eyes.

"What do you mean?"

"What I say."

TT looked uncomfortable. A state he's not usually in and even he couldn't sign a' mumbled' "alright."

"Just alright? "I queried.

"All these questions, you a copper or something?"

I raised a placatory hand and indicated, *"sorry."*

I watched him roll a cigarette and light up.

He looked around the garden, up at the trees, scratched himself, puffed on his cigarette, squirmed, and then finally, after a few more twitches, pulled out his notepad and began writing. He handed me a filled page.

"She's a nice girl," he had written." I'm meeting her here

after her class this afternoon. We're going for a coffee.

I've never met a girl like her before and to be honest I don't know how to behave when I'm with her. I told her of my past and she said she already knew about me. Yet she still wants to see me. I don't understand! Do you think she's just another, 'do-gooder' wanting to 'save me from myself'? "

I wrote, *"No I don't. Give her a chance to get to know you and from what I saw I think she really likes you. Just behave yourself that's all – you know what I mean."*

He looked up at me, nodded his head that implied "thank you," and tore up the scraps of paper.

"Now let's do some work, "he signed.

*

It was my first official lesson as a married man and I was breaking all the rules, as I don't think students are supposed to kiss their teacher on arrival – well, not fully on the lips anyway!

Then Jo and I sat in our usual chairs of teacher and student and just grinned at each other.

After a companionable silence Jo said,

"Reg, I don't think it's a good idea for you to kiss me like that at the beginning of our lessons, as it confuses me, and I'm not sure if I'm in the bedroom or the classroom."

"Didn't you like it?" I signed.

"Yes, that's the point. I liked it too much and it's er well, it's too disturbing."

"Ah, yes I think I understand." I signed, wriggling in my seat, *"I find it disturbing too."*

"Good. Now today, we are just going to talk. You will write down what you want to say and then with my help you will repeat it by signing. Do you understand?"

I nodded a *"yes."*

Jo raised an enquiring eyebrow?

I signed a, *"yes."*

"What do we talk about?" I wrote.

With one correction from Jo, I signed, *"What do we talk about?"*

"Anything you like, why don't you ..."

And that's what we did. For two hours, with prompting and help from Jo, I "talked" about what I knew best, Waaree and cattle. I really struggled with my signing and mouthing, and in trying to give the right emphasis to some words, my hands would get so mixed up and entangled, that Jo, \with all the patience in the world, had to come to my aid and help me out.

In the end, I was exhausted, and I knew the lesson was over when my teacher said,

"Darling, on your way home would you get some milk, I think we're out."

* * *

I arrived home and was greeted by the mess in the kitchen. In our rush to get to school this morning, there hadn't been time for the washing up to be done, and dirty plates, saucers, knives and forks littered the kitchen table.

I made myself a mug of tea and sat out on the deck and watched the kids playing footy in the field beyond.

It would be hours before Jo got home, so there was plenty of time to clear up and have everything 'just so'.

Good time for me to also do a bit of painting and earn some money.

I found the best light on the deck for my easel and the

landscape I was working on, poured my self another mug of tea, then just sat and studied my half finished painting.

"When you sit in your room in front of your canvas, Reggie, you will find it hard to start painting, even though you have photo, magnifying glass, and drawing of what you want to paint. You will not be able to remember clearly or feel what it was like then in the bush, and you will need a 'magic carpet' to take you back to that time.

The magic carpet that you need is 'the dreamtime stories of the Kalkadoon tribe'. In your mind, listen to my voice, and pick one out and remember that story as I told it when we went walkabout in the bush. For a little time be one of us and think like a Kalkadoon aborigine."

Dear Lily, how I miss your voice and your wisdom. So many stories you have told me, from when you held my hand as a little boy to that of a grown man. Some of the names come back to me – Mila Takujan, Milumanu, Jullen and Tankin, Kali's Journey, Malkanuru.

I chose Malkanuru.

I closed my eyes and cleared my mind, *as Lily taught me,* and conjured up her soft mesmerizing voice as she told the story.

"Long ago in the dreamtime there were seven beautiful sisters who were known as 'Malkanuru' and whose beauty was unmatched by any living creature. They were born from the night sky and they wandered the lands and skies with their long flowing hair floating behind them, their beauty was such that every man who gazed at them fell in love and lusted after them. Every attempt by man to marry them was fruitless as they came from the night sky and their hearts were as cold as ice ..."

As her voice continued in my mind I studied the half finished painting on my easel and slowly I began to remember,

176

in detail, what it was like when I was there. Then I mixed my colours and started painting.

Jo stood at the door leading onto the deck and watched her husband. He was so immersed in what he was doing that he hadn't heard her entrance or her 'hello.'

She was sure that he had gone to the place that the faraway look he so often had took him to. It was a place where she couldn't join him and she felt a twinge of jealousy of not being able to share something that was so special to him.

She stepped back into the kitchen and put the kettle on.

It was the slight sound of cup and saucer that intruded into my dreamtime story. It must be Jo. Damn – I had intended to do so many things before she arrived home.

I put down the palette, wiped my hands and headed for the kitchen.

Jo was sitting at the kitchen table having a cup of tea. She looked up as I entered and smilingly said, "Hello, husband."

Sometimes, when I see Jo, I am so overwhelmed with an emotion of love for her that it makes me feel helpless in not being able to, with my hands, fully express it, and my mind screams out in frustration for a 'voice' that I do not have.

"*Hello, wife,*" I signed, and gave her a lopsided grin.

We met in the middle of the kitchen and kissed.

"Would you like a cuppa?" she whispered.

I hadn't really thought of tea but I nodded a "*yes.*"

While she poured my tea I sat down at the table and wrote in my notepad, "*We must come to some arrangement about paying the household bills.*"

I handed it to her.

She glanced at it, gave me a winning smile and said.

"I thought we'd just split everything down the middle."

"Is that fair?" I wrote, *"I, as your husband, should be paying all the bills."*

"What a quaint old fashioned thing you are Reg. No, the modern way is that we share. We're both working, you with your paintings and me with my teaching. You must keep an account of all monies you spend on the house. I'll keep some kind of expenses book and we can settle up at the end of each week, fortnight or monthly, whichever suits you best. What do you think?"

I hated talking about money with Jo, but she obviously had thought about it and if she was going to look after the accounts that suited me fine.

I nodded a *"yes."*

"Good, then that's settled then. I thought we might have steak for dinner. I bought some on the way home, as I don't think I could stand another night of leftovers."

There was no particular innuendo attached to the word "steak" when Jo said it, but it did bring a smile to my face!

* * *

Chapter 15

The morning sunlight streamed through the windows into our room and with it came a feeling of well-being, of it's 'good to be alive' and I snuggled closer to the reason for all of this and in reply got an answering snuffled sound of contentment.

I lay there loath to break the cocoon of warmth that encased us. Outside the world was waking up, dogs were barking, birdsong came from the trees in the yard and the sound of traffic could be heard in the distance.

Reluctantly I arose, showered and did all those things one does in the bathroom and then headed for the kitchen to make some coffee. I was on my second cup and I hadn't done anything except stare off into the distance and think of nothing, my mind a complete blank. I can hear Lily saying.

"Let your mind go walkabout. Clear out all the rubbish and start fresh and clean. Then you think clearly."

Yeah, right – now what do I do about TT.

He's been preying on my mind for weeks. I wanted to do something for him, to get him out of the rut he was in, which was virtually being a prisoner on probation, if there is such a thing! He'd class me as another bloody 'do–gooder'. That didn't bother me, if I could in any way be successful. He was too talented to waste his life as he was doing now. He would make a great teacher. The Institute for the Deaf could use those talents, but I always come up against the same brick wall – where or how are deaf mutes gainfully employed? Who employs them – how can they fit into the workforce?

I didn't hope to solve that problem. I'd have enough on my plate organizing TT.

TT was a convicted felon and if he wasn't a deaf mute, he'd be serving his time in prison just like any other crook that got caught. But the prison system didn't have the facilities to cope with deaf mutes, so TT copped it sweet by being allowed out to serve his time. His only strictures were travel and reporting weekly to his Probation Officer.

I would have to somehow get them to 'swap' over what he was doing now, in exchange for attending a teacher's college for the deaf and mute.

To find out if this was at all possible, I would have to have a chat to his Probation Officer – the one whose knickers he was trying to get into – pre Bridget Rose.

Jo's petite Maid of Honour would be my 'ace' in the pack. Get her onside and TT would be like putty in our hands and could easily be moulded into whatever 'shape' that was required!

All very iffy, but it was a start.

"You've got that faraway look on your face again – where's it to this time?" Jo said, as she put her arms around my waist and nuzzled into my back.

I was surprised by her presence, as I can usually sense when somebody enters a room.

I turned around and signed,

"I was thinking of TT. I want to help him. We have so much. He has so little."

"And how does my cowboy want to help him?" asked a smilingly Jo.

"I'm serious Jo. He would make a great teacher, don't you think?"

Without hesitation, she replied, "Yes I do, and how do you propose to get past being labelled a 'do-gooder' and being rubbished by our friend TT?"

"I want you to talk to Bridget Rose and convince her that TT should be encouraged to try and get into a teacher's college. We need her help as I think at the moment he's so besotted with her that he'll do anything to please her. We can stay in the background and do whatever we can to make it happen."

Jo stared at me for a few moments.

"Do you know what you've just done?"

Nonplussed, I shook my head.

"You've just signed that whole speech without too much difficulty."

I looked at my hands that had instinctively reacted to her question – *at last, a bit of light at the end of the tunnel* – and signed,

"I did it without thinking."

Jo, put her arms around me, gave me a hug and said, "and that's how it should be.

Yes of course I'll help you. When Bridget Rose and I have finished with TT, he'll think it was his idea."

* * *

TT was waiting for me in the garden on this particular morning when I arrived for my lesson. By now both of us had accepted the routine of this daily, unpaid lesson that he so generously gave. The light at the end of the tunnel that I now so often saw was due mainly to him. I knew it, Jo knew it and he knew it.

He wasn't sitting in his usual place, but nervously moving around, hands in pockets, cigarette hanging from his lips and after a curtly nodded 'good morning' went back to staring at the sky, trees or anyplace but me. All of this twitchy behaviour was, I knew, a preamble to getting something difficult off his chest.

I waited, keeping my eye on him, as I casually pulled out some papers from my school satchel, ready for today's lesson.

Finally he stopped in front of me and signed,

"I want to better myself."

I raised an enquiring eyebrow, *'Oh, how?"* I signed.

"The only skills I have are thieving and signing. Thieving is out, as I tried that without success. I kept getting caught and now I am permanently on probation, a prisoner on the outside of a prison. But I know I am good at signing and maybe I could use that somehow to better myself. I could teach."

Here he stopped signing and watched me. It was the look of a little boy who had lost his way and was asking for help.

I nodded and with as much enthusiasm as I could put into my hands and face, agreed with *his idea* of being a teacher – *mentally blessing Jo and Bridget Rose as I did so,*

"I think that's a great idea of yours TT. You'd be a fine teacher. I'll vouch for that, and Jo and I will help in any way we can."

Here I paused and as tentatively as I could, signed, *"Would you like us to approach your Probation Officer, you*

182

know, the one whose knickers you were trying to get into?"

TT stared at me as his face slowly suffused with a crimson coating.

I kept a serious straight face and stared back.

"Are you taking the piss?"

I slowly and very seriously shook my head.

I don't think he believed me for one moment, but eventually he signed,

"I'd be grateful if you would. I'll give you, her name, phone number and address."

* * *

Probation Officer, Muriel Erwood's office was attached to the main Brisbane police station and Jo and I, after following two vague directions, found ourselves outside Room 25 – Probation Offices.

We straightened our shoulders and entered into a reception area. The receptionist was in her mid forties, plump and smiling a welcome. Her name tag said, ' Martha.'

"Yes, can I help you?"

"We're here to see Probation Officer Erwood. We have an appointment. Mr and Mrs Brady."

That was the first time we'd used our married name. *Mr and Mrs Brady* had a nice ring to it and brought a smile to my face.

"Oh yes, she is expecting you, "and Martha pressed a button on a small machine, speaking as she did so."Mr and Mrs Brady are here."

The door of one of the two offices leading off the reception area was eventually opened by an ash blond woman neatly attired in a dark pant-suit. She looked to be in her mid thirties. Her features, free of make up, gave her a well-scrubbed look that went well with her slim build and athletic movement, which bespoke of jogging and gym. No wonder TT was trying to get into her knickers – it showed he had good taste.

"I'm Muriel Erwood, TT's probation officer," she said, reaching out to shake our hands and usher us into her office.

Like her, the office was neat and tidy. Her desk free of clutter, everything *just so.*

Once settled in our matching chairs, there was no upstaging by Muriel Erwood, Jo was the first to speak.

"I need to tell you that my husband *(that also had a nice ring to it)* is mute but can hear."

I became the centre of her attention and received a smile of sympathy and words that I couldn't take offence from.

"Oh, I'm sorry to hear that."

She looked back at Jo and asked.

"Now, how can I help you?"

"We've come to ask you, if it is at all possible to help with the rehabilitation of Ted Tyson, one of your probationers?"

"TT?"

"Yes. We feel that with his talent for signing the deaf mute language he would make a splendid teacher, if given the chance. He has been teaching my husband daily on a volunteer basis and I have used him a couple of times to fill in for me with the adult classes. He has refused any payment or any overtures by us 'do-gooders' to help him in any way. I think he is lonely and just grateful for the companionship of the other students."

Muriel Erward thoughtfully studied Jo.

"How do you propose to er rehabilitate him then?"

Jo spread her hands out in front of her and said,

"Not us, you!"

"Us?"

"Yes, The Probation Board. If, instead of being on probation, he could somehow attend a teachers college and get that piece of paper that said Ted Tyson is a qualified teacher.

His signing is of such a high standard that he already now much better than most of the teachers so there would be no problem with his ability ..." here she paused and very quietly said ..."only with his record."

When Jo had finished, I could have swept her up into my arms and hugged the life out of her and Muriel Erwood had not been immuned to her impassioned speech. There was now a brightness or sparkle on her face that hadn't been there before. Then as I watched, it clouded over and she slowly shook her head.

"Ted Tyson is a convicted felon. He should be in gaol paying for his sins.

You must know the reason why he is on probation and outside the goal. He was convicted in a Court of Law and he must be under surveillance.

We, the Probation Board are responsible for him."

She rose from her chair and walked to the window and stared at the brick wall, which was her view of the outside world, then she shook her head, clasped her hands in front of her, then at her back, did a circuit around the table and finished up from where she had started from.

She studied me for a lengthy time and then Jo go her share.

"Would you both be prepared to take on the responsibility of TT, if by any chance he could attend a teacher's college?"

I didn't actually fall off my chair but I came bloody close.

I signed to Jo, *"Does she mean like foster parents – like his mum and dad?"*

"What form would our responsibility take?" asked Jo.

Muriel Erward shook her head.

"I don't know for sure. This is all very problematic. I will talk to my boss and find out if this is at all possible. But first, I must have your assurance that you are prepared to be responsible for him. That would mean keeping him on the straight and narrow, see that he attends school and generally behaving like a model citizen. What you'll be taking on is the welfare of this young man, his future, his life." She paused for a moment to let all of that sink in.

"His rehabilitation will be your thanks. What do you say?"

Stunned, I looked at Jo.

She reached out and took my hand and smiled a smile I couldn't fight.

I smiled back, my head behaving like Noddy's.

* * *

Chapter 16

"Well?"

I'd barely reached my seat in the garden before TT was waving his hands in front of my face asking questions.

"Well what?" I signed.

"How did you go with the Probation Officer?" he signed.

I wrote, *"TT, we only saw her yesterday. Give the girl a chance. She has to talk to her boss to see if it is at all possible. This is a first time for something like this and it's going to take time. You have to be patient. I think Muriel Erwood is on your side, and by the way, I can understand you wanting to get inside her knickers. She's a very attractive young lady."*

He looked at me balefully and signed,

"I wished to bloody hell I'd never told you that."

Whenever I now mentioned the words 'knickers' and 'probation' they had salutary effect on TT – ever since the appearance of Bridget Rose!

"Anyway, Jo was absolutely marvelous. She put your case to her so eloquently and convincingly that Muriel

Erwood could not, but be convinced that you were worth rehabilitating. She assured your Probation officer that you would have no difficulty in getting into the Teachers College for the Deaf or TAFE, as your signing was already better than most of the teachers. The big problem is your criminal record."

Here I paused and handed him the note, there didn't seem to be anything else to say.

As he read a cloud of despondency washed over TT's face and his shoulder's sagged when he moved away from where I was sitting. He pulled out the makings and started to roll a cigarette, and not too successfully.His hands that were usually so eloquent and fluid were now clumsy and shaky. He gave up in the end and threw the half rolled fag away. He looked back at me. His eyes shiny with unshed tears. He slowly signed,

"I'm always going to have that criminal tag aren't I? It's on my record and it'll never leave me. I thought for just a moment there, I was in with a chance to *be* somebody."

He cynically shook his head and signed,

"I should have known, I was living in a dream. But we all need to have dreams and fantasies don't we, and this time my dream was more real because there was somebody else involved – Bridget Rose.

To be somebody and gain her respect and maybe, maybe one day, ask her to marry me. Was that too much to wish for?"

He imploringly asked me, wiping away the tears that were now unashamedly coursing down his cheeks.

I felt like hugging this young man to ease his pain.

I wrote,

"Don't give up so easily TT. The steeplechase has just

started so don't fall at the first hurdle. We're all on your side.

Jo and I were asked to give our assurance that we'd be prepared to be responsible for you, if and when you attend the Teacher's College. This we gladly gave. We'd be a cross between probation officers and foster parents. She said, because of your record, you still needed to have some form of surveillance and Jo and I would be her unobtrusive watchdogs."

A subtle change came over TT after he had read what I had written – I could see it in his face as he watched me. He pulled out the makings again and this time his hands were steady and sure as he deftly rolled a cigarette and lit up. He signed,

"You and Jo'd do that for me?"

I nodded a *"yes."*

"Why?"

I didn't want to go down this path as it was getting all too serious and might get maudlin. I tried to lighten it up with his favourite hate and smilingly wrote,

"Because we're a couple of do-gooders who want to save you from your self. Your premise of 'robbing the rich to give to the poor' went out with Robin Hood – who, by the way, never got caught by the Sheriff of Nottingham – 'cos he always had a plan B."

There was no answering smile from TT.

I kept trying,

"And maybe it was also because Errol Flynn was so much taller than you are."

TT, puffing deeply on his cigarette, studied me for some time, his face showing nothing of what he was thinking. Eventually he signed.

"Right, mister smart arse, lets do some work then."

* * *

I'm never sure whether it's cloud seven or nine that very happy people were supposed to spend a lot of time on, but whatever cloud it is, I was on it. I wandered through the days in the euphoria of married bliss. Doing what I was supposed to do and smiling as I did it. Jo called it "that dopey grin" I called it my *"I love Jo look."*

The days went into weeks as we nervously waited to hear from the Probation Department and even that could not mar our happiness – some of which rubbed off on TT and Bridget Rose who openly now had become an 'item'.

The four of us would often dine together at Jo's house. TT and I would do the honours with the steaks and Jo and Bridget Rose the other bits and pieces. I needed the steaks, but their supply of energy I think was wasted on TT and Bridget Rose, who I don't think had reached that stage yet of exerting themselves as Jo and I were apt to do!

The change in TT was remarkable and all because of our demure Maid of Honour, who without any apparent effort had turned the infamous 'free spirit' into a courteous charming and considerate suitor. There was a positiveness about him now, in place of the tentative puppy on a lead bit he had at the beginning of their relationship and Bridget Rose, smart girl that she is, took a step back and allowed him to take the lead in so many things and she happily followed.

But we worked bloody hard. TT was using these lessons to hone his somewhat considerable teaching skills. He didn't just focus to me as he used to, but now would encompass the whole garden with his signing, it was as if he was in a classroom full of students and he was their teacher.

Dear God, I hope he isn't disappointed.

It would destroy him!

* * *

It was on a Tuesday morning that the news from the Probation Department came.

TT was in full flight with his signing and I was struggling to keep up with him, when Jo's sudden appearance turned both of us into a frozen tableau of expectancy, which was a mixture of fear, relief and hope.

Jo spoke and signed at the same time.

"The Probation Board want to see us all next Friday at 10 am. I said we'd be there. TT, I want you to bring Bridget Rose along as well."

TT smiled and nodded, while I hugged and kissed the pretty messenger.

It was difficult to work after that. So much depended on the outcome of the interview on Friday, that even the cool TT was distracted and called for an early lunch.

For the next two days we all went through the motions of normal behaviour, but I don't think I made any progress with my signing, as my mind was on the possible scenarios that I kept playing out in the forthcoming meeting with the Probation Board, and there was an uncertainty about TT's teaching that didn't help. Nor did the sudden appearance of Bridget Rose at these morning sessions. Her presence was a big distraction for my teacher, who spent more time looking at her than me – *what's that saying? Two's company three's a crowd!*

Friday eventually arrived – the waiting was over.

Jo, clucked around me like a mother hen, picking *invisible things* off my one and only suit, making sure that I was presentable. Then thoughtfully stepping back to take a better look saying,

"The hat."

I got the hat.

She grinned.

"That's better."

I made the front seat and we set off to pick up TT and Bridget Rose.

I'd never seen TT in a suit before, but he was in one now and I must say 'he scrubbed up pretty well'. He'd make a great model. Bridget Rose complimented his appearance and the two of them made a very attractive couple. They looked like two young well off professionals on their way to the office, rather than a convicted felon and his girlfriend on their way to the Probation Board!

We all nodded a greeting, squared our shoulders and headed west to fight for the future of a friend.

Martha in reception greeted TT like an old friend. His weekly visits over the years to see his Probation officer had endeared himself to softhearted Martha who felt sorry for that 'nice young man in trouble who couldn't hear or speak'.

"They shouldn't be too long," she informed Jo, "please take a seat."

The reception was a sparse area in need of some tender loving care. Its grey walls did nothing to lift the spirits and the two depressing landscapes of drought scenes didn't help either.

Jo, TT and Bridget Rose were already in full flight, talking, and their signing and mouthing had Martha fascinated, as they conversed and seemingly understood each other!

Martha, eventually, smilingly approached us.

"They will see you now."

She led us to a door marked 'Interviews', which she

opened and announced to those inside, "Mr and Mrs Brady, Ted Tyson and Bridget Rose Arnold," closing the door behind us as she left.

Confronting us were four people sitting behind a long table. Muriel Erwood, two suited gentlemen and another female, with some form of recording equipment in front of her.

Muriel Erwood beckoned us forward.

"Would you please take a seat," indicating the first row of chairs lined up in front of them.

We all sat. I took off my Stetson and placed it on the empty seat beside me.

Muriel Erwood spoke,

"Mr and Mrs Brady, with me are two senior members of the Probation Board and a stenographer to record this interview. Do you have any objection to that?"

Jo quickly signed to TT who shook his head.

"No, not at all," replied Jo.

"Good. Now I presume, as Ted Tyson is a deaf mute you will be speaking on his behalf. Is that correct?"

"Yes and No," Jo answered.

"Pardon?"

"I think we should let Mr Tyson speak for himself. Let him tell you why he wants to, as he puts it, ' better himself.' He can do that by signing and I will interpret what he is saying for you – it would be a sort of transcript. Would you agree to that?"

Muriel Erwood looked at the two, by now, bemused Board members who glanced at each other and nodded.

"I need to stand behind you so I can see TT while he is

signing," said Jo, getting up and moving around to the back of the group at the desk.

She smiled and signed to TT, who nodded and looked at Bridget Rose. She reached out a reassuring hand that he held for a moment.

It was like being in the theatre. The room went still and quiet – it was that special moment before the curtain rises.

TT, for several seconds, studied the people who would decide his fate with a calmness that I had often seen in him. *A quality he no doubt needed when he was silently moving around in the darkness of a house relieving the owners of their valuables!*

He began to sign and Jo's voice followed,

"My name is Ted Tyson and my address is Number 25 Harben Road, Kingston. I live with my mother who is a widow. I am also a convicted felon on probation and a deaf mute."

He paused for a moment and looking directly at the two senior officers continued,

"Do you ever wonder what it's like to be unable to hear or speak, to watch other people laughing and talking, listening to music and all the other pleasures that being normal brings them? As a teenager I was never able to follow pop groups like The Beatles and The Rolling Stones or hear Frank Sinatra and Bing Crosby sing. Simple things, I know, but they were not for me. I was in a world of silent signing and sometimes, grotesque mouthing and over the years a resentment built up inside me against the God that made me a deaf mute and the world in general. I thought I could even things up a bit by stealing from the rich and giving to the poor. It was a mistake, it was wrong, I know that now, and the poor didn't want what I tried to give them anyway."

What we were all witnessing was TT brilliantly showing,

with his expressive hands and mobile face, how signing should be done and the actress in Jo's interpretation only enhanced the mood and emotion that he portrayed. The Probation officers eyes were glued to TT. He was like a snake charmer and the soft cadences of Jo's voice in their ears was the music that they heard.

"Being on probation has proved to me the futility of the life I was leading. That feeling sorry for myself was a waste of time and effort. I want to be a better person – to do something worthwhile.

To use what talent I have to get a decent job and be a responsible member of the community. As good as they are, I don't want to work in a Sheltered Workshop on a disability pension and a small wage funded by the Government. I want to be independent.

I would like to be a teacher at the Deaf Institute or TAFE. For this I need a Teacher's Diploma – a piece of paper saying that I am qualified to teach.

I am asking you, if somehow I could use this probation time, still under surveillance, to study at a teacher's college and get my diploma. The rehabilitation of prisoners is a high priority on the list of many institutions. I would be one of your success stories."

He turned and looked at me for a moment, then paid attention to Jo.

"Mr and Mrs Brady have offered to be responsible for me. For that I am humbly grateful. I would never let them down. Thank you."

In the utter silence that followed Bridget Rose gently laid her hand on TT cheek, he slowly turned his head and kissed it.

It was such a poignant moment from these two attractive, impaired young people, that it had the stoic Probation department shuffling papers and *doing things* to hide their reaction.

* * *

The wheels of bureaucracy still apparently turn slowly and the days, once more, went into weeks, as we cooled our heels and waited impatiently for news from the Probation Board.

TT was losing the positive attitude, that had always stood him in good stead, and now there were the beginnings of a despondent approach to almost everything he did. He would, every so often, break off in the middle of our lessons, imploring for reassurance, and sign something like,

"They're gunna turn me down aren't they? That's why they're taking so bloody long. I knew it. It was a bloody waste of time. Yeah – they'll turn me down for sure – I know it."

"You know bugger all TT," I patiently signed."*Yours is a unique case and it'll take time. Those two members of the board were won over by your speech, I could tell. We all thought you were great, seriously, now stop farting about and let's get on with the lessons."*

"Won them over, do you think?"

"Yeah, won them over."

Mollified by a bit of praise – it was back to work – until the next time – in, I should say, about ten minutes time!

* * *

It was nearly five weeks before word came from the Probation office and a smiling Joanne Newton delivered it to the two of us, working in the garden. We saw the smile, stopped signing, and waited for the good news.

Jo signed,

"TT. They have agreed in principle to you using your probation time in attaining a teacher's diploma."

TT punched the air and gave a silent shout, "Yeah."

I hugged and kissed the pretty messenger.

She extricated herself and continued.

"But the two senior probation officers feel that this could be achieved by you being a sort of, an apprentice, a student teacher. They were most impressed by your signing and our working together at the meeting. They think this should continue, which would solve the problem of surveillance. It means working five days a week with me. Doing exactly what you're doing now, except that you'd be getting credit for it and some form of remuneration. What do you think?"

TT, eyes suspiciously shining, spread his arms wide in a gesture of humility and thanks.

"Now go and tell Bridget Rose the good news."

He took off running.

"Well Reg Brady," said Jo, "you should be proud of yourself. It was your idea."

"Maybe," I signed, *"but you made it all happen. It would never have got to where it is now without you."*

"Come on then, let's go and celebrate by having lunch."

"What kind of sandwiches did you make?" moving off towards the buildings.

"Vegemite and lettuce." I signed.

"Wow. Lucky me!"

* * *

I always felt good after my morning session with Amanda and Co. Five cheerful little deaf mutes knocked aside any thoughts of self-pity or depression I may have had before

I entered their classroom. A new world of communication was opening up for them and a negative attitude from me had no place in their spontaneous laughter as I was greeted with high-fives that made me feel ten foot tall.

This mood was usually still with me when I greeted TT and he must have often wondered why I was always so bleedin' cheerful! Well, how could I not be, after being in the contagious company of Amanda, John, Luke, Dorothy and little Carol!

Over the past weeks there were subtle changes taking place in TT. His clothes were looking different. He was taking a little more care with their presentation – like, he was now ironing his t-shirts – and he never ever wore his cap back to front anymore – so what was left to change!

On this particular morning I surreptitiously watched him – there was something odd about his behaviour – jerky – twitchy, and he was marching around the garden as if he was on patrol – so what was it?

I was just about to give up, when – good god! There was no cigarette dangling from his lips and his hands were in his pockets! Not a fag in sight.

I smilingly signed a cheerful, *"Good morning."*

"What's so fucking good about it, I'm trying to give up the fucking fags," he signed.

"How long has this been going on?"

"Since last fucking night. She says it's bad for my health! I mean how fucking worse can it get – I'm already deaf and dumb!"

"Well, you could be a deaf mute with lung cancer!" I signed.

"Trust you to take her side," he angrily signed.

"Are we talking about Bridget Rose?"

198

"Of course we're talking about er Bridget Rose – who else! She says I shouldn't smell of cigarettes when I start next week as a student teacher."

"Well I'm sure she wouldn't mind you having the odd one as you ease into the first day of your withdrawal period!"

He shook his head adamantly and signed,

"No, it's got to be *cold turkey*. It's the only way I can do it."

We seemed to have reached an impasse, as I painfully remembered the problems I had in giving up the fags.

We sat and just looked at each other.

"Could I have something to eat now do you think?" he tentatively signed.

And that's how we started the day's lesson. TT munching on his lunch – two hours before lunchtime!

* * *

Chapter 17

Monday, and TT was waiting in reception ready to start work on his first day as a student teacher. Jo and I had driven in tandem to the institute and her arrival had him on his feet and the two of us followed her to the classroom.

Five little deaf mutes greeted Jo and I as we entered, with high fives and silent laughter. They veered around TT, not quite sure what to make of him.

He didn't do anything. He just stood there, like a statue, quite still, not moving.

His stillness eventually drew the little ones complete attention and when he had it, he simply raised a hand in a gesture of a high five and waited.

It was tiny Carol who trotted over and gave him a high five. Then there was a concerted rush as the rest of them joined her and TT smilingly using both hands high fived them back.

I looked at Jo who shook her head in wonderment.

It had taken TT just two minutes to win over five little deaf mute strangers.

I wandered out into the garden on my own, TT was with Jo, watching and learning as she worked with Amanda and Co.

After about an hour he thoughtfully appeared and slowly shaking his head signed,

"They put things in the right perspective don't they?"

I nodded.

"Okay. Let's see what you've learned this morning."

The three of us later had lunch together. TT had insisted in bringing his own lunch – as he was now a student teacher – and what he was eating had Jo and I enviously watching. *I must bring better food I thought, and not cut the bread so thick!*

TT and I worked for one hour while Jo did some paper work. This came to a halt on the arrival of about a dozen adult students – the elite, in their last year at the Institute.

They all waved a welcome to Jo and looked with interest at TT and myself as we entered the classroom. There was an arrogance about some of them and I could sense the hackles on TT's neck rising.

Jo signed,

"I have with me today a student teacher, Ted Tyson, who will be sitting in on all our lessons."

She pointed to TT who raised an arm and nodded. He turned to Jo and signed, "I would like to say hello to the students."

Jo nonplussed, signed,

"He wants to say a few words to you."

The students gave TT a bored look of disinterest and waited.

And TT, as with Amanda and Co, stood quite still and looked at them and waited – and waited – until the shuffling stopped and he had their full attention.

He then treated them to an exhibition of such high quality signing, the like of which they had never seen before. The speed and clearness of his signing was too fast for me to read. He involved them all by pointing at each of them in turn, his face asking a question and getting a shake of the head and a sheepish shrug in return. This went on until they were all sitting upright, with eyes glued to him as he showed them how far they had to go to reach his standard – and when he had finished he had their respect.

It reminded me of a scene from the film "Reach for the Sky'. Douglas Bader the new Co of a recalcitrant Canadians squadron didn't make a speech. He just hopped into a Spitfire and gave an exhibition of aerobatics and low flying that had the Canucks shaking their heads in wonderment and respect.

It was also a salutary lesson for me as I crept out of the room and went shopping at the supermarket.

*

Jo was late! She usually gets home just after five. It was now 5-30. Probably discussing things with TT after his first day as a student teacher. Yeah that'd be it.

I studied the landscape in front of me and then carefully signed my name in among the leaves and twigs at the base of the tree. Not having Lily around to comment on its quality, left me in the limbo of not knowing if it was any good or not. I needed Jo's opinion.

6.00 and she's still not home – hope she's all right!

She wandered in at around 6.30, and smiled up at me as I kissed her. I led her to the landscape and signed, *"What do you think?"*

202

Smiling vaguely at the painting she tilted her head this way and that finally saying, imitating Lily, "bloody good".

She still had this strange vague smile on her face and she moved as if in dream – what was wrong with her?

"Are you all right?" I signed.

She grinned and replied,

"Yes, we're both fine."

"What are you talking about Jo?"

"We're going to have a baby."

Stunned – I couldn't quite comprehend the news – a baby!

"But I thought you were on the pill?" I signed.

"I was. But it must have been one of those nights when I forgot and you crept up on me. Why, aren't you pleased?"

If Jo was happy, I was happy. I opened my arms and enfolded this dear, sweet, women into my body and held her tight – that answered her question.

"I'm hungry," she whispered into my chest, "and I have to feed the little one."

"Well the little one will have to cope with heated up casserole and steamed carrots and cabbage," I signed, *"now, find a bottle of wine for a celebratory drink, while I do the meal."*

And that is how we celebrated the news that we were going to be parents.

It was only when I was lying in bed that night that the full impact of what was going to happen hit me. Jo and I had always skirted around the talk of 'babies,' as there was always that niggling thought that they might inherit my genes of being mute.

But now, we are going to gamble that this wouldn't happen

and the child would be like Jo and not like me?

Was it fair to bring into the world a child that couldn't speak?

Would the child thank us?

I remember as a little kid the frustration of not being able to talk and the tears of anger as I stared in the mirror with my mouth open, looking to see if I could find out what was stopping me from making a noise.

The years of growing up as a 'dummy' and the bad times when I wallowed in self pity and anger

But there were also the good times.

There was always the enjoyment of the book I was reading – the sound of Lily's voice as she told me the dreamtime stories of the Kalkadoon tribe and the days of driving the herd with the feel of a horse under me and the wind in my face, as I galloped in pursuit of wayward cattle. Then there were the nights around the camp fire, with the sounds of lowing cattle intermingling with the gentle crooning of the aborigine stockmen as they settled the herd under a star studded sky.

And at the end of a long drive the enjoyment of the many cold beers, with Jack, in the pub.

There were other times, when my mind floated free of reality and I would lose myself in the perfect fantasy of being able to talk – in the landscape world I had created on canvas.

Then I met Jo and we fell in love and got married.

I was content.

But no matter how dire I thought things got during my life, there was never a time when I wished I hadn't been born.

* * *

We entered into a period of subdued excitement now that

a baby was coming. It seemed to influence everything we did and when we told TT, he gave Jo a hug and me a high five.

So far there was no sign of a baby bump and Jo admonished me for,

"Always staring at her tummy. It's early days yet and babies can't be hurried."

The other thing that was affecting our lives was TT.

His empathy with the students, from Amanda and Co to the elite class, was changing the way of teaching. He knew how they felt, their problems, their hang-ups, their frustrations, because he was one of them – a deaf mute. And he used this knowledge to reach them in a way that other teachers, like Jo, who can hear and speak, never could.

Jo told me, "he is so innovative, that I just sit there, full of admiration as he creates in the class an enthusiasm that I could never attain. He is a born teacher and the classes are always fully attended – nobody takes a 'sickie'. The students are receiving the full benefit of his presence and because of his methods we are getting through twice the amount of work. I just wonder how I can do him justice in my monthly report to the Probation Board."

* * *

The months dovetailed and our lives developed into a pattern. Saturday morning was usually earmarked for housecleaning and gardening.

I was a lousy gardener and a green thumb, *that*, I didn't have.

"I think I'll go and see George and Arthur to see what they think of my latest landscape," I signed to Jo. *"If they feel it's up to scratch I'll leave it there with the others. By that time it'll have cooled down a bit and I can catch up on the gardening."*

Jo gave me what I can only describe as an 'askance' look. I did check on that word once. It said, "to regard suspiciously."

"I see, give them my regards."

Left me in no doubt that she did 'see' what I was up too

It's money for the little one," I quickly signed.

"Yes money for the little one." She smiled and went back to cleaning the kitchen stove.

*

George and Arthur always had the 'Welcome' mat out for me and after the offer of tea, coffee, gin, white, red or maybe a beer! I settled for coffee and unwrapped my latest offering.

They both thoughtfully studied my landscape. Going through the same routine that I'd seen them do a dozen times – stepping in close, moving back, to the side, making small noises, putting their glasses on, taking them off. When they had run through the full gamut of moves, they turned to me and held out their hands.

"Very good Reg, very good, up to standard," they effusively said, "well done."

I wrote, *"Thank you. I'll leave it with the others in the strong room then."*

"Yes that's a good idea," said George."Now, Arthur and I wanted to talk to you about the Spring Water Colour Exibition."

I gave them an enquiring look.

"Reg. It's an annual event that has become very popular and attracts artists from all over Australia – the good and the bad. It's a chance for new talent to be seen and discovered. We would like to make several of your landscapes the centerpiece of the exibition."

I held up my hand and then wrote,

"But I thought we'd agreed to withhold my paintings and not flood the market?"

"Five of your paintings will have a red dot sticker on them, indicating they are sold. Two will be open to offers and those two only will go on the market. What do you think?"

So that's how dear sweet kind George and Arthur control the market and keep the prices up!

I nodded in agreement.

After all I have to think of 'the little ones' future!

* * *

Chapter 18

George limped his way up to a small raised platform and tapped his walking stick for attention. The well-heeled room of patrons and sponsors obediently hushed and waited.

"First, I would like to thank you all for all coming here today." he said.

"The Spring Water Colour Exibition has now become, I am proud to say, a very popular event. It gives us here at the Gallery a chance to discover new artists and take it from me there is a lot of outstanding talent out there. These artistic people create on canvas and paper their vision and allow us to escape for a short time the ordinariness of our lives and share with them their dreams as we look at their work on display.

Such an artist is Reg Brady, whose sole exibition of landscapes here today will enrich your lives with the colours, energy and love that he has put into his paintings. Reg was taught to paint, when he was a small boy on a lonely cattle station in the far north. His teacher was Lily, an aborigine elder of the Kalkadoon tribe and his paintings have a strange quality that only an affinity with his surroundings can come from."

Having said that he pointed in my direction and as one the viewers followed his finger. He had talked me into wearing my Stetson, which made me stick out like a sore thumb, said it added colour to the proceedings, and what a right country bumpkin I felt as all the eyes took me in.

And as I sheepishly nodded, smiled and shuffled with embarrassment, trying not to look like the Marlborough Man or John Wayne, my eyes locked onto one particular person giving me the once over.

She was a tall, willowy blonde with all the curves in the right places and after she'd slowly looked me up and down, I felt completely naked. The only thing covering my body seemed to be goose bumps. Even my manhood woke up and took notice!

What was there about this woman that she could suddenly affect me like that – a happily married man!

It seemed that my being married was no protection against this thing called 'lust,' and that is what she was oozing from every pore of her attractive body. Not that I was fighting it. Instead I was rather flattered that I should be on the receiving end of such attention. It had never happened to me, 'so openly' before. Usually I was on the receiving end of being ignored.

It would seem churlish not to acknowledge such attention, so I ambled over in what I thought was the nonchalant approach that John Wayne might use in such a situation, except by the time I reached her, my 'cool' walk had developed a bit of a self-conscious hop!

Wait until she found out I was mute – her attitude would change and 'she'd' be 'hopping' from one foot to another with embarrassment.

What I had seen from across the room was only enhanced by her nearness and whatever she was oozing was hitting all the right spots on my masculinity and my 'coolness' was taking a hammering.

I reached into my coat pocket and brought out pad and pencil and wrote, *"Hello, my name is Reg Brady. I'm mute but can hear."*

I tore off the page and handed it to her.

She read it, looked up at me and in a husky voice said,

"Yes I know who you are and that you are ..." and she started to say 'dumb', caught herself in time and went red in the face as she whispered, "mute."

I wrote, *"For years we were referred to as being 'dumb'. They changed it because they thought it was derogatory, but whatever word you use, dumb or mute, we still can't talk. And you are?"*

"Sarah Wells."

She beckoned forward the two men were with her.

"Greg Strauss and Michael Ingram."

I reached out, shook their hands and nodded hellos.

Greg Strauss was a short, expensively dressed, rotund, middle-aged man and his companion Michael had the same expensive look but was thin and looked like he was in need of a good feed!

"Greg and Michael own art galleries in Sydney and Melbourne."

I smiled and nodded.

Greg stepped forward.

"We like your work very much Mr Brady and please call me Greg. We must entice you down South to show your landscapes sometime and may I call you Reg?"

I nodded and smiled a *"yes."*

"They would get a larger exposure down there and be in greater demand. You could make a lot of money."

I wrote, *"I'm doing very well in Brisbane Greg. I can't keep up with the demand here."*

"Yes I can see that, five already sold and two under offer. Well done. Arthur has promised me first refusal if any of the offers fall through."

He smiled and jokingly said, "I don't suppose you've got a couple hidden away that you might like to get rid of?"

I sadly shrugged my shoulders and shook my head.

Already lying – welcome to the 'art world.'

"Pity" he said, eyeing me thoughtfully.

I got the feeling that he didn't believe me – maybe I was a bad liar and it showed!

Sarah stepped forward and rested her hand on my arm.

"Reg we're all going back to Michael's place for cocktails. A lot of patrons of the arts will be there and I think it would be a good thing for you to meet them. You never know – it could enhance your career in knowing the right people at some future date – what do you say?"

There was a persuasiveness and appeal about Sarah that was hard to resist and her low husky voice plus the slight pressure of her hand on my arm made me well aware of her physical closeness.

"Do come Reg. I'm sure it will be well worth you while."

Was I reading something else in her invitation, other than 'enhancing my career'! Whatever it was I felt quite safe – a happily married man with Jo sitting on my shoulder.

I nodded a *"yes."*

"Good," she enthused."Do you have transport?"

I nodded again.

"May I borrow your pad and pencil, I'll write down the address for you in case you get lost."

I handed her pad and pencil and as she scribbled she said.

"If you like to follow us, we'll be off in a few minutes after we say goodbye to George and Arthur. What kind of car do you have Reg?"

I took the pad and pencil from her and wrote,

"A yellow campervan."

"How nice, a yellow campervan," she smilingly said after reading my note, "we shouldn't lose you then."

George and Arthur walked me to the door as I left and Arthur jokingly said as he shook my hand, "Watch your back with all those rich people Reg."

I kept thinking about that as I followed the big, easy to follow, chauffeur driven BMW in front of me – was it some kind of warning?

The surrounding district we were now driving through set the tone for this affluent area with trendy up-market boutiques and expensive restaurants.

The Brisbane River on our right was fronted with beautiful restored mansions of a bygone era – the homes of the early industrialists who had made their fortune and after leaving their mark and name on the City centre had moved on.

The large imposing automatic gates swung open as the BMW approached them and I followed closely with 'Aloha', along a graveled drive lined on either side by manicured lawns and herbaceous borders and parked my lovely bright yellow machine between a Mercedes and a nondescript Range Rover.

My three new friends watched me as I locked the van and joined them. We all hesitated for a moment as they looked back at my campervan. They seemed rather intrigued with it, or maybe they had never seen such a bright yellow one, with bull bars and a tow bar, in a setting such as this before and very quietly murmured, "yes, nice, lovely, really stands out doesn't it!"

'Aloha,' towering above all the other vehicles in the drive seemed as if she'd got confused with the parking and had mistakenly ended up with the limousines.

The house in front of me looked as if it should have been in a different country. It was a diamond, lead-lighted paned English mansion, which had no doubt helped some homesick overseas migrant, who had built it, to feel at home in this new land where he had made his fortune.

It was as out of place in this setting as my van was in the driveway!

The heavy dark wooden front doors were open, allowing the Australian sunshine to spill into the large oak beamed hallway where groups of casually, expensively dressed animated people twirled flutes of champagne that waiters kept refilling.

Sarah took me by the arm and eased me through this polished floored entrance hall and out on to a deck that overlooked the Brisbane River. More lawns and flowerbeds ran down to the water's edge, where a large sleek motor cruiser was moored and chairs and umbrellas dotted the garden as more waiters floated about making sure that nobody held an empty glass.

The popularity of Sarah among the male guests was very apparent. They made it their business to say hello as she weaved her way through their midst and only backed off on seeing her arm linked possessively through mine as she shepherded me down to an umbrella covered table and chairs.

A sign on the table said RESERVED.

A waiter hovered nearby with a tray of drinks.

I quickly wrote a note that simply said BEER and handed it to Sarah.

She took a glass of champagne from the attentive waiter and then sent him scurrying off to get me my beer.

We settled ourselves in the chairs and I took off my hat.

"I do like you wearing your Stetson Reg, it suits you. Goes with your image of an Australian stockman. You should always wear it."

I nodded and smiled, as I didn't quite know how to reply to all of that!

They say that clothes maketh the man. Well with me it looks like it's me bleedin' hat!

"Reg, I have to be honest with you. There was an ulterior motive in inviting you here. I work for Simon Lever, a film producer and director – you may have heard of him?"

I shook my head.

"Simon read your article in the Art Gallery magazine and thinks your life story has all the ingredients to make a good semi-documentary/feature film and that you would be ideal to play the lead – which of course is you."

I was too stunned to reply.

"He should be here any moment and can explain it to you better than I can, but initially how do you feel about that?"

I wrote, *"Sarah, I'm no actor. I wouldn't know how to begin. My wife is the actor in the family she belongs to a theatrical group. But I am mute and my face mirrors what I'm signing. She says I wear my heart on my sleeve."*

Sarah read my note and looked at me for a few moments.

"But those are the qualities we would need and who better to play you than you!"

The waiter arrived with my much-needed beer and was followed by a small, smiling, untidy, roly-poly man, with a magazine hanging out of his jacket pocket, who, literally bounced into our midst. He stood on tiptoe to kiss Sarah and then turned his full attention on me, thrusting out his hand as he did so. I shook the outstretched hand.

"I'm Simon Lever and you of course are Reg Brady. Would you mind standing up and putting on your hat for me."

Not a request but an order.

Nonplussed, I rose, reached out for my Stetson and stuck it on my head.

He stood there watching me, and as he watched he grinned and slowly shook his head from side to side murmuring something that sounded like,

"Move over John Wayne."

"Thank you Reg."

I sat down, took off my hat and paid attention to my beer.

Simon produced the magazine from his pocket with a flourish and waving it before my eyes said,

"I read your condensed life story in this and I think it would make an excellent film which I would like to produce and direct. But first I need your approval and your commitment to play the part of Reg Brady. Your lack of experience is not a problem, it's a bonus and your ability to read and do the sign language is another plus. It would take us months and months to teach an 'actor' those skills and the constant rehearsal on the set would be time consuming and prohibitively costly."

Simon paused for a moment, but his enthusiasm was so infectious, it was difficult not to like this little man who now stood in front of me with an expectant grin on his face.

"What do you say Reg?"

Me a film actor – my life story for the whole world to see – money for our future – money, he hadn't mentioned money.

I wrote one word on my pad and showed it to him.

"MONEY?"

"Once you agree in principle, I'll talk with your agent. Do have an agent?"

I didn't, but I wrote, *"Yes, George and Arthur from the Art Gallery."*

"Good. I'll talk to them on Monday and when we're all happy, I'd like to bring a scriptwriter to see you. I need to have a screenplay done so as I can do the costing and start pre-production."

He waited for me to speak.

"You haven't answered my question Reg?"

My head was in a turmoil of ifs, buts, doubts and sheer bloody panic – I needed Jo or TT for help – but I was supposed to be a big boy now and head of the family – so, did I have the courage to wear the pants and make a momentous decision that would change my life forever!

I nodded a *"yes "*and Simon hugged my tummy and Sarah kissed my cheek.

"Welcome aboard," enthused Simon, "you won't regret it."

* * *

When I got home Jo wasn't about – *she must be still rehearsing her play 'The Importance of Being Ernest'.*

If I were to do this film she'd be a great help – she could

216

give me a few pointers on acting.

I got a beer from the fridge and went out onto the deck and began to watch the inevitable game of junior rugby taking place on the field at the back of the house. Jo's call of,

"Darling, I'm home," had me out of my chair and saved me witnessing my team's inglorious defeat.

I met her in the kitchen where we kissed and hugged. She leant away from me, wrinkled her nose and sniffed the air.

"Smells like Chanel No 5."

I grabbed my pad and wrote,

"When I agreed to allow them to film the story of my life the Producer/director, Simon Lever and his assistant, Sarah Wells, hugged me. One of them must have been wearing perfume."

Jo read my note, looked at me and then studied what I had written again, "maybe it was the Producer/director," she said.

My puzzled expression made her smile.

"Only joking."But what's this about, making a film of your life?"

I wrote,

"That's what they want to do, with me playing the lead - which is me. They said there was no one better to play me, than me. I thought it was a chance for us to get some kind of security for your baby bump, which I can now see, so I said that if the money was right, I would agree. Also it would give me lots of publicity for my paintings. I told them George and Arthur were my agents, what do you think?"

A stunned Jo smiled her lovely smile, slowly shook her

head and cod proudly said, "My husband the film star."

"You don't mind? 'I signed.

"Of course I don't mind darling, I'm proud of you." And then very quietly said, "maybe the chap upstairs keeping score, is on your side now and is trying to make up for things!"

I nodded a *maybe* and signed, *"I would like you to ring George and Arthur first thing on Monday and tell him the news. Tell them they are my agents, but not to agree to any final figure until they've spoken to us."*

"Yes sir," said Jo, snapping to attention and giving me a very military salute.

"Now, would you like a gin and tonic?"

I nodded a *"yes"* and signed, *"how was your rehearsal?"*

"Good, it went well. I didn't fall over the furniture."

* * *

Monday morning brought with it a subdued inner excitement that I could barely contain, as I half listened to Jo talking to George and Arthur about the film.

What with babies and films, even my making the sandwiches for lunch couldn't bring me back to reality, as the air around the Brady household seem to buzz with a new strange energy that was to forever change our future.

Jo finished on the phone, came over and put her arms around my waist.

"George and Arthur have agreed to be your agent. They think it's splendid idea, the film, and that they'll look after you."

She peered around to see what I was doing and gave me a gentle squeeze.

"Do you think we should get sliced bread in future – you know, the sandwich size?"

I looked down at my sandwiches. I must admit they did look a bit thick!

*

While Jo told TT about the film, I high-fived Amanda and Co, and their happy infectious contact was contagious.

This is where my real world is and it would always be here. No matter how often I ventured outside its perimeter, my muteness set me aside as a stranger, and the isolation it brought with it made sure that I would always have to return to this silent world.

We all need human contact. We all need it because we are human.

Jo and TT took over the class.

I wandered out into the garden to do some work, but my mind was full of films and babies – I really needed TT to keep me focused.

In my mind I was already casting the film.

Who was going to play Jo and what about TT? Jo was an actress and a pretty one at that – as a couple people had often said that we look like John Wayne and Maureen O'Hara – which can't be bad – and nobody could play TT as well as TT. It would take a lifetime for an actor to learn to sign like TT as the signing would have to be authentic – no TT would have to play himself – and then there's Bridget Rose – she'd have to play herself. For the other normal parts they could get actors, but with people that had to sign they'd need the real McCoy.

While I was mulling all this over in my mind TT arrived, slapped me on the back and signed, "So, who's a big film star then?"

I wrote,

"If it's a story of my life, you and Bridget Rose will have to be in it, the same with Jo. Who better to play yourselves than yourselves!"

He read what I had written and signed,

"And what about the Probation Board?"

With all the excitement I'd forgotten about the bloody Probation Board!

I scribbled,

"We'll figure out something. I'll turn the producer loose on them. He'll have an angle or as the gangsters do in the movies, "make them an offer they can't refuse!"

"They also do it in real life," signed TT.

"Really?" I signed.

TT nodded a knowing 'yes they do' and signed, "now, lets do some work, I have to earn my wages."

* * *

I was in a slow moving queue at the Commonwealth bank, with my cheque for $18,000 and a deposit slip in my hot little hand. I kept looking at the cheque and shaking my head in wonder at how fortunate I was. But I'm not a cockeyed optimist and with *'so much luck'* negative thoughts began to invade my mind.

Where is the downside to all this luck that I'm having?

And when does the shit begin to hit the fan?

It can't go on like this. Even the law of averages must come into action soon and disturb the level of the playing field.

I considered myself lucky when I met Jo and TT. Now I'm told that I'm a celebrated landscape artist and the soon to be subject of a feature film. All this achieved without any apparent effort on my part and put down to the luck of the draw!

Bullshit!

I'm a great believer in luck, but even I knew there are limits.

Jo keeps telling me that the guy upstairs, keeping score, is trying to square things up for my muteness!

I would like to believe her, but naïve, I am not!

Even George's phone call saying he had turned down Simon Levers initial offer of $200.000 and had asked for $250.000 – but had agreed in principal to my playing the part and permission for me to be interviewed by their scriptwriter – had all the earmarks of cloud cuckoo and Lotto land.

Still, 'go with the flow' as they say and this I will do.

And you never know, giving Lily''s stone an extra rub, I might be able to turn off that bloody fan before anything hits it!

"Next."

And I stepped forward and presented my cheque to the teller.

* * *

"TT is so much a part of our lives, that it would be impossible to do the film without him and who better to play TT than TT!"

Jo's impassioned plea to the probation officer was pressing all the right buttons and Muriel Erwood was shaking her head like a punch drunk fighter.

She came back with,

"TT is a convicted felon and already has been given permission to do a teacher's course. Now you want him to play the second male lead in a feature film."

She paused for another shake of her head and continued,

"Where does his punishment for all his misdeeds come in? When does he pay the price for robbing half of Brisbane's affluent society of their jewelry?"

"But, don't you see. TT can be your success story. His rehabilitation will be your benchmark for all other probationers wanting to go straight."

"Yes I do see, quite clearly and I don't need to be reminded how to do my job."

An admonished Jo replied.

"I'm sorry. I didn't mean ..."

Muriel Erwood waved a placatory hand.

"Not to worry – no offence taken, but I'm finding it difficult to see how we can combine TT's teaching course, his probation period and now his filming, all in one package and make it work."

"Surely we just carry on as we're doing now," said Jo "with the added responsibility while he's filming?"

Muriel Erwood gave a wry smile and shook her head.

"Leave it with me. I'll talk to my boss and see what he's got to say. It wouldn't surprise me if I didn't end up asking TT for his autograph!"

* * *

Chapter 19

Once more we settled down to wait, while the wheels of bureaucracy slowly turned. But now we had the distractions of the proposed film, and the arrival of Simon Lever with his scriptwriter on the forthcoming Saturday.

TT, thriving in his new role as a teacher, was practically running the Institute and the students followed him around as if he was the Piped Piper of Hamlin. His, innovations, charisma and talent had them doting on every word he signed and the girls practically wetting their knickers as carnal thoughts distracted their signing and concentration!

I was now spending a couple of hours with TT in the morning, then after lunch, he would go and take over the adult class, while Jo devoted her time to me. That meant, that for five days a week, I was getting a full day's private tuition. This was reducing my learning time by half and increasing my ability to form sentences and converse with TT and JO, without having to use that bloody note pad.

A lot of sweat, but the light at the end of the tunnel was getting bigger and brighter.

Saturday arrived and Jo had me dusting and cleaning a

house that already looked spotless. I was dusting off dust that I couldn't even see and I have 20/20 vision!

I just hope the big producer/director and his scriptwriter like the smell of Mr Scheen and lemon smelling floor polish – 'cos that's what they've got.

*

Eventually the doorbell chimed. There was a quick flurry from the kitchen and a breathless,

"Would you get it Reg," from Jo.

Which I did, and was confronted by Simon and his scriptwriter who was a tall, thin, middle aged man, wearing, jeans, t-shirt and oversized horn-rimmed glasses, that gave him the look of a distracted owl.

Simon was dressed in a myriad of colours that went with his flamboyant gesture as he thrust out his hand to be shaken – which I did.

At the same time introducing me to his scriptwriter.

"Reg, meet Peter Oldham, who will be writing the script."

I reached out to shake Peter's offered hand and nodded a hello, at the same time stepping back to allow them to enter the house.

Jo was waiting for them in the hallway and looking like a million dollars.

"Hello. I'm Joanne, Reg's wife, but everybody calls me Jo."

And from that moment onwards Simon Lever never took his eyes off my wife.

He looked like he had run into a wall!

Instinctively I moved to stand besides Jo.

Simon, unmoving still stared.

The new Maureen O'Hara and John Wayne ran through his mind.

He shook himself into action and thrust out his hand.

"Jo, how nice to meet you," shaking Jo's hand and introducing Peter.

"This is my scriptwriter Peter Oldham."

Introductions over we all moved into the lounge.

Jo had arranged armchairs around the large coffee table so that everybody would be comfortable.

As we settled in our chairs, Simon said,

"Jo, would you consider playing yourself in the film, Reg's wife?"

A nonplussed Jo stared at him.

"Me? You want me to be in the film?"

"Yes. Who better to play his wife than his real wife! Have you ever acted?"

"Only in the theatre. I belong to the local drama group. At the moment we're doing The Importance of Being Ernest. I'm playing Gwendolen. We open next Saturday."

Simon was another head shaker – which he was doing like a puppy.

"This gets better and better," he said unbelievingly.

"Would you give me address of your theatre and times of performances?"

"Yes of course," said a rather flattered Jo, getting up, "I'll get you a dodger." She disappeared into the kitchen and returned with a colourful sheet of paper, that was under the windscreen wipers of half the cars in the local car parks and sticking out of all the local letter boxes.

The 'interview' was a prolonged repetitive affair, which

seemed to make my colourful life story – a dull boring litany of events, by the time Peter Oldam got it down on paper.

The routine was that, Peter would ask me a question, which I would answer, by either writing it on my note pad for him to read or by signing it to Jo who would then relay it to Peter.

My answers, in the cold print on paper, didn't have the same feeling of what I was trying to convey. And even when Jo repeated some of my answers, they didn't have the emotion I felt, when *I* was talking about the bush, the cattle, and heat and dust of the outback.

It was all very dull and after three hours of this I think we all had had enough and the scriptwriter's, "Well, that should about do it. I think I've got enough here to be going on with." signalled the end of the interview.

While all this had been going on, Simon, who had been listening, was busy doing something on page after page of a sketchpad that he had with him.

There were lots of hugs and kisses as Simon and Peter took their leave.

Kissing and hugging seemed to be the 'norm' with show biz people!

Simon's final, "we'll be in touch," left Jo and I looking at each other in a bemused sort of way, wondering where our normal life had gone too.

She came over to me, put her arms around me and said.

"Well my husband, what did you think about all that?"

All I could do was shake my head in a nonplussed way.

"Now darling I must dash, we have a run through this afternoon," and she plonked a quick kiss on my cheek and was gone.

The house was suddenly very quiet and I was alone with the turmoil of my own thoughts.

To calm myself down I turned to the only thing that would get me back to reality – my painting.

I lifted the sheet off the half finished landscape that I had been doing the night before and studied it for some time. It wasn't right, there was no energy in the colours, no movement, and working by the artificial light of an electric bulb hadn't helped.

Lily would have said,

"Leave it Reggie. Come back when your mind be fresh, and then think back to the feeling you had when you first saw the picture you wanted to paint. Second best painting no good – only best is good."

I took her advice and replaced the sheet.

* * *

EPIC DRY CONTINUES IN QUEENSLAND

87 PER CENT OF STATE DROUGHT-DECLARED

'Since the current dry began, the Queensland Government has provided more than $120 million for drought relief measures.'

'This is the fourth failed wet season in a row for many communities.'

'The latest drought map shows the extent of the epic dry in Queensland.'

'A fourth failed wet season for much of Queensland has led to little improvement in the state's official drought declaration list.'

And so ran the headline in the newspaper of the troubles

that were now besetting the cattle farmers of Queensland.

Jack would be among them.

I had been so taken up with my own affairs, that life at Waaree had been pushed into the background and had lost some of its importance in my life.

Jack and I had run Waaree, it seems, since we were kids. We had gleaned our initial knowledge of cattle from our dads and the aborigine stockmen.

We read books, questioned old-timers and backed it up with days in the saddle of sheer bloody hard work and trial and error. We had bounced ideas off each other some good some bad, and so far had found solutions that helped run the station at a profit.

The droughts, fires, floods and other troubles that a cattle farmer faced was shared by the two of us – what's that saying ..." a trouble shared is a trouble ..." well whatever it is, it had worked for us.

Our brotherly companionship helped. From the misery of the drought-ridden days, to the peaceful tranquility of the star studded sky of the nights, while we sat around the campfire and listened to the muted lowing of the cattle that was brought in by the soft soughing of the wind.

I should be with him now sharing his problems and hopefully helping him solve some of them.

When I think back to when I was a confused nine year old, who had just been told his father was dead, thrown from his horse while mustering, and Jack's mother taking me in her arms in a comforting embrace and murmuring words of sympathy and solace.

Then after my Dad's funeral the sudden trip to Cloncurry in my best clothes, to be inspected by some very serious looking gentlemen who later told me that Jack's parents were now my legal guardians.

"They will be like your parents Reg, like your mum and dad."

And they were. They took me into the big house and treated me as their son.

A 'mute son' who brought with him his own set of problems, which they uncomplainingly handled.

So while I now sit on my butt, in my nice cosy little house, on a roller-coaster ride of good fortune, my mate is doing it tough on his cattle station up north and needs all the help he can get.

But how the hell can I help?

I got up from my comfortable armchair and went to the fridge for a cold beer – *how often in the heat of the day had Jack and I wished for a cold tinnie to wash the dust out of our throat* – and thoughtfully wandered out to the back verandah, enumerating in my mind, the many reasons of why I couldn't get up north to help Jack.

First, I was a married man with a pregnant wife who was doing a play with the local amateur group. I was in the middle of a language course subsidised by the government. I was responsible to the Parole Board for the behaviour of a convicted criminal out on parole, and to top it all off, I was committed to the making of a film of my life!

Each 'reason' demanding my time and commitment, so what bloody chance did I have!

While ruminating on this Jo arrived from dress rehearsal, all hot and bothered.

"The dress rehearsal was a disaster," she cried," I dried twice and I *did* trip over the furniture. I caught my heel in a piece of carpet that hadn't been nailed down properly and landed in Ernest's lap. He thought it was funny."

I tried to look sympathetic and took her in my arms and

gently pecked away at her lips until they were reduced to a small murmur and silence.

"Mmm, you're so nice to come home to," she whispered, "but if you keep doing that I'll have my way with you and nothing will get done. It's opening night tomorrow night and I've got so much to do," prising herself out of my arms and backing away.

"What have you been doing, sitting around reading the paper ..."she stopped suddenly, her eye catching the headline on the front page.

"Oh, I see. It's this terrible drought isn't it – all those poor people – how hard it must be for them to watch their cattle and sheep die ..."she trailed off and thoughtfully came over to me.

"And Jack will be in the middle of it won't he?"

I nodded.

She studied me for some time.

"You'd like to be with him wouldn't you?"

I nodded.

"Then we'll have to find a way for you to get there?"

"How?" I signed.

"The play will be finished in a week and the school holidays start on the following Monday. We'll get permission for TT to go back to his weekly reporting to his Parole officer and then we can catch a flight to Cloncurry and hopefully Jack can pick us up from there and take us to Waaree. It'd be like a holiday. We need to get in touch with him now and see if it's all right for us to come. There, problem solved. Now I must do some sewing, my dress was torn when I fell and I need to run through my lines. Will you get the dinner."

Just like that – problem solved! Why didn't I think of that!

* * *

I'd never been to a live theatre performance before and the Chatham Community hall this Saturday night was packed to the rafters. There was a buzz of nervous excitement and chatter from the audience that consisted mainly of the relations and friends of the actors in the play, from the very old to the very young.

I found my seat, a moveable wooden chair and waited like the rest for the play to begin. I was nervous for Jo. Simon might be in the audience and I'd like him to be impressed with her performance, but no matter what *he* thought, she could do no wrong in my eyes – I just hope they'd nailed that piece of carpet down!

The lights dimmed and slowly the chatter died down. When all was quiet, the curtain rose on 'The Importance of Being Ernest.'

There was that special moment, just before the curtain rose, when the theatre was dark and quiet, which brought me out in goose pimples. It was a new and strange sensation for me. I'd often heard people talk about the 'magic' of live theatre – maybe this was it. I had never felt it in the cinema or a concert hall before and I can't explain it. There was an odd expectancy in the feeling, of what I wouldn't know – strange!

For the next two hours I was transported into the world of Lady Bracknell, period costumes and cucumber sandwiches. The only jarring notes, that brought me back to reality, was recognizing the local butcher who was playing Ernest and Algernon being played by the barber in the High street who cut my hair.

But most of the time all my attention was on Jo. She

looked gorgeous, spoke her lines with clarity and feeling, was absolutely edible and I couldn't see the baby bump.

The play ended to a standing ovation. Each member of the audience all had their favourites or relatives in the cast, and the ladies got bouquets of flowers while the men continually bowed to the bursts of applause. Jo was presented with the biggest bouquet of all by one of the stagehands – its size was more in keeping with the leading lady of an opening night at the State theatre than a cast member of local amateur group at the community hall. Jo looked surprised for a moment, but bent down to graciously accept it. It wasn't from me – I didn't know you did such things – it had be from Simon – who else!

But he hadn't stayed to the end. What did that mean!

Finally after the last curtain call, I fought my way back stage to find Jo, which wasn't hard, as the huge bunch of flowers she'd received signposted her whereabouts.

And there she was, half hidden by flowers, surrounded by friends, her face simply glowing as she animatedly talked to the group around her. I paused for a moment.

It was to count my blessings and wonder how it was that, that beautiful creature in the period dress holding the flowers was my wife – but she was and I had a piece of paper to prove it.

We made eye contact and moved towards each other like two homing pigeons. I enveloped her, flowers and all in my arms, kissed her, nodded, smiled and indicated without words, that I liked her performance.

Trestle tables appeared, along with casks of wine, trays of food and audience and cast hoed into the after opening night party.

I don't think I ever felt 'so out of it', so dumb. I was sort of an appendage to Jo and people spoke to me because I was 'there' and when they found out I was mute, they smiled in sympathy and moved away. Jo tried to draw me into the conversation a couple of times, but what was the point, I couldn't bloody well talk and she ended up telling them that I was mute, which caused embarrassment all round. It was easier for me to nod and smile a lot, which I did I think to everybody in the hall. By the time we left I felt like bleedin' Noddy – all I needed was a little bell!

When we got home, Jo was still on a high from her performance and the glasses of Chateau cardboard she'd consumed, that going to bed was out of the question – she wanted to party on. That was fine by me. So while I popped the cork on a bottle of champagne, that just happened to be in the fridge, she found vases and jars to accommodate Simon's flowers and turned our home into a florist shop.

She showed me the card that came with the flowers.

Absolutely lovely – well done. I don't need to see the second half.

Will be in touch, Love Simon.

"Do you think he really meant that?" Jo queried.

"Of course he meant it. You were great." I signed.

I was finding out that actors had to be reassured all the time about their performance, appearance, voice and everything else associated with their role.

"I know I can do better tomorrow at the matinee. We're having notes from the director about tonight's performance before the show so I'll get a few home truths then. But he's already warned us about 'speaking up', because our audience will all be from the local retirement villages and nursing homes and most of them have got a hearing problem."

"Well you don't have to worry." I signed.*"After all the years of teaching people with a hearing problem and enunciating*

clearly for their benefit they'll hear every word and syllable."

"I hope so ... and you really couldn't see our baby bump?"

"No Jo, please believe me," I signed, *"I really couldn't see our baby bump."*

We sat on the verandah, watched the stars and Jo slowly wound down from her high, to just being tired, a bit pissed and had run out of questions about the performance and hers in particular.

She got up plonked a kiss on my head and slurred,

"I'm going to bed, I'm so tired, night, show tomorrow ..." and wandered off towards the bedroom.

I was left with the remnants of the champagne and my own thoughts.

Watching the actors tonight, I began to think of my own upcoming venture into the acting world.

How do I convey what I am really thinking and feeling, when I sign my lines in a scene that will be subtitled in cold print for the audience? It has to be a mixture of body language and facial expression. I'm one of the lucky ones because I can hear and I have a pretty fair idea of how words are pronounced. But mouthing words can be an unnecessary distraction, as the audience will be reading the subtitles. All I can do is to really believe and feel what I am signing and hope the combination of that and my facial expressions conveys as truthfully as possible as to what I am saying and feeling.

The champagne was gone and so were any coherent thoughts that may have helped solve the problems of my upcoming career as an actor. My learning, no doubt, would come on the word 'Action' and how I handled my nerves on my first day of filming.

Later when I, all lovingly, crept into bed and snuggled up

to Jo's warm comatose body, all I got was a wriggle and a sleepy, "Hello" ... and a dismissive "night night."

* * *

TT's reaction on Monday, to the news of his return to visiting the Parole Officer once a week for several weeks was one of anger.

"Why the bloody hell do I have to report to the Parole Officer again. I've just got used to being a 'free' man and now it's back to being a crim on parole ... shit happens doesn't it," he signed, "makes you want to take up the fags again."

I signed, *"It won't be that long and Bridget Rose will be there to support you and keep you on the straight and narrow."*

"Yeah, she won't be too happy. She'd just got used to me being a law- abiding citizen ..." he paused for a moment, "and I didn't need *her* to keep me on the bloody straight and narrow, I did that myself," he angrily signed.

"Okay okay." I signed in a placatory manner.

He studied me for a moment.

"Do you know what you have just done?" he signed.

I shook my head.

"You have not used your notepad once during this conversation – well done."

I looked at my hands as if they didn't belong to me.

"I did it all without thinking." I signed.

"And that's the way it should be," he signed, "now lets to work."

* * *

Jo was in the throes of ringing Waaree that afternoon

after school, which was quite a business as her voice had to be relayed by radio and picked up on the station's own frequency.

"The phone is ringing there now," she said.

"Hello, this is Jo Brady, Reg's wife. Who am I talking to? Oh Mary how nice to say hello to you. Yes he's fine. The reason I'm ringing is that Reg and I would like to come and visit you in the school holidays. Reg says that he can be a help with the cattle and take some of the load off Jack's shoulders. Are you sure? We'd like to come next Monday. There's a flight getting into Cloncurry at 11.10 am. That would be wonderful. Looking forward to meeting you and Jack then. Yes I will, Bye."

"There, all done and dusted," she said, putting down the phone."She sends her love and says Jack will pick us up. Now, Monday morning we'll, get your pet taxi driver to take us to the airport. Our flight is at 10.10 and we have to be there a half an hour before take off, so he could pick us up at around 8 .45. How does that sound to you?"

What could I do except smilingly nod my head and continue to marvel at – how things seemed so easy when you had a voice.

* * *

The week dragged by. It's always the same when one is looking forward to something that you think is good. Sometimes it doesn't quite live up to your expectation and if you've experienced it before, you forget the downside and only remember the up side.

Already I think my mind and body had made the trip to Waaree as I could feel the heat and dryness of the outback on my body every time I thought about it. But it didn't seem so bad as I sucked on a cold beer in the comfort of the back verandah of our house in Brisbane. I knew that the harsh reality would soon change all that and then I'd wonder why I ever thought that working cattle in the outback during a prolonged drought was ever good. But when I wasn't doing it I hankered after it – so ingrained with the grit of the red dust was a love of the outback that I couldn't explain.

Maybe it was Lily's teachings – the days and nights in her company – her stories – of going 'walkabout' and listening to the wind and rain. And as I watched the stars and animals, she would tell me of the 'dreamtime' and had me thinking like an aborigine.

It was then, that I daubed my paint brush on the canvas I was painting.

Maybe that was it – maybe!

TT got over his sulks and things got back to normal. Eventually the end of the week did arrive and Mick Maloney our pet taxi driver was on time and we were on our way to the airport.

* * *

Chapter 20

The flight to Cloncurry took about three hours, enough time for the plastic meal on offer and a couple of beers, before stepping out into the heat of the day.

A smiling Jack was there to greet us and his reaction on seeing Jo was the same as every other man's reaction on meeting her – *how can a mute guy like me get such an attractive women like Joe Newton to marry him!*

"Hello Jack. It's nice to meet you at last," was Jo's warm greeting as she held out her hand.

Jack's bemused look from me to her as he shook the proffered hand was a picture and his stuttered,

"The pleasure's all mine Jo," was in keeping with his look.

For the 35 minutes it took to fly to Waaree, Jack pointed out the various landmarks to Jo, while I just stared out the window of the Cessna and savored the bush-land as it unfolded beneath us. It looked brown, dry, hot and dusty and you wondered how any animal could exist in such conditions. But exist they did as it was usually balanced by the 'wet season' in a climatic cycle that enabled the breeding of some of the best beef cattle in the world to thrive there.

The homestead soon came into sight. It was a green oasis in the middle of a brown landscape that stretched as far as the eye could see. The home paddocks were partly filled with cattle that were being hand fed and two windmills were busily turning, pumping bore water into troughs for their drinking.

A big well established station like Waaree had been able to withstand the fires, floods, droughts and fluctuations of the market that was part and parcel of life on a cattle station, but it still required all its resources to fight and recover each time it was put to the test.

Jack and I and his aborigine stockmen had mustered this vast property each year by horse, but now had come the time to change and be more competitive, by adding the use of motor bikes and helicopters.

The two Yamaha motor bikes leaning against the wall of the hangar were the first things that Reg sighted as he stepped out of the plane.

"There's our work horses for tomorrow Reg, all fed and ready to go, take your pick," called out Jack.

I walked over to the machines. They looked brand new – all shiny and clean. I swung my leg over the saddle of one and straightened it up and sat there thinking – *now how the bloody hell, do you ride this thing!*

"You get your first lesson tomorrow. It will be like the blind leading the blind – should be fun!" said Jack.

I gave him a doubtful smile, and as I stepped away from the bike I ran my hand along its shiny surface and instinctively gave my new 'horse' a pat on its padded leather rump!

Mary gave Jo a welcome hug and I got the same and while Jack attended to the luggage I signed to Jo,

"I'll see you all up at the house. I just want to say hello

to Lily, won't be long," and headed towards the aborigine houses.

Lily, I think was expecting me. She was sitting outside her house in her favourite chair poking the earth with her digging stick and as I waved and approached her she rose and I was swamped with a Lily hug that only she can give.

"You good man to come and see me so soon – not wait for days."

I smiled and nodded.

"You bring your woman to see me when we can have time together yes?"

I nodded and signed, *"How are you?"*

"Older and my bones hurt."

She held up one of her hands. The fingers were twisted and slightly deformed with arthritis.

"But okay – not whinge like men," and she roared with laughter, giving me a friendly thump on the arm.

"Now go back to Boss and his woman Mary. She very good for Boss and will be good mother. Go now."

* * *

Mary, starved of female companionship for so long, latched onto Jo like a long lost sister and the buzz of female chat and laughter that concerned mainly their pregnant condition and baby bumps boded well for our stay at Waaree. Jack and I relaxed and sipped our cold beer on the verandah to a background of happy kitchen noises.

All my hard work at the college in learning the correct language went down the drain as I instinctively reverted back to my old signs so Jack could understand me.

"Bloody hell Reg, that new stuff's like double Dutch. But I'll have to learn it, otherwise you're gunna' revert back to the old ways."

"No I think I'm far enough advanced to be able to switch when needed and I'll have to talk to the stockmen as well so it'll be back to the old ways while I'm here."

We hadn't mentioned the drought or the way things were at the station as we'd been too busy with the euphoria of meeting up again and we'd shied around what I knew was worrying Jack. The distant view from the verandah of the packed holding paddocks strewn with bales of hay was enough for me to see how bad the drought was affecting Waaree.

He must have been reading my mind.

"You can see how things are Reg and there's a lot doing it much harder than me. I feel for those poor bastards and hope they get the rains soon.

I'm preparing to sell some cattle early, decrease the numbers of stock, in preparation for the year ahead. And I've got two mustering camps going. Peter, the head stockman, with 7 ringers has got one about 20 miles from us and I spend a lot of my time going from one to the other. That's where the bikes come in handy.

Tomorrow, if your up to it, we'll get on our Yamahas and bring what cattle we can find down to where the stockmen can take over. Learning to ride the bikes doesn't take long. They're not very heavy – it's just a matter of balance and to begin with you use your legs either side like an outrigger canoe."

He made it all sound so easy that I couldn't help but nod my head in agreement. I wasn't quite sure what I was agreeing to because there was a little doubt in my mind as to the connection, to begin with, between riding motor bikes and outrigger canoes!

"But nothing beats the stock horse for working cattle Reg,

241

you'll find that out. Bikes may be all right for sheep, but give me a horse, stock whip and a cattle dog. That combination has it all over the bike in rocky gorge country and scrubby locations – where dogs are able to flush out cattle from low brush. I use the bike mainly to get to the mustering camps in the morning and to get home at night."

Bikes, horses and canoes were put on hold as Mary and Jo joined us.

"I thought we'd all have a drink together before we eat," said Mary."Then afterwards, while Jo and I clear up, you men can settle down and have a good old worry about the drought," she continued cheerfully.

"You see what I'm up against Reg – a cheerful optimistic wife who wont allow me to wallow in self pity and pessimism. She always has me looking for that elusive silver lining that apparently is in the darkest of clouds." He wryly shook his head, "and usually with her help I find it."

The warm loving relationship between Jack and Mary was to be envied. I looked at Jo and the small smile and look she gave me said it all and I was content.

*

Next morning Jack showed me how to ride my Yamaha."It's all so simple," he said, "just a matter of balance."

And he did make it look easy, except for my first effort, when I gave my machine too much throttle and it shot out from under me and I landed in the dust. But after that with some trial and error and using my long legs as outriders for balance I got the hang of it and sort of farted along behind Jack as I set out on my first day of mustering on a motor bike!

One mustering camp had been set up about a half an hours ride on the bike and all the aborigine stockmen that I knew so well were saddling up for the days work.

Lots of "G'day Reg, how yer goin' "were called out and I shook their hands, smiled and nodded to them all. There were several strangers but each gave me a G'day and a big smile of welcome.

Jack picked out a horse for me and as I settled in the saddle the months slipped by and it was, as if I'd never been away. It was a good feeling.

Twelve hours later I could hardly bloody move. A long day of drafting, branding and castrating in the heat and dust took its toll on a body that hadn't done any physical exercise since it left Waaree. I ached from top to toe and my butt was so chapped and sore that every bump on the padded seat of my Yamaha on the way home was agony. Then there was tomorrow to look forward to!

"A good hot bath will work wonders," said Jack, "tomorrow will be like a walk in the park."

I soaked in a hot bath filled with perfumed bath salts, that Jo insisted I use. Then smelling like a big Sheila – in some clean clothes – joined the others on the verandah and immediately fell asleep. Too tired to eat, I begged forgiveness, made my apologies and headed for bed.

And to think that I hankered after this life in the outback! To have a good horse beneath me during the day and spend the nights beneath the stars and to go to sleep on the hard ground to the soft sounds of the hobbled horses in the distance and the muted noises as the cattle settled down for the night – bollocks – It hurt like hell just turning over in a soft bed on to my left side.

The alarm went off at five o'clock. I'd had ten hours sleep and I felt like death.

I staggered out of bed, somehow found my work clothes and got dressed – *I think I was still asleep* – and went along to the kitchen where Jack thrust a mug of tea in my hand, with the words, "we'll have breakfast at the camp."

I numbly nodded, burnt my mouth on the firs gulp of tea and followed him out to the bikes. He kick started his and waited while I sorted myself out with another sip of tea.

I got on my 'pain machine' turned the key, gave it a kick, and I must say I was surprised when it roared into life. I followed Jack away from a house, that I should think by now was very wide-awake.

Tomorrow morning I will wash and clean my teeth before going to the kitchen!

At this time of the morning there were a lot of roos hopping about and were a danger to man and beast. Hitting a 'big red' on a motor bike could spell the end of all three of us, bike, rider and roo. I was now wide awake.

Chops and damper around the campfire was the fare for breakfast. Charlie Wright saw to the supplies for the mustering team. He used a four wheel drive truck that he handled like an expert – where the mustering team could go he could go!

I had the same horse as yesterday and I was working with three of the aborigines and a couple of dogs in the rugged gorge country and scrubby areas where the dogs were able to flush out the cattle from the low brush.

The aches and pains were easing and the effort of keeping my end up with the other stockmen took all of my concentration. The heat, dust, sweat, branding, castrating, mustering and drafting took care of the rest of the day.

After twelve hours in the saddle, it was a mug of tea and back on the bike for the long haul home!

I'm not too sure about this to-ing and fro-ing, because each day the mustering team got further and further away from the homestead. About three hours were spent on a Yamaha. This time could have been used just sitting around the camp fire sipping iced cold beer that Charlie may have brought and going to sleep underneath a star filled sky and getting up an hour later. It was the stockman's life I'd been used to and I think I could handle it again.

Over the meal that night Jack voiced my thoughts.

"The mustering camp is getting too far away to be commuting of a day so I'll be staying with them for about four or five days. There's no need for you Reg to be away, you could help Charlie and some of the girls with the hand feeding in the home paddocks."

I shook my head and signed,

"No, I could be more use mustering, I'll stay with the team."

"Reg, you don't have to ..."

I firmly shook my head and signed a big *"No."* and looked around the table. I got an understanding shrug from Jack, and a smile from Jo and Mary.

Later, in bed, as Jo snuggled into my back, she murmured, "how's my man?"

Her man was very sore and very very tired!

* * *

Working the difficult gorge country at the top end of Waaree brought different problems daily. From recalcitrant bulls, broken trap yards, extreme heat or the extra large numbers to be castrated, ear marked, or branded. Then if only part of the mustered mob was wanted, the selected animals had to be 'drafted away' from the mob while contained in a large enclosed area.

This all took time and it was where the riding skills of the aborigine ringers were never more apparent than when cutting out, drafting and handling large mobs of hungry thirsty cranky cattle. The beef industry at the top end would not have been able to function without them.

Jack had been away three days at the other mustering camp and had left me in charge. Giving orders or instructions to my stockmen was quite unnecessary as their knowledge and skills needed on a cattle station far outweighed mine. The antics that I had to get up to to make myself understood, had them practically falling out of the saddle with laughter – but it had always been like that – I was still the light relief of the mustering team!

Their never ending cheerfulness seemed to make light work of the hard live they endured and to see them work the cattle with horse, dogs and stock whip was one of admiration and envy.

The days were hard, long and hot. In the evening I'd hobble my horse for the night, see to it that it was watered and fed and sit next to a couple of the aborigine stockmen, who'd say nothing at all.

We'd sit like this for some time, staring into space, breathing in the ambience around us. A fire is built, the dogs are fed, a mug of tea is thrust into my hands and food appears on a tin plate – I don't bother looking at it – I eat because I need to and by 8 o'clock each night I'm struggling to keep my eyes open long enough – to watch the shooting star show in a star studded sky high above my earthen bed.

I wave my hand in the flickering light of the campfire with a gesture that I hope says *"goodnight"'* and get back various cheerful voice noises from my friendly workmates.

Often before sleep claimed me for the night the image of Jo would appear and her warm smile would wash over me like a balmy breeze that also brought with it the soft lowing of the cattle along with the quiet soothing noises made by the aborigine stockmen who kept them company and calm during the hours of darkness.

*

It's 5am again and the outback sky is cloudless, with a colourful display of pinks as the sunrise takes over and it promises to be another hot scorching day.

I scan the horizon that is now being blurred by the heat it's ripples covering the land in waves of shimmering mirages. My shirt, already clinging to my back is wet with sweat as we move the cattle out of the holding yards. They were fast losing condition and if the rains didn't come soon we were in danger of losing the entire herd. I could see that they were barely surviving on what little pasture they could find and stayed close to the remaining water holes, filling their bellies to make up for the lack of feed.

The days seemed endless as the cattle slowly moved back in the direction of the home paddocks to be watered and hand fed.

The herd grows as feral cattle and stragglers are added and the large mob in their desperate search for food continually move in all directions searching for what little pasture there was. Their restless movement keeps us all on the move, patrolling the edges of the mob, trying to contain and calm them down. This goes on night and day and even my resilient uncomplaining ringers are exhausted from lack of sleep.

My continually scanning of the skies for rain clouds brings no relief or hope – if and when the rain did come it could be too little or too late.

*

Heavy dark clouds had been gathering during the afternoon and now hung down to the horizon in the distance. I'd been watching them as they slowly spread across the sky, but I'd seen this many times before. And so often my hopes for rain had disappeared, as the water-laden clouds continued on their way, to shed their load on somebody else's parched land a hundred miles away.

But something was different today. I could feel it in my body. Goose bumps prickled my skin and the hairs on my arms rose as the wind dropped and an eerie stillness covered the land. Even the cattle sensed a change and paused in their foraging.

Then I heard it. A low rumble in the distance and beyond the ridge flashes of light behind the clouds. Lighting.

Men, horses, dogs and cattle formed a tableau as their cocked heads listened and waited.

And it came with the wind out of a cloud-laden sky in a heavy down pour that soaked men and beasts as they stood there, letting the longed for rain wash over them.

It continued for the rest of the day and all through the night, solving our water problem but not our immediate one – fodder. The grass would take two to three weeks to grow and somehow we had to keep the cattle alive until then. They were still hungry and the stockmen tired, wet and uncomfortable.

It was a morning dawn that was dark and wet as I rode around the restless herd until I found Billy the head stockman.

With difficulty, a mixture of signs, pad and pencil, I explained that we had no choice but to let the cattle go back to the trees and scrub to get what feed they can. It had taken days to ferret them out and now we were putting them back again!

Billy nodded his head in agreement saying,

"Good boss, take mob alonga bush, get feed alonga bush."

I signed, *"After we put them go back in the bush, let most of the men eat, sleep and try to get some dry clothes. I'll stay with the rest of them and watch the cattle."*

"Okay boss."

*

For days and nights the rain came out of the grey sky in a steady stream that soaked the once parched earth. Puddles of water dotted the land, the rivers flowed and the dams and soak holes were filled. The drought that had plagued the country for months was broken.

I stank to high heaven!

My clothing after another night of rain and sodden bedding was wet and clinging and every time I moved it gave it off odours that only a lot of soap and hot water would eliminate. I longingly thought of the homestead and a bath tub full of steaming water laced with Jo's smelly salts.

Like me, Billy and his men hadn't washed for weeks and now our clothing, bedding, horses and even our food had no protection from the incessant rain. Nobody whinged. I counted my blessings, the aborigines thanked their rain god and Jack, wherever he was, was probably doing a rain dance with Peter and his men.

I missed Jo. I missed her companionship, her presence, her love. I missed 'talking' to her. I haven't had a real conversation with anybody since I joined the muster. The antics that I get up to, to get Billy and his ringers to understand me I don't think can be put under the heading of 'conversation'. It's more like a cabaret act with them as my audience.

I watched the wind move the branches of the trees hoping that it would blow away the clouds and let the sun warm the earth and speed up the greening of the land.

It was towards evening when Charlie arrived with the ute full of dry blankets, clothing, rations, waterproof sheeting, petrol for the bike and the news that,

"Jack was back at the homestead organizing the home paddocks, thinning out the herds so that the muddy ground would not be spoilt, for future pasture, by thousands of hooves churning up the soil.

Also a road train of hay had arrived, which everybody, including your Jo, were now busy unloading and filling the barns and spreading the feed from trailers around the paddocks. Your wife said not to worry, she feels great and the exercise is doing her and the baby bump the world of good."

All this delivered at machine gun speed.

I nodded and signed my *"thanks."*

Charlie, always in a hurry, was busy unloading the ute and with his help we improvised a leanto with the waterproofing to keep the supplies dry. A quick mug of tea and he was ready for the off.

"Reg, any messages you want to write?"

"No. Everything's fine, I signed, *I'll be back in a couple of days."*

*

The morning dawned grey and rainless. A cool wind had risen and was chasing the clouds across the sky, leaving small patches of blue as they scudded by.

Moving the herd through the scrub and trees towards the home pastures was a difficult exercise for men horses and dogs. The lack of feed sapped the cattle of energy and they continually stopped to fill their bellies with water to sustain them.

A couple more days of this and hopefully we'd be in sight of the home pastures and the thought of seeing Jo and luxuriating in a hot bath and having a decent meal, had me day dreaming, which is a dangerous thing to be doing, when herding cattle in rocky and scrubby land.

Three weeks of the school holidays had already gone by

and I'd hardly seen Jo or anybody else for that matter. Seven aborigine stockmen had been my constant companions and in a weeks time I'd be back at school as a student.

A different world from the harsh one I'm in now – but this was the one I hankered after! I just didn't realize, how spoilt I had become after my stay in Brisbane and being married to Jo.

Escaping into the fantasy world that I had created in my landscapes, when the going got tough – was a whole lot different to the harsh world of reality, and how silent a world it would be at Waaree.

When mustering, I can only 'speak' to anybody with my 'home made' signs, a language the aborigine stockmen understood, and apart from Jack, their pidgin English and animal noises are the only sounds I hear.

*

Back on my Yamaha, I rode ahead of the herd, to find out where Jack intended to water and feed them.

In the distance I could see the faint line of fencing – the start of the huge home paddocks that were measured in square miles not in acres and for a moment I indulged myself in the luxury of thinking about my creature comforts that awaited me.

My indulgence didn't last for long as I spotted a dot and a puff of dust heading towards me – Jack on his bike.

He pulled up near me. Then, grinning, backed off with his words of greeting,

"God you stink. Don't go anywhere near Jo, otherwise she'll be off you for the rest of your life."

I smilingly signed,

"And it's good to see you to."

He acknowledged this with a wave of his hand.

"I'll take over now. You go straight to the house and have a bath. Don't stop and talk to the girls – get rid of the pong first."

And he unnecessarily over-revved his machine and was gone in a cloud of exhaust fumes – big skite – just showing me how adept he was on the bike now!

* * *

Chapter 21

I sipped my beer and watched two kids kicking a ball around on the footy field at the back of the house. The rugby season was over for the summer but the kids yonder were still honing their skills in the 'off ' season – either that or they'd been told by their mum to go out and play.

Jo was busy inside unpacking from the trip to Waaree and maybe like the kids, I'd been shooed out of the way and told, "Leave the bags to me. I want to sort out the washing that needs doing. You did enough hard work at Waaree, and remember, it's school tomorrow so get ready for that."

'There's school tomorrow.'

God, that world was a long way from the one of mustering cattle at Waaree. But already the memory of the harsh uncomfortable past few weeks was quickly fading and no doubt in a few more weeks time – in hindsight – I'd be dreaming and thinking how romantic it all was and hankering to ' do it all again.'

Which in reality is a load of bollocks. It's hard bloody work, except for that short period at night besides the camp fire, when the stars are so low you feel you can reach out and touch them and you close your eyes to the soft sounds of the cattle settling down for the night and hear the snort and chink of the hobbled horses in the distance. That's the nostalgic romantic bit that you think about and you even forget the hard bloody ground that you're lying on.

* * *

Amanda, Luke, John, Dorothy and Carol, my lovable little group of classmates seemed to have grown in all directions, in the months that I had known them.

And the four weeks holiday had done nothing to dampen their enthusiastic greeting as they rushed towards me and I did the mandatory high fives with both hands, which now became intermingled with the small signs they had learnt from Jo.

For the half an hour I enjoyed their company I felt uplifted as I watched their happy faces and from open mouths their silent laughter.

And I do believe that sometimes I could hear that joyous sound.

TT was the other end of the spectrum as there was nothing consistent with his moods and I was liable to be greeted with any one of them from the throes of quitting smoking to the euphoria of being in love with Bridget Rose. Today it was 'love'!

"I want to get married," he signaled, before I had a chance to say hello.

I didn't have an answer for that statement, except a query, *"So?"* I signed.

"Well, what do you think?'

"Have you asked Bridget Rose?" signing the obvious.

"No, not yet."

"Don't you think you should ask her first."

"Do you think I should?"

"Well of course you should, I signed, she's the one that you want to marry – isn't she?"

"Of course she bloody well is."

"So then for God's sake marry her."

"There's no need to get angry, I was only asking for your opinion."

"Well if I was Bridget Rose I'd run a bloody mile at the thought of it," I added.

"Very funny," and he lapsed into his little boy sulky 'silence' by sitting on his hands.

After an uncomfortable couple of minutes of this, I signed,

"TT, when you see Bridget Rose today, just tell her that you love her and want to marry her ASAP."

"That's it?"

"Yep, that's it and if she says 'yes', then the four of us will put our heads together and organize it."

Mollified, he doubtfully looked askance at me and tentatively signed,

"It's, that easy?"

"Yep. It's that easy."

He thoughtfully drummed his long artistic fingers on the table – *and for a moment there I thought he was going to ask 'what if she says no' I was ready with the answer ' then we'll get you a gun and you can shoot yourself.'*

"Right, so let's do some work," he signed, now all businesslike."I want you up to the mark as you'll be my best man and will have to make a speech."

Shit, make a speech! I'd forgotten all about that and I was appalled at the thought of standing up in front of all the mature students and signing a speech that they would understand – I wasn't good enough – I couldn't do it – I'd make a fool of myself – I was feeling sick already. Jo would have to vocalize it for the normal guests ... TT as my best man did it for me – but I'm no TT – oh God ...

*

"We'll write a speech which you will learn and then we can rehearse signing it until you've got it off pat.

Besides it'll be good practice for you – you may have to do something like that when you're filming."

That seemed to have solved my problem and I gave her a big 'thank you' hug.

"I don't want to put a damper on things, but you do realize that TT will have to get permission from the Parole Board."

Bloody hell, in the rush to get him to the altar, I'd forgotten all about them.

"TT is a convicted felon, "continued Jo, "And already they have allowed him out of gaol on parole, take a teacher's course at the College, act in a film and now he wants to be allowed to get married! They will quite rightly ask,' when does he pay for the crimes that he committed'?"

I signed, *"But he would be the benchmark for their rehabilitation programme. He'd now be a married man with a responsible job and a respected member of the community. Isn't that what they advocate? Wouldn't he be their success story?"*

Jo nodded her head and added,

"We can but try. I'll make an appointment and we'll take TT along with us. We'll let him put his side of the argument to them. As you know he can be very very effective."

*

Muriel Erwood, TT's probation officer, stared in disbelief at Jo, TT and myself and in a no nonsense voice said,

"My probationer now wants to get married! And when may I ask is he going to pay his debt to society for the crimes he has committed?"

Jo gave me a look that said 'I told you so,' and turned her attention to the Parole Officer.

"Officer Erwood, TT would like to talk to you about why he wants to get married. As, before I will interpret his signing for you."

Muriel Erwood gave a long suffering sigh and replied,

"Yes, all right then," and waited.

Jo nodded to TT who knew what he had to do. He raised his hands slowly in front of him in a gesture of humble sincerity and began.

He did not have a *baton* but he conducted Jo's voice as if it was an orchestra. He drew the words out of a dear face that clearly showed the myriad of emotions that flowed across it and I could tell that she was now mesmerised by TT's flow of hand movements and in a different world as she softly told his story.

"I love Bridget Rose and I want to marry her. You have already given me so much and it seems greedy to ask for more, but the only way I can repay you and my debt to society is by being a model citizen and a credit to you and your rehabilitation programme. I don't know what else to do or how else to repay you. Not being able to speak or hear is a drawback that Bridget Rose and I are determined not to allow it to stop us from having some form of normal life.

I will have an honours degree when I finish my course.

That is not conceit. That is fact. I know my ability as a teacher of Auslan and I ask no favours in the exam room."

Here he paused and studied his hands. Then slowly lifted his head and looked directly at his Probation Officer. After a moment his hands moved and Jo's voice began.

"I beg of you to allow us to marry and form a small unit that normal people will point at and not pity, but in some way feel proud that we are a member of their community – not on Welfare but holding down responsible jobs with The Deaf Institute of Queensland. We will pay our way and not 'bludge.' We ask to be given the chance to do that."

Muriel Erwood didn't speak or move for a full minute, then shook her head as if to clear her mind and bring her back to earth.

She turned her attention to Jo and said,

"I have no problem with Ted Tyson's wish to get married and lead as normal a life as possible. I also applaud his determination not to be a burden on the community."

TT watched Jo's hands and 'read' the signing of the Probation Officer's words.

"But I wonder if being a 'good citizen' now is repayment enough for all of his previous misdeeds. He said it is the only way he knows how to repay his debt. I'm inclined to agree. As a convicted felon he should be in gaol. It is not his fault that we have no facilities to cope with him in prison. I for one would feel justly proud if he became the success story of our Rehabilitation Programme.

I cannot begin to comprehend what it would be like to be deaf and mute, and to achieve what he has in such a short time is worthy of out further trust. To lead a normal life is such a simple wish. Let us try and allow him to fulfill his dream.

I will speak with the Parole Board."

TT slowly looked at Muriel Erwood with eyes that were now suddenly shiny and raised his hands in a supplicatory gesture.

Their eyes met and held for a moment.

She gave a small nod and quickly left the room.

* * *

Chapter 22

Once more we waited on word from the Probation Board, and as days turned into weeks TT's despondency and pessimism became more apparent.

"They're taking too bloody long," he signed." We should have heard by now – I'll bet there's something wrong – what do you think?"

"I think you're getting your knickers in a twist for no good reason." I signed.*"Give them a chance. They're a Public Service for God's sake and you know how long they take to do things. Besides you're driving us all crazy. Just relax - and anyway I need more time to improve my signing for my speech as your best man."*

As before we all settled down to our normal routine while we waited. TT's wedding was just another event to be added to the mix of his graduation, the forthcoming film and our 'baby bump – which was now making an appearance – so we all had something to think about.

* * *

TT, one morning gave me some bad news.

"I told some friends who ran a catering and car hire business that I might be getting married soon. They insisted that they to do the catering and hire me a white stretch limo at 'mates rates.' I said, I'd let them know."

I knew by now that the only friends TT had, apart from the school, were his 'friends' from the underworld and the thought of him turning up in a white stretch limousine with a chauffeur for his wedding was not a good idea. His Parole Officer and the police may wonder where he got the money to pay for it from. They might think that he still had some of his 'loot' hidden away and was cashing it in when he needed it.

I signed,

"*I don't think that's a good idea. If your Parole Officer knew that you were still associating with your past 'work mates' you could be in dead trouble.*"

"It's a legit business and my Mum would be paying for it."

"*I still think it's a bad idea,*" I signed, "*I thought I might take you in my nice yellow campervan.*"

"From a white stretch limo to a nice yellow campervan! That's quite a jump isn't it?"

"*Only joking.*"

"Good."

He shuffled around for a bit and then finally,

"Okay, but they'll really be offended."

I gave a noncommittal shrug.

"Aw shit," he signed, "all right let's do some work then."

I always thought the signing of that 'swear' word was obscene and I still do.

* * *

Since they had become an item, Bridget Rose had now

261

taken it upon herself to bring TT his daily lunch and she fussed over him like a mother hen. TT relished all this attention he was getting and I could tell he was already luxuriating in the thought of the lovely pampered life that lay stretched out ahead of him. All he had to do was to get Bridget Rose to the altar!

I wasn't sure if he'd actually asked Bridget Rose to be his wife. This quiet demure young lady was ' in charge ' of the relationship and she would be the one to say if and when their marriage would take place. I think TT hoped that if the Parole Board allowed him to get married, he would then, armed with their approval, pop the question.

Meanwhile time went by and his usual laid-back demeanour had now changed to one of aggression and this he took out on me. I don't think I've ever worked so hard. Repetition and more repetition was his whip and TT drove me without letup until he was satisfied that I knew what I was doing and my signing would pass muster.

The plus side to all of this was that I was learning very quickly and the light at the end of the tunnel was getting bigger and brighter. I could now, with a little difficulty, hold a conversation without the use of pad and pencil.

*

The long awaited news came on a Friday.

Bridget Rose was 'setting the table' – *she had now taken upon herself to bring a small tablecloth, condiments, serviettes and plates daily so the four of us could lunch in style* – and Jo's arrival was always met by an expectant TT who positioned himself so that he'd be the first to see her as she came out of the side door of the main building.

It was Jo's smiling face that foretold him the good news and brought him to his feet.

"I've just had a call from your Probation Officer, she

signed, "the Parole Board has agreed to you getting married. There are a few restrictions but nothing to worry about. An official letter is on its way with all the details."

TT and Bridget Rose looked at each other and the sheer wonder and joy on the faces of these two impaired young people was poignantly heartwarming.

TT held out his hand and as Bridget Rose clasped it they turned to Jo, took a couple of steps and hugged her.

TT eventually extricated himself, came over to me and smilingly shook my hand. Then the three started talking and laughing at a speed that was way beyond me.

I just nodded and smiled a lot.

* * *

The organization of TT's wedding had taken centre stage and he and I were more or less relegated to the background as the ladies took over, lead by Betty Arnold, Bridget Rose's mother, who was also paying for the wedding.

Already they had decided that the wedding, with a pink motif, would take place with a celebrant in the garden of the bride's home. There would be a marquee over wooden flooring, in case it rained, and the ceremony would be conducted underneath an archway of roses at the end of the garden. There would be sit down meal laid on by the caterers and each guest would be greeted on arrival with a flute of champagne with more to follow.

A list of invitations had been drawn up, checked, rechecked, crossed out, added to, double-checked, mulled over, until finally after numerous phone calls and just before everyone I think went crazy, the number and names were agreed upon.

Muriel Erwood, TT's Parole officer, was among the fifty invites.

Jo was going to be The Maid of Honour and I would be Best Man.

The only instructions that TT and I were given, was to turn up on the day, on time, with a ring and wearing a pink tie.

All this without ever having met the parents of the bride and groom!

"We must have them over for a BBQ," said Jo.

"The wedding is in three weeks time and it seems odd that we haven't all met up before now – we are all just voices on the phone! I'm going to do something about it. I'll ring them and ask them over for next Sunday, so clean the BBQ."

* * *

The BBQ was spotless, the sausages, chops and steaks had been bought and the parents of the bride and groom were due any moment. Jo had been busy doing salads, platters of nibblies and some small white potatoes were in the pot ready to be boiled. Sarah Lee had also been invited and would be doing the ice cream and cheesecake for dessert!

"And remember cowboy man you are not in the bush cooking for the stockmen. Our guests may not like their meat burnt black on both sides, gently does it."

I love my wife dearly, but I'd been cooking meat all my life and there'd never been any complaints. All you did was to get the fire going, wait for the hotplate to get to the right temperature, throw the steaks and chops on and after a lot of hissing steam and smoke do the other sides the same – done. Maybe the outsides were a little black but the meat was nice and tender on the inside.

The first to arrive were the Arnolds. Bridget Rose signed them in as Larry and Betty Arnold. They were a shorter, plumper, rosier, jollier version of their daughter and would not have looked out of place in the flowerbed in our front garden. I shook their hands and nodded hellos. They smilingly spoke to Jo and myself and signed to Bridget Rose. In the end Jo, Betty and Larry were signing and talking all at the same time and Bridget Rose was replying.

I'd never seen anything like it and stood there like a stunned mullet. How they all understood each other was beyond me. They were unperturbed by it all and carried on as if it was an everyday happening.

TT, having scrubbed up rather well and in his best 'suitor' mode, arrived with his mother Frances who was a tall smart attractive friendly woman in her fifties. After introductions and without missing a beat she joined in the conversation.

I could not help but admire Betty, Larry and Frances who, on learning that their child was deaf and dumb had studied and learned Auslan at the institute, so as they could make contact and 'speak' with their offspring as they grew up.

Their standard of signing was way ahead of mine and to watch these six people signing, talking and laughing, was a lesson on how adversity had been overcome by years of hard work, love and the determination to give their child a life.

TT took over as barman and with a few deft signs got their orders and the 'conversation' slowed down as they sipped their drinks.

On viewing the cooked steaks, chops and sausages, Jo gave me a nod of approval and the meal progressed right through to the dessert with the conversation coming mainly from the parents.

TT and Bridget Rose, their hands busy with knife and fork couldn't 'talk' that much and the parents carried on chatting quite normally without making any allowances for their offspring.

If the BBQ was Jo's idea – that the people involved in the wedding should get to know each other, then it really worked. Betty, Larry and Frances seemed to get on like a house on fire and there was never any indication of dissent or mention from Betty and Larry that their daughter was marrying a convicted felon out on parole!

TT and Bridget Rose sitting on this cushion of friendliness between the two families counted their blessings and the days before they'd be man and wife.

My 'best man' speech would be a short one, as there were only so many good things you can say about a crook and I didn't want the guests, who knew TT's record, to wonder whom I was talking about.

The best man in his speech usually gently 'roasts' the groom. In my case I couldn't make jokes about a deaf mute that regarded himself as a modern day Robin Hood who kept getting caught because he was unable to hear dogs barking, police sirens and burglar alarms. It might get a few cheap laughs but the majority of the guests were deaf mutes and they might not appreciate jokes about being deaf.

Although TT was an expert in rendering alarms harmless and held in high regard by the underworld, the Security companies now were one jump ahead of him. They had a back-up alarm system that would cut in once the main alarm was dismantled and notify the Security headquarters. That had been his downfall.

A bemused head detective and three constables had crept up on TT in the dark and watched him 'working' for some time – picking out by torchlight only the best pieces from the owners jewelry box – and wondering why he hadn't heard them and reacted to their presence.

It was a shift in the air movement that spun TT around to be confronted by his captors.

The police torches lighting him up like a neon sign and the four guns pointing at him had deterred him from making a break for it and the shouted orders of,

"On the floor, on your face, hands behind your back." meant bugger all to TT as he reached for his top pocket.

"Hands away from your pockets," screamed the detective, waving his gun.

Unperturbed TT extracted a piece of notepaper and handed it to the now red faced policeman who by the light of his torch read,

"I am deaf and mute."

The detective stared at him.

"You mean you can't hear ..." then realized what he was saying and tried to cover up his embarrassment with a loud,

"Cuff him."

I stood in front of the full-length mirror, tried to strike the right pose – that cool relaxed look that TT always had when he was signing and started to rehearse my speech again.

"When TT asked me to be best man, I inwardly quailed at the thought, but smilingly accepted. He was my best friend and had stood by me when I married Jo. The least I could do was to return the favour. There was only one problem – my signing was not up to your standard or especially TT's and I stand here wondering if you all know what I am talking about."

I would pause here and wait for some reaction from the guests.

Hopefully faces would smile, heads would nod and the hands signing 'applause' would encourage me to go on.

* * *

The wedding was Saturday, in two days time, and the prospective groom and myself were both becoming nervous wrecks.

TT with the prospect of marriage and me with my ' best man ' speech which I had rehearsed so many times with Jo that she too was getting more nervous than me.

"That's enough, "she said."I think we're overdoing it. It will lose all spontaneity if we do it anymore. Relax until Saturday morning and then we'll run through it again before we go to the wedding."

Classes were a waste of time. TT was thinking of marriage and I was mentally going through my speech. I was like dog with a bone – I wouldn't let it go – *I would have loved to have had TT run me through it ...*

"Your signing is rubbish," he signed, "what's wrong with you?"

That's all I needed to be told – that my signing is rubbish!

"Nothing." I signed.

He watched me for some time.

"I'm calling it a day," he signed, "I'm sending you home to do some painting. You need to relax and think of something else."

TT, astute person that he was, knew my problem and the fix I needed.

* * *

The landscape in front of me was nearly finished. It now needed those little touches that made all the difference and brought the painting to life.

I willed myself back to the time and tried to remember what was it that made me choose this scene. What was it that caught my eye and had me sketching madly before the image in my minds-eye disappeared?

I could hear Lily's soothing voice.

"You and me Reggie have traveled so many miles together. We have seen things that only an aborigine can see. We have watched the trees bend with the wind and the rain make the rivers run. We have looked in wonder at the animals that are our friends. Close your eyes and be the river and the wind Reggie, feel its power and the strong waters of the river and when you are part of the picture then pick up your brush and paint."

I closed my eyes and retreated into the fantasy world of my landscape. I wandered along the banks of the river and watched the willow tree sway and white caps come and go on the river wavelets as the strong wind came down the valley and brought everything to life.

I retreated further into my fantasy world until I felt and thought like an aborigine," be part of what you see "said Lily, and it was only when I could feel the energy of the river and the power of the wind coursing through my body, did I pick up my brush to paint.

For two hours I lost myself in my landscape and now it was finished. Jo came up behind me and kissed the top of my head. I waited for her opinion.

"You clever husband, you've done it again," she said, "baby bump and I are very pleased."

I kissed my wife, put a sheet over the painting and went to the fridge to get a cold beer.

Painting for me is therapeutic. It mentally and physically calms me down and as I settled into my favourite chair on the verandah, to watch the never-ending game of kids kicking a ball about, I thoughtfully thanked TT for giving me an early mark.

* * *

Chapter 23

The day of the wedding had arrived and I struggled to get the bloody pink tie that Jo had bought for me to sit right. What with that and a pink handkerchief sticking out of my top jacket pocket, I looked like a great big galah!

On Jo pink was fine. She looked absolutely gorgeous.

She wore a perky little pink hat, a neutral coloured dress that I'd never seen before, a pink frilly thing around her waist hiding the baby bump, pink shoes and pink gloves with matching handbag. She was irresistibly edible.

That thought distracted me for a moment as my mind wandered off in that direction.

Standing together we looked like we might have stepped off the icing on top a wedding cake.

"Well husband mine are we ready for the fray?"

I nodded and the butterflies in my gut woke up!

*

I was driving Jo's car and we were in one of the up-market suburbs of Brisbane. I looked at Jo and gave her a shrug to go with the look that hopefully meant, *"are you sure you've got it right?"*

Jo studied the map spread out in front of her.

"Yes, I have got it right. Keep going until we come to the next roundabout, than turn left and then first right and we're in Darcy Avenue, Number 16."

I slowly drove past a high brick wall and came to the entrance of No 16.

There was a man standing by the imposing gates checking invitations. I wound down the window and handed our invitation to him. He glanced at it, took a look at us and said,

"There's a place reserved for you Sir. Just follow the driveway to the front of the house."

All rich houses seem to have mandatory gravel drives, herbaceous borders and neatly trimmed lawns, No 16 was no exception. I found a sign that said – BEST MAN & MAID OF HONOUR.

The house was modern, very big and the music issuing from the open front door was one of my favourites, Frank Sinatra's 'Come Fly With Me'. It was something for the oldies – as they were the only ones that could hear!

I remember TT telling the Probation people, that being deaf, he was never able to enjoy the songs of Frank Sinatra. Well he missed something there. I was brought up with Sinatra and had whiled away many a night in my cups listening to his songs.

The long polished floor hallway led through house to the back patio and lawns where groups of people were busy talking and laughing silently.

Betty Arnold, looking rosier than ever, rushed to meet us, kissing Jo and shaking my hand.

"Welcome, it's so nice to have you here. I think you know everybody so I'll leave you to circulate," and she moved off to greet more arrivals.

A waiter appeared with two glasses of champagne.

"I must say the Arnolds do it in style," remarked Jo, looking around and sipping the French champagne.

Seats had been arranged on the lawn with a centre ailse that lead to a rose covered archway. Beyond the archway was a swimming pool and gazebo. To one side there was a large pink and white marquee.

But I'll bet Bridget Rose would swap all this just to be able to hear or speak

I saw TT and his mum having an animated conversation with a bemused Muriel Erwood, TT's Probation officer.

I nudged Jo and indicated I was going to join TT.

"I'm coming with you," said Jo.

And Muriel, "do call me Muriel," she had said, was once more treated to a an experience of how deaf mutes and normal people, capable of reading the sign language, carried on a conversation. Jo interpreted the signing of TT and herself, while his mum spoke as she signed

Muriel and I smiled and nodded a lot.

TT and I stood waiting by the archway with the Celebrant, a pleasant young woman in her thirties, for the Wedding March music to begin.

Four times TT had signed,

"Have you got the ring?" and four times I had mouthed and nodded a *"Yes."*

The music started and Larry Arnold with his beautiful daughter Bridget Rose on his arm began the slow walk down the centre aisle.

I must say Bridget Rose looked a picture, she was a vision in pink, and I could feel TT visibly swell with pride as his future bride walked towards him. I think I did the same as I watched Jo, the Maid of Honour walk behind them.

Larry stepped back and left the four of us with the Celebrant, who must have attended the same school as the one that did Jo and I, because she said all the right things with a simple sincerety, that Jo, who was interpreting for the guests had no trouble conveying.

I watched TT's face as I purposely looked for the ring. I searched my right pocket – it wasn't there. I felt my left pocket – felt again – ah there it is and I it handed over to a relieved TT who looked like he might have killed me there for a moment!

TT kissed the bride and they were now man and wife.

There was a lot of rice throwing, kissing and silent celebration from all the deaf mutes as we headed for the marquee.

Muriel Erwood singled Jo and I out,

"I'm going to leave," she said, "My presence here is a constant reminder to Ted Tyson of his past and I think that today he can do without that. Would you say goodbye to the Arnolds for me. Being here has been an eye-opener. It has shown me another side to life that I didn't know existed. I thank you for that."

"I'll walk you out," said Jo.

The inside of the marquee was like a very up-market restaurant. TT and Bridget Rose were already seated at the top table. I found my seat next to TT, gave his arm a squeeze and a nod of, "well done".

He smilingly signed.

"You bastard, you did it on purpose, didn't you, that bit

with the ring?"

I gave him my most innocent look and the appropriate shrug and shake of the head that conveyed, *"what are you talking about or what bit with the ring ..."*

It was after the main course that TT slipped me a note.

"I cased this joint once," I read, "it was on my list of likely places to be done over. What if I'd knicked one of Mum's nice rings and then given it back to Bridget Rose for our engagement and Mum had recognized it!"

I got the giggles and couldn't stop. TT kicked me under the table and Jo plied me with water. I excused myself and went to the loo.

When I returned I was back to normal and ate my apple pie and ice cream without mishap.

I don't know how many glasses of red wine I'd had but by the time my 'turn' to speak came around I was nice and relaxed or to be more truthful – a bit pissed.

I stood up and Jo rose beside me, ready to voice my signing. She gave me a smile on encouragement and when I turned to TT, he gave what I can only describe as a grin of good-natured gloating – *a rather you than me look!*

I looked out at all those expectant faces knowing that 99% of them could neither hear nor speak and I would just be the dummy that Jo worked with her voice. It would be like a ventriloquist act.

"When TT asked me to be best man at his wedding, I inwardly quailed at the thought, but smilingly accepted. He was my best friend and had stood by me when I married Jo ..."

And so I went on, remembering what had been written and if I faltered Jo, who knew the speech backwards, come to my aid and spoke over my stumbles. I praised TT's talent as a teacher of Auslan and eulogized over his importance in the upcoming movie of my life and finished up with,

"The movie could not be made without him and when the film is finished and released, the people who see it will have a better idea of the life of deaf mutes, of how they behave and live like normal people in a world of silence."

I turned to TT and rested my hand on his shoulder.

"And I ask you all to be upstanding and raise your glasses to TT and Bridget Rose – the Bride and Groom."

This they did and refilled their glasses.

Normally at a wedding reception there's always a few guests getting well and truly sloshed.

Not so at this reception, as most the guests were deaf mutes, and had to use their hands to 'talk', which meant of course that they couldn't hold a glass.

So – no glass – no drink – no drunk!

I couldn't believe what I was seeing.

We were all out in the front driveway, with handfuls of rice, to see TT and Bridget Rose Tyson off on their two-day honeymoon.

A beribboned shiny white stretch limousine with attending uniformed chauffeur was waiting there, in all its glory, to convey them to the bridal suite at the Hilton Hotel.

I looked closely at the chauffeur. There was something very familiar about him and I'll swear to God he was the leader of those 'friends' that TT had spoken to on that street corner – when we were trying to trace my stolen paintings.

TT had told me about the hotel being a 'pressie' from his mum, but not a dickie bird about the limo!

I caught his eye just before he got into the car and gave him a questioning look.

275

He replied with a happy smiling nonchalant shrug and disappeared as the chauffeur closed the door behind him with a soft expensive 'clunk'.

We circulated for a short time, then claiming 'baby bump' was playing up, said our goodbyes and left.

With Jo driving we soon found ourselves back on our own verandah, sipping champagne, holding hands, getting maudlin, repeating out wedding vows and then happily staggering off to the bedroom for a second honeymoon.

* * *

TT arrived Monday morning after two days of honeymooning and he looked a mess.

Faint blue bruising beneath his eyes told of the lack of sleep and his lethargic body movements and signing pointed to sheer and utter physical exhaustion.

Sweet, demure, gentle, innocent looking Bridget Rose had really put him through the wringer!

Her perky arrival at midday with the lunch basket was in complete contrast to her new husbands but as always the table was laid and the food displayed, this time, looking very much like the best of the leftovers from the wedding. We tucked in.

None more so than TT, who ate as if it was going out of fashion or if the truth be known hadn't found time to eat on his honeymoon!

Jo feeds me steaks for energy. I must get her to have a word with Bridget Rose. If you want the engine to keep running well you must put the best fuel in it!

*

Tuesday morning and TT was early and looking better.

"My wife," *I think that was the first time he may have*

signed those words and I could see the pleasure on his face as he did so, "has gone for her driving licence test. Her parents have promised her a car if she passes."

"That's great," I signed, *"I didn't know she was taking lessons."*

"Yeah, she wanted too keep it a secret, she thinks it's bad luck to tell people."

He thoughtfully lapsed into 'silence' and closed his eyes.

I thought he was asleep for a moment and then he signed,

"They've given us a two bedroomed unit in that posh area. It was all ready and waiting for us. We moved in early this morning."

"That's fantastic TT." I signed.

"Is it? What the fuck is there left for me to do – water the pot plants!"

He angrily got up and agitatedly moved about signing,

"I don't want their handouts. I know they mean well but I want us to do it. All right, so we'll have mortgages and all the problems of paying things off but they'll be ours, something we've done – not a handout." He dropped his hands and sat down.

"I may sound ungrateful, but that's the way I feel." He got up and mooched about.

"What do I do, hand it back and then where do we live – it'd be either her parents home or my mum's home and that's not the way I wanted to start married life. I feel trapped somehow. I'm beholden to her parents already and I've only been married three days!"

He stopped signing and then started again.

"My friends offered me a unit, no strings attached, but that's a big no no as far as everyone else is concerned, especially my Probation Officer."

I shook my head in horror and signed,

"TT, you would lose everything and I mean everything, including Bridget Rose. Why do your 'friends' keep giving or doing things for you?"

He studied me for some time and then slowly signed,

"Because I didn't squeal. I didn't name names."

I knew then that those 'friends' would always be there for TT and that there *was* something in that much bandied around expression, 'honour among thieves.'

I gave him, what I hoped was, a gentle understanding nod – *I really liked this man* – and slowly signed,

"Give it time TT, give it time, things will work out."

"Yeah."

* * *

I could hear Jo on the phone to Mary. Ever since they met they'd become bosom pals and spent a lot of time talking to each other – at least a couple of times a week. What they found to talk about God only knows, but talk they did, with Jo's voice being relayed by radio to Waaree from Cloncurry.

I was on the verandah sketching the outline of a new painting when Jo came out.

"How do you feel about going to Waaree in the school holidays?"

"But what about the baby bump?" I signed.

"Its not due to put in an appearance for another eight weeks. We could spend a couple of weeks there and be back here with four weeks to spare."

"Do babies arrive on time?"

"Usually. Sometimes they are a bit early or a bit late, but

no more than a couple of weeks. It 'd be a nice break. Jack is working from the homestead so there'd be no staying away overnight if you wanted to help him."

It sounded like a good idea. Whiling away the time sipping cold beer in my old chair on the verandah and going walkabout with Lily.

"If you really want to go Jo we'll go," I signed.

"Give me the dates so as I can tell TT, who'll do his nut. Also you'd better check on the weather report, it's not the wet season yet but there's usually the odd cyclone hanging about and you'll have to inform Muriel Erwood to."

"I'll do all that, "she said, coming over and giving me a big thank you hug, "and what a nice husband I've got."

*

"Ah shit, not again," was TT's reaction to the news.

"It's only for two weeks TT – two visits that's all," I signed, *"Besides your Probation officer is a very nice lady and has done you a lot of favours, so stop whinging and get on with it."*

"Okay okay," he signed, holding up his hands in a placatory gesture.

"So how is married life?" I signed, changing the subject.

A dreamy look washed over TT's face and he signed,

"I didn't know one could live this kind of life. Being deaf and mute, I never expected to be able to have these feelings of happiness. Being in love with the person you live with changes all that, don't you think, and you forgive God a lot of things you accused him of. The anger inside you subsides and you count your blessings when you wake up each morning and reach out to the person you love. You sit at the breakfast table – she is there, and knowing all the time she is in the house brings a contentment that you never knew you could feel. Maybe it's the newness of married bliss but for now it is there and Bridget Rose and I intend to make the most of it."

He gave me a sheepish grin.

"Well you did ask."

* * *

Chapter 24

Mick Maloney, my pet taxi driver, was on time and we loaded up and set off for the airport.

I had insisted Jo book Business class with Qantas for the short journey, as I didn't want my very pregnant wife all squashed up in economy. Also I could have a few beers in comfort to while away the three hours it took to get to Cloncurry.

Jack and Mary were waiting there to greet us and after lots of hugs and kisses, we headed off to the private plane sector where Jack's Cessna was.

Jo and Mary hadn't stopped animatedly talking since our arrival and the short hop in the Cessna to Warree failed to stop them.

It was good to be back in my old room and as I slowly walked around it, I touched things, here and there, and moved them slightly to where they used to be – remembering.

The girls were in the kitchen doing what girls do in kitchens when Jack called out,

"Come and have a beer."

I went out onto the verandah and there was my old chair waiting for me.

The beer was cold and we raised tinnies to each other in a toast.

"It's good to see you in your old chair with a beer in your hand Reg."

I signed, " *Yeah, I miss all this. It was so much part of my life.*"

We sat in companionable silence for a moment, when the crackle of the radio intruded.

Mary called out,

"It's for you Reg, somebody called Simon."

I went to the radio room taking Jo with me.

"Hello Simon its Jo, Reg is here."

"Reg, the head money man for the film has arrived in Brisbane. He's here for two days at the Hilton. It's imperative that you see him.

He won't release the production costs until he's seen you and given his backers his approval. It would only take a day, there and back Reg, but if you don't see him we can't start pre-production."

I looked at Jo and signed, *"I'll have to go. I could leave in the morning and be back by the evening."*

Jo didn't look too happy with this sudden turn of events but nodded.

"Yes, don't worry I'll be fine."

Jack had heard the last of Simon's message.

"I could run to Cloncurry now if it's any help. You'd be in Brisbane tonight and back here tomorrow afternoon."

"That'd be great Jack. I signed, *"The sooner I get there the*

sooner I'm back."

* * *

Sometimes I'd catch Sarah looking at me the way she had the first time she saw me at the Gallery and the intensity of her gaze stirred an unwanted feeling that I didn't need right now.

My thoughts were with Jo and how to make a quick exit. I needed to get to Waaree in case cyclone Betty changed direction and brought the centre of the storm over the cattle station. The cyclonic rains would make it impossible to get through to the homestead.

Some instinct was telling me that all was not well with her and the regret of leaving her to see the big American investor was overwhelming.

I singled out Simon and wrote,

"I'm leaving now Simon. I must get back to Jo. I've seen your money- man, Mr Steinberg, who just looked me up and down and made the remark ' Yeah, looks good, pity he's dumb,' then turned all of his attention to Sarah and ignored me completely."

An apologetic Simon was all over me like rash.

"Ah that's just his way Reg. He thinks you're great for the role – he doesn't mean to be rude – it's er just his way ..."

I hurriedly wrote, *"Say my goodbye to them all, I'll be at Waaree,"* and I quickly shook a nonplussed Simon's hand and headed for the door.

* * *

The first thing I saw below the 'DEPARTURES' sign at Brisbane Airport was,

ALL FLIGHTS TO CLONCURRY IN OR OUT CANCELLED

DUE TO CYCLONE BETTY

Shit – it must have changed direction – now what do I do?

Helicopters would also be grounded.

The girl at the Information desk, after reading my note, saw my problem and was very helpful.

"Go to Jetstar, counter 5 and ask for Louise. Give her this," scribbling on a note pad and handing it to me." She will see that you are booked on the first available flight out of here to Cloncurry."

I joined another queue and Louise did exactly that. She was all sympathy and understanding, after I had parted with $245.

I wandered aimlessly around with all the other stranded passengers, joining food queues for something to do and eventually finding a seat near the Departures indicator and waited.

The airport concourse had now taken on the appearance of a refugee reception centre. Bodies wrapped in blankets, handed out by the airlines, littered the floor and seats and fractious children were testing the patience of their cranky parents.

I dare'nt go home to get some sleep and a shower in case I missed my flight, so I waited with the rest of the un-showered passengers and prayed that the eye of cyclone Betty got a move on and quickly passed over Cloncurry.

Getting to Cloncurry was the first leg of my journey to Maaree but how the bloody hell do I get the rest of the way?

* * *

'CLONCURRY MUSTERING COMPANY'

That was the big sign that greeted me. I had a list of four and it was the first on the list.

It was a hangar-like building with a small block of offices attached to the front.

I entered the door that said 'enter' and was welcomed with a cheery

"Good morning sir, how can I help you," from a rather plumb young woman behind the counter.

I handed her a page from my note pad.

A little nonplussed she took the piece of paper and read the note.

She looked up at me, gave me a look of sympathy and then read the note again … we were interrupted by the entrance of a young man who looked about sixteen. He was wearing thongs, shorts, a t-shirt with a helicopter emblazoned on the front and a baseball cap back to front. He was chewing a toothpick, looked like a short TT and was probably the office boy.

The young lady handed him the note!

He read my message, curiously looked up at me, slowly gave the toothpick a few extra chews and said,

"Just had a report in. The winds dropped and it's okay to fly."

I was given another perusal and then eventually after more chewing,

"Alright," he looked at the note, "Reg, you're on. I'll take yer."

This child is going to take me to Waaree – did I have a choice!

"Waaree isn't on our list of clients so maybe in the future you'll give us a bell if you ever should want a copter."

I vigorously nodded and signed a *"yes"* – *anything to get to Jo*

"My name's Aaron," he said, offering a handshake.

We shook hands, which I overdid a bit, because he comically counted his fingers afterwards.

"I'll take number three Ruth. Be with you in moment Reg," and he ambled off into the hangar.

By the time I had signed several documents and parted with a lot of money a small helicopter had been wheeled out to the take off area. It looked like a toy.

"It's the copter he uses for mustering cattle, there's room for one passenger. Have a safe trip."

I nodded and signed my thanks and headed out to Aaron who was strapping himself into his seat at the controls. I jumped in and sat in the passenger seat next to him. He handed me a headset that was plugged in to socket above my head.

"So that we can chat."

Realized what he had said and gave me an apologetic shrug.

I put the headset on anyway and strapped myself in. There were no doors on either side, just open spaces!

Aaron pressed a few buttons and with lots of shuddering the propeller above my head slowly turned, then gathered speed, and we slowly lifted off the ground.

I'd never been in a helicopter before and this little one did nothing for my sense of security. All that seemed to be between me and the outside world was a thin sheet of Perspex!

We gained height and I presumed turned in the direction of Waaree leaving Cloncurry quickly behind us.

Aaron didn't seem to be doing anything at the controls. He looked like a small boy that had been allowed to sit in the pilot's seat. One hand was loosely on the control column and all his attention was on the ground below. He had discarded his thongs!

I was now on my way to Waaree with a barefooted pilot who looked about sixteen and wasn't looking at what he was doing!

Suddenly we dipped towards the ground, leaving my stomach somewhere in mid-air, and Aaron's voice came into my headset,

"Reg, I show you how we muster cattle. It'll give you an idea how we operate and the advantages a chopper has over horses."

Being 'shit scared' was putting it mildly. We were now flying below the level of the trees and practically sitting on the backs of three cows that were being shepherded by Aarron like a cattle dog. He wheeled and turned them at will and gave me an exhibition of dexterity with his helicopter, that left my heart in my mouth and my sphincter muscle very tightly closed.

His *piece de r'esistance was* actually nudging one of the cows with the landing gear of the helicopter, getting it to go in the right direction!

After this exibition, he glanced over at me, saw my white knuckled reaction to his skills, raised his hands in a placatory gesture (now no hands on the control column) and flew at a *safe* height the rest of the way to Waaree.

He dropped me gently on the front lawn, shook my hand, gave me a cheeky grin, then took off backwards and was gone in a gust of wind that stripped the last of the blooms from the flower beds.

Lily was standing at the top of the steps waiting for me.

When I reached her, she didn't welcome me with open arms nor did she clasp me to her ample bosom. Instead she gave me a filthy look of silent disapproval that eventually was broken by,

"You like son to me Reggie, so I can tell you. You behave like arsehole."

Well what did I expect – the return of the Prodigal Son – hugs and kisses!

I nodded a *"hello."*

We stood there like two stuffed dummies in a window.

"Boss and his woman both in Cloncurry. They have baby girl, called Rowena."

I was pleased for Jack and Mary – when did they go to Cloncurry?

I impatiently signed,

"Where is my wife?"

"Maybe your woman not want to see you – but she in your old room – mother and daughter both good."

I managed to sign a grateful *"thank you"* for Jo had got her wish – a girl.

"Mother and daughter are both good ..." I could feel the prickles start behind my eyes – aw shit, not again – always bawling!

I stood outside the door for a couple of minutes – readjusting my clothes and my mind – before I tentatively tapped on the door.

No response. I tapped again and gently opened the door and stepped into a florist shop and immediately thought that all these flowers were bad for my daughter's and wife's breathing – *I'd read that somewhere* – too much pollen!

Jo was watching me from the bed. She had a bemused unworried look on her face and there was no hate, no anger, just a look of relief – *maybe that's wishful thinking on my part – I was now clutching at straws.*

"How's my cowboy?" was her familiar greeting.

That took me across the room and I fell on my knees at the edge of the bed and my right hand went out to Jo, who took it into the warmth of her breasts and held it there. My body just fell apart and I could hear her soothing sounds as she gently stroked my shoulder and head.

After awhile I was finally down to gulping hiccups. She whispered into my ear,

"Don't you want to meet the other member of our family?"

Dear God I'd forgotten about our daughter.

Jo rang a little bell and Lily appeared.

"Lily, I think my husband wants to meet his daughter."

I started to tidy myself up. Jo laughed,

"You're wasting your time, I don't think she'll even notice."

Lily arrived with, what looked like, a small wrapped parcel. It could have been a loaf of bread, except that there were two small pom poms hanging out of one end of the bundle.

Lily went to hand the baby to Jo who shook her head and indicated me.

Now, baby rabbits, lambs, chicks, piglets, poddy calves, kittens and puppies I could handle, but a baby 'person' was a different ball game.

No nonsense Lily plonked the baby into my arms and in a voice loud and clear, reminded me, "to hold the baby strong – they like that. They tougher than you think, but that don't mean you drop them." And left me holding my daughter.

Jo propped up on her elbows looked at her family.

"What a beautiful picture, I must get it ..."scrabbling around the drawer of her bedside table.

"Lilyrose will always be able to show it to her friends."

She came up with one of those new digital cameras and happily clicked away.

In the back of my mind something was not quite right. Lilyrose? I couldn't ask Jo, as my hands were full so I did the only thing I could do, I gently put our baby in the bed beside her mother and quickly signed,

"Lilyrose, has our daughter been named already?"

Jo looked up at me and slowly nodded her head.

"I wasn't sure when you were coming back and when I was in that 'no mans land' between living and dying, it was Lily's soft voice talking and crooning her dreamtime songs and stories that helped with the pain and kept me alive. When the baby was born the first face that I saw was Lily's. It was only right that we name our child after her."

Lilyrose began to cry and it didn't impinge on my subconscious for a moment. Then the sound slowly began to eat into my brain as I listened to the wonderful cranky noises she was making. My daughter was not mute. She had not inherited my genes and by the sound of her, she would be able to talk.

I looked at Jo.

"Thank you for bringing into the world this beautiful child." I signed.

She smiled and softly whispered.

"No problem."

I knelt down beside the bed.

290

"I love you Jo and I can't begin to apologise," I signed. *"I should not have left you – the film could have waited."*

My wife reached out her free hand and stroked my cheek.

"Oh Reg, it's so good to see you say that again. The last few weeks have been so empty. You often seemed to be many miles away in your thoughts and distant with your physical contact that I began to doubt your love, but now when I see the way your hands and face say those words again my world is complete, and I know I couldn't love you the way I do without you loving me back."

We stayed like that until mother and child closed their eyes and slept.

I watched over them for a long time and counted my blessings.

* * *

A grim-faced Lily was in the kitchen waiting for me and her voice went with her demeanour.

"You be like a son to me Reggie and you let me down. You treat your woman very badly and when she needs you, you not here. You away with your rich new friends."

Ashamed – as only Lily could make me – I spread out my arms in an empty gesture ... *there was nothing I could say in my defence.*

"Sit down and I will tell you about your woman and child."

I sat on the nearest kitchen chair.

"After you dumped Jo – yes Reggie, dumped – 'cos that's what you did, you here one day, same day gone, you couldn't get away quick enough to join your big friends back in Brisbane."

I didn't try to explain to her why I left.

"Boss had to take his women to hospital – something

291

wrong. He could not get back for your women. The wet season it come along with big cyclone so fast, that the rains and storms come down harder than ever before and suddenly, all land round us was flooded. It was the worst it's ever been, we couldn't get out and the weather was so wild the copters had no place to get in.

Your wife became ill with the damp and mosquitoes. Then her baby started to move six weeks before it's time and had somehow got stuck and was badly the wrong way round. They call it 'breech'. She needed surgery to save her and the child. The Flying Doctor was waiting in Cloncurry, giving us what little help he could over the radio.

The pain must have been terrible and many times she called out your name in agony, but you not here ... you with your friends ..."

I could feel the prickles of tears starting behind my eyes ...

"The night we thought Jo would die. I sat beside her, with my hands on the bare skin of her tight swollen belly. I would help her and the baby 'passing' into their 'dreamtime' life of the next world.

All through the night, I sat and sang my songs that you know so well, and I called upon our Gods that roamed with the wind and lived in the land and water for help. After long time I slept ...

Then, I felt tiny movement under my hands ... then I felt it again ... the baby was on the move ... and this time was movin' and turnin' in the right way. It was as if it was sayin', "as nobody else is doin' anythin' about it, I'm not givin' up," and the movements kept goin' on towards the dawn and were getting deeper and stronger – that baby was a real fighter. In the half-light Jo and I looked at each other in wonder.

"I think there's a baby coming Lily," whispered Jo.

I called out to the house for lights, towels, basins, hot water, cold beer and anything else I could think of, and when the baby came it came into the world in a big slippery rush, and I just bloody lucky to catch it before it hit the end of the bed.

"It's a girl," I called out.

"A girl?"

"Yes, a beautiful brown haired girl," giving it a smack on its backside, and getting back a yell of protest.

I tied up the cord and handed over daughter to mother and as I did so, your beautiful woman, all covered in sweat, looked up at me and said,

"We shall call her Lilyrose."

"I be very proud … you very brave woman …"

She looked at me for long time and then whispered, "no, it was like shelling peas."

Lily watched me squirm and bawl for some time – I couldn't stop bloody crying.

"You very lucky man to have woman like Jo

Come, the girls will watch over your woman – we go walkabout."

She rose and collected her digging stick by the kitchen sink.

"We can find a log, then you can sit and write me your sorry story of why you such big arsehole."

* * *

Chapter 25

The homestead was a sudden hive of activity. Two new babies and their mums, a nurse from Cloncurry hospital, the Flying doctor, two bewildered new fathers who always seemed to be in the way, no matter where they went, and Lily with her whole tribe was out the front doing an aborigine ritual dance that would keep away the 'bad spirits' from the newly-born babies. Well if that wouldn't, the dust created by their stamping feet would!

Jack and I found a secluded corner on the verandah and helped Lily keep the evil ones at bay with cans of 4X!

After the doctor and nurse had checked on babies and mums they departed leaving long lists of instructions of what to do and what not to do.

Lily kept on dancing and waving her branch of leaves around in the dust and only when Jack had decided that the evil ones had been well and truly banished did he give Lily a six pack. She, then with entourage in tow, happily departed.

*

"We've got a little stranger in our room." I signed to Jo,

who was propped up in bed reading a baby book.

"You better get used to it my cowboy, she's going to be with us a long time."

I peered closer at Lilyrose who was in a cot in our bedroom. She was so still – was she all right – I nudged her with my finger – she reacted to my touch – yes she was okay.

"Reg will you stop prodding Lilyrose and come to bed. You'll wake her up and it'll take ages to get her to sleep again," whispered Jo.

"I was just checking."

"Now come to bed, there's a good boy."

I snuggled into Jo and she said,

"It's the two o'clock feed, will you get her for me."

I opened my eyes – I'd just got into bed – what happened to all those hours ...

I could hear crying noises coming from the cot.

I peered closely at the bedside clock – it said 2.10.

Half asleep I staggered over to the cot and picked up our baby and took her back to Jo's milk bar.

When I next awoke Jo and Lilyrose were both fast asleep, the nipple of Jo breast half hanging out of her baby's mouth. It was a lovely picture of mother and child. Now what do I do. As gently as I could I eased Lilyrose away from Jo, who, still asleep, slid back down under the sheets.

Each time I put Lilyrose down and she felt my hands leave her body she started crying. I did this four times and in the end, gave up and starting walking up and down silently singing, *My Mabel Waits For Me*, hoping the vibration in my chest would send her to sleep. How long I did this for God only knows.

Finally Lilyrose, now weighing a ton, was fast asleep and she didn't react when I put her down. Once more I staggered back to bed.

I had just closed my eyes when Jo shook me awake.

"Come on my husband, time to get up. You said you wanted to help Jack with some fencing."

I signed, *"But I just got in ..."*and gave up.

That was my first night of being a father and a whole month of bleak nights stretched out before me – maybe we could wean Lilyrose off that night feed – then we could all get some sleep – or take it in turns of getting up – or what do other people do ...

Jo was bright and chirpy and was changing Lilyrose's nappy. My nose was telling me she had done 'jobbies'. That was the cute name Jo and Mary had given No 2's, poops or craps. Jo said,

"Lilyrose has done jobbies, sounds much nicer than, Lilyrose has done a crap." Well whatever term is used it's still on the nose!

By the look of Jack he hadn't fared any better and we both had that Johnson's baby powder – sicky – milky smell about us. We ate breakfast in thoughtful silence.

Digging post-holes and stringing wire was hard going and at lunchtime, with food uneaten, we both fell asleep under the shade of a gum tree.

We stayed another week and our daily routine got easier with the doing of it. Taking turns at night was a big improvement. Picking up a bundle of warm soft baby-person at 2 o'clock in the morning didn't seem so bad and I never got tired of watching her in the soft night light at Jo's milk bar.

Sometimes my heart would be so filled with love for these

two people that I would have a little cry and the tears would spill down my cheeks unchecked and unnoticed.

* * *

Jack's Cessna was packed to the gills. For one little person Lilyrose seemed to have a lot of gear and we were travelling light!

Jo and Mary had hugged and kissed several times, with little Rowena getting squashed in the middle, before Jack prised them apart and got everybody into the aircraft.

Mary, Rowena and Lily waved us goodbye.

"We'll be back next holidays – that's a promise," said Jo to Mary."I'll ring you when I get home."

The flight with Qantas from Cloncurry to Brisbane was uneventful. Lilyrose behaved herself and slept most of the way. I was rather proud of her. I had dreaded the thought of the trip as most kids from my experience spent their time bawling or if they could move, their over indulgent parents allowed the little darlings to crawl all over you with their sticky fingers.

Not so our child I smugly thought – our child is a good child.

It hadn't taken me long to join the indulgent set!

* * *

Our first family outing was to the Baby Shop as Lilyrose had arrived early and we had nothing prepared for her. A room at the house had been emptied and turned into a nursery, which now apparently had to be refilled with baby things – starting from scratch.

A smiling salesgirl named Rita, according to her nametag, danced attendance on us and as she ticked off her suggestions and our purchases her smile became broader – *I'll bet she was on a sales commission.*

297

The first thing that was bought was some kind of harness that was strapped around my chest and Lilyrose was inserted into it. I was told mothers in Asia and the Indians of America carried their babies like this.

Well maybe it was fine for the mothers in Asia and the Sioux Indians of America but it looked a bit odd on a six foot three Australian male wearing a Stetson.

I self-consciously trailed around after them until eventually Jo called a halt.

"All done," she said, with a smile of satisfaction. "Now you wait here with Lilyrose, while Rita and I put her baby seat in the car."

I sat down on the nearest chair in the nappy section and looked down at Lilyrose whose big brown eyes stared back at me and she squirmed in her halter. She must be wondering what happened to the soft comfy breasts that she usually has to rest against and where's the hell's the milk bar! She nuzzled her face against my shirt – looking.

I shrugged an apology and felt inadequate.

Lilyrose quietly studied my face with a thoughtful look and then she smiled at me ... I'm sure it was a smile ... her beautiful little lips had curled into ...

That's when my nose caught a whiff of 'jobbies.' I bent my head for a closer sniff and that made my eyes water.

Ah no!! Not that. Not in a shop. Now I've got a baby strapped to my chest with a nappy full of stinking jobbies!

Shoppers walking past, stopped, sniffed, looked back at me, and then hurried on. I think I cleared the area I was in, in two minutes flat, mother's deciding suddenly to get their disposable nappies elsewhere!

Eventually we did get home but things didn't improve. Jo

loaded down with the smaller shopping called out,

"Darling will you change her nappy, while I sort this lot out. Her things are all there by the little table that I change her on."

Change her nappy!

I went into the new nursery and found all the gear, Swipes to clean her with, baby cream, powder and disposable nappies – *shouldn't be too difficult.*

I laid her on the table and took off her nappy – Ah God, what a smell! How could a sweet little thing like this create such a pong. Averting my eyes, which had begun to water again, I cleaned her up with handfuls of Swipes, gave her little bottom a good coating of cream and threw Johnsons powder all over her. Now she smelt like our baby.

The disposable nappy was no problem and I velcroed her into it until she was as snug as a bug in a rug.

Well I thought, that wasn't too bad – *once you got used to the smell.*

I proudly took her into Jo to show off my handiwork.

"Darling that was quick, "she said, taking Lilyrose, "and doesn't she smell nice."

She then started laugh.

"What's so funny?" I signed.

"You've put her nappy on back to front."

Bugger and I thought I was being so clever.

"Never mind darling, you'll be better next time," and she deftly flipped Lilyrose over and put right the recalcitrant nappy.

So this wasn't a one off – there were others to follow!

* * *

I was back at college in my new class and Jo was 'Mum at home' looking after baby.

It was all very new to her and she was taking some time to get used to it. I was doing what I'd always been doing but Jo was finding, that coping with housework and motherhood all day wasn't all it was cracked up to be!

She missed the daily interaction with the students and teachers and was already trying to find ways and means of getting back to college and what to do with Lilyrose!

She had been adamant – in collusion with Mary – that she would breast feed Lilyrose for a year but already she was talking about weaning her on to the bottle and that was after only six weeks!

"It would give me more freedom, don't you see," she said, "but there's still the problem of who's going to look after her if I went back to work?"

I couldn't come up with any solutions and signed,

"Are you sorry now that you had a baby?"

"I cannot believe you asked that," was her angry reply.

"Of course I'm not sorry. You know very well she was a surprise and very much wanted. She just arrived earlier than planned that's all."

"I'm sorry Jo, I didn't mean to question your love for Lilyrose, but I don't know how I can help," I signed and continued, *"I should finish college in a year's time. I should by then be proficient enough to cope with other deaf people in the outside world. Then I will take over and be Mum at home while you go back to work.*

I will find time for my painting when Lilyrose is sleeping or in her playpen. There problem solved."

Jo didn't share my smug solution of 'fixing' the problem.

"And what about the film?" she asked.

I'd forgotten all about the film.

"Right," I signed."

"I want you to get onto Arthur and tell him that we'll require a full time Nanny for the duration of the shoot. Tell him to have that in the contract. No Nanny, no actors."

Jo looked at me as if she was seeing me for the first time.

"When will I ..."

"Now," I signed firmly.

"Yes sir," she said, saluting, and left.

I heard her on the phone talking to Arthur.

She returned smiling,

"No problem, said Arthur."

She put her arms around me, giving me a squeeze.

"Oh, "she said, playing a 1920's vamp, "I do like a strong man," batting her eyelids at me.

* * *

It was special day today. Jo was bringing Lilyrose into college for all to see, staring off with Amanda and Co.

I always did my mandatory visit to the little ones each morning and was continually amazed at their progress. Their lack of inhibitions as they made contact with strangers and their interplay with each other was a lesson that we adults, in adversity, could all learn by.

TT was their teacher and every so often he would come out to lunch with tears streaming down his cheeks and would wave away my concern.

But always Amanda and her group would have some affect on him. Be it, crying, laughing, frowning or the shaking of his head in wonderment.

Today he had told them Jo was bringing in her baby to see them.

I was in the room for this special occasion and their little faces were glued to the door, waiting. The air hummed with expectancy and when Jo did open the door with her carrycot, I think they all stopped breathing.

Jo walked over and placed the carrycot at their feet and stepped back.

I looked around. TT was sitting on top of a desk watching. Jo joined me and we waited.

Nothing happened for quite some time, then Amanda tentatively stepped forward. She slowly stretched out her hand and a little fat fist came out of the cot, opened and took hold of one of her fingers and hung on.

Amanda threw back her head in sheer utter silent delight and the others crowded around wanting a turn.

It was such a poignant moment that only the most hard-hearted would fail to be affected. I could hear Jo sniffling besides me, and when I looked, TT had gone.

* * *

Chapter 26

All was quiet as I entered the house and I couldn't as they do in the movies call out "Darling I'm home "and the little women would answer with.

"Did you have a good day at the office dear?" putting my slippers by my chair and a cold beer on the side table for me.

First of all I was mute and secondly I don't think that happens in the real world, only in the movies.

What actually happened was Jo calling out,

"I'm here on the verandah."

I went out and Jo was reading and rocking Lilyrose in her rocker with her foot.

I kissed my wife, chucked my baby under the chin and got a smile from both.

She waved a manuscript in front of me.

"This arrived today. It's the first draft of the screenplay of the film. I've just finished it. They sent it for our approval."

"What's it like?" I signed.

"I'm not going to tell you what I think. I don't want to influence you in any way before you read it."

"*Right,*" I signed, "*be like that. I'll get myself a beer and start reading.*"

"While you're doing that I'll get the meal ready."

I sat in my favourite armchair and opened the beer and the manuscript.

Scene 1:

A kaleidoscope of aerial shots of Waaree cattle station, showing the vastness of the property – herds of cattle – wildlife – rivers and forests – finally zooming on to the figures of a aborigine lubra, Lily, and a small towheaded white boy of about eight walking through the bush.

The faint sounds of a didgeridoo will be heard faintly in the background each time Lily appears – it's her music.

She is talking and pointing with her digging stick, obviously explaining something to the small boy ...

That boy would be me.

It took me two hours to read the screenplay and at the end of it I was exhausted. I had played all the scenes in my minds eye. Some were wrong and would have to be rewritten but mostly they had done us proud. They had covered all the important events in my life with the right amount of humour and Jo, TT and Bridget Rose would be justly chuffed with their sympathetic characters. TT would win best supporting actor without a doubt and if they could capture the soothing voice of Lily as she talked of the bush and told her dreamtime stories of the Kalkadoons, with the faint echo of the didgeridoo in the background, it would lend a degree of authenticity to the film that would be unique.

If only I could play my scenes the way I thought they should be played I'd come out smelling of roses – but I had never acted before and to portray the right feelings with all the nuances without a voice was a daunting task – it frightened the life out of me. Gregory Peck might be able to do it, but I'm no Gregory Peck!

The cold print of sub titles, are not a match for the emotional cadences of the human voice.

Still, it was a film about *my* life and I was playing me, a real character, who was mute, allowances would be made for that.

"Well, what do you think?" asked Jo.

"I think I'm hungry," I signed.

"Right. I'll get your dinner. I kept it warm in the oven."

Jo put the meal on the kitchen table and took the cover off. It looked like some sort of casserole.

I signed, *"You tell me what you thought while I eat."*

Lilyrose, bored with being ignored started crying.

Jo picked her up and sat down opposite me and began breast-feeding her.

So, while I ate my meal and Lilyrose was at her favourite milk bar, Jo gave me her opinion.

"Overall I think it's very very good. Our scenes I like very much, they have the right amount of humour and are not maudlin or over sentimental, just right I thought. The mustering scenes and work on the cattle station I found exciting – real cowboy stuff – you come out of it looking like John Wayne. The scenes between you and Lily are lovely. They have everything, affection, poignancy and one is aware of the special relationship that obviously you and Lily have.

The bush fire with Blackie the bull is nail biting drama.

The art world and your landscapes are given a lush background in contrast to the cattle station and Arthur and

George are lovely characters.

TT will probably steal the picture. He comes out of it as a mixture of Robin Hood and the Dead End Kids. His scenes between him and Bridget Rose are delightful – especially when he proposes to her.

You and TT work well together and the comradeship that develops between you two becomes very apparent.

The boarding house scenes are very funny especially the Indian – the Peter Sellars character.

It's surprising the amount of humour in the film.

If we all can do justice to this screenplay then we will have a very good film. But can a feature film consisting mainly of non-actors be a success?"

"I wish I knew the answer to that," I signed.

"The big hurdle is getting the audience to accept us as real people without swamping our characters with too many layers of sympathy because we are deaf and mute. The only way I see we can do this is by humour. I don't mean belly laughs – I mean a quiet humour. We must be able to laugh at ourselves in spite of our afflictions. A couple of scenes need rewriting – they are over sentimental and should go in the opposite direction.

But like you I think they've done a great job. My gut turns over at the thought of trying to bring it to life and doing it justice."

"Mine to," said Jo.

She reached out over the table and took my hand.

"But we have each other. We're in this together and if we do go down we'll go down with all guns blazing."

"We'll talk to Simon before we start shooting," I signed, *"he's the director and if he sees it the same way we do then*

we're halfway there."

Jo and I were on the same page and with our optimistic outlook the insurmountable hurdles were already getting smaller.

* * *

As I pulled into a parking space at the college car park a shiny new car parked beside me. Out stepped TT from the passenger side and Bridget Rose from the driver's side.

I hopped out and signed, *"Good Morning,"* to them both.

They returned my greeting.

I walked around the new car, nodding in admiration at its shiny surface.

Bridget Rose, proudly signed, "It's my new car. Daddy bought it for me after I passed my driving test. It's an automatic Corolla."

"Very nice." I signed, *"don't you agree TT?"*

TT didn't bother taking his hands out of his pockets, to reply, but just nodded.

"Don't take any notice of him at all this morning, "she signed," he's grumpy because he didn't buy it for me. He said his 'friends' had offered him a good deal on a nearly new car but I said NO. It's probably one of those that had fallen off the back of a truck – if you know what I mean!"

Yes I did know what she meant. Good girl, she'll keep him on the straight and narrow.

"You two have fun. I'm off to do the shopping. Must feed the brute," she signed, getting back into her new car and smartly backing out with a toot of her horn

TT gave a shake of the head, a non-committal shrug and slouched off towards the buildings.   .

Well he was grumpy for all the right reasons. He cared for her so much he wanted to buy her everything.

"Must feed the brute," she had signed. *I wonder if she's buying him steak!*

Amanda and Co had snapped TT out of his grumpy mood and involved him in a made up game that he must have devised. He had Dorothy on his back and was ' cantering ' around the classroom, in the attitude of a horse, chasing the others who were dodging him and silently laughing fit to bust.

He was probably playing the games he never played as a child – who would want to play with a deaf mute kid – only other deaf mute kids like Amanda & Co.

I left them to it and retreated to the garden to do some work. I needed to put in the hard yards with this film coming up.

The mere thought of which gave me palpitations.

* * *

A possible start date for the film with the working title of 'Silent Signs' was in six months time and changes to the script arrived weekly via different coloured pages of A4 for our approval.

TT was virtually running the college and taking beginners to the senior classes without missing a beat. Such was his charisma with teachers and students, that attendance at the college had never been higher. He spent all day at the college doing something and always in demand.

Now that Jo wasn't there, who was going to write his monthly report! The other teachers, senior to him, had stepped aside in deference to his talent and leadership qualities and TT had just carried on doing things the way he always did them. He had more to offer than they did and the other teachers without any jealousy on their part acknowledged this and now looked upon him as their leader.

TT, without asking, receives this kind of loyalty from a cross section of the community, beginning with The Royal Institute of the Deaf, to his nefarious 'friends' at the other end of town!

TT and Bridget Rose were our constant valued visitors and would spend a lot of time nursing or playing with Lilyrose. They would make great parents but they never mentioned 'babies'.

The 85% chance of having a normal child probably wasn't good enough odds for them to take the gamble. And how would two deaf mutes bring up a normal child anyway!

* * *

"Reg, she's taken her first step," called out an excited Jo from the nursery.

I quickly left my painting to watch this special occasion.

When I got there Lilyrose was trying to claw her way up the side of the playpen to get on her feet to have another go.

I couldn't call out encouragement to her. All I could do was clap. By now she was getting used to it being the only sound that ever came from me. She didn't understand why I didn't talk to her and every so often she would stop what she was doing and stare at me with questioning look on her face.

It was the same when she first started to crawl and the despair I felt when I tried to come to terms with the fact that I would never be able to 'talk' to my daughter.

I had picked her up to hug her and there was a look of puzzlement on her face when I didn't say anything 'like Mummy did.' She had studied me for some time and then had reached out her chubby little hand and touched my lips – where the sound should come from.

I had choked up and blindly put her in the playpen and rushed from the room, followed by Jo, who enfolded me in her arms and held me while I sobbed my heart out.

And I still inwardly scream out in anger and frustration because I don't have a voice to talk to my daughter.

But no matter how dire things got in our small world, the contentment of married life and the love we had for each other, levelled out the playing field and Jo and I shrugged off the problems that arose and counted our blessings.

That fan was still whirring away at my shoulder, but nothing had hit it so far!

Maybe the chap upstairs keeping score was still on my side.

Maybe – only time will tell!